His hands mov...
stilling t...

"How dare you?" she gasped. "You have no right to touch me!"

His pale gaze slid to hers. "We have already been through this, but I'll remind you as you seem to have forgotten. Until we reach London, you are under my control—completely and absolutely."

She glared at him. Her heart was racing and it seemed that the skin on her ankles still tingled where his fingers had touched.

"Your feet are cut to ribbons."

"As I have already said, sir, it is none of your concern."

Rosalind's heart was fit to burst and her stomach was a small tight ball of fear. She watched him with the wariness of a trapped animal.

He released her hands, then took hold of her left foot and began to unwind the binding.

"Sir! What on earth do you think you are doing?"

* * *

Unlacing the Innocent Miss
Harlequin® Historical #1016—November 2010

London, 1814

A season of secrets, scandal and seduction!

A darkly dangerous stranger is out for revenge, delivering a
silken rope as his calling card. Through him, a long-forgotten
scandal is reawakened. The notorious events of 1794, which
saw one man murdered and another hanged for the crime,
are ripe gossip in the *ton*. Was the right culprit brought to
justice or is there a treacherous murderer still at large?

As the murky waters of the past are disturbed, so servants find
love with roguish lords, and proper ladies fall for rebellious
outcasts until, finally, the true murderer
and spy is revealed.

Regency Silk & Scandal

From glittering ballrooms to a Cornish smuggler's cove,
from the wilds of Scotland to a Romany camp—join
the highest and lowest in society as they find love
in this thrilling new eight-book miniseries!

Margaret McPhee

UNLACING THE INNOCENT MISS

HARLEQUIN®

TORONTO • NEW YORK • LONDON
AMSTERDAM • PARIS • SYDNEY • HAMBURG
STOCKHOLM • ATHENS • TOKYO • MILAN • MADRID
PRAGUE • WARSAW • BUDAPEST • AUCKLAND

Recycling programs
for this product may
not exist in your area.

ISBN-13: 978-0-373-29616-3

UNLACING THE INNOCENT MISS

Copyright © 2010 by Margaret McPhee

All rights reserved. Except for use in any review, the reproduction or
utilization of this work in whole or in part in any form by any electronic,
mechanical or other means, now known or hereafter invented, including
xerography, photocopying and recording, or in any information storage
or retrieval system, is forbidden without the written permission of the
publisher, Harlequin Enterprises Limited, 225 Duncan Mill Road,
Don Mills, Ontario, M3B 3K9, Canada.

This is a work of fiction. Names, characters, places and incidents are
either the product of the author's imagination or are used fictitiously,
and any resemblance to actual persons, living or dead, business
establishments, events or locales is entirely coincidental.

This edition published by arrangement with Harlequin Books S.A.

For questions and comments about the quality of this book
please contact us at Customer_eCare@Harlequin.ca.

® and TM are trademarks of the publisher. Trademarks indicated with
® are registered in the United States Patent and Trademark Office, the
Canadian Trade Marks Office and in other countries.

www.eHarlequin.com

Printed in U.S.A.

Dear Reader,

I was reading a book about the history of the English police when I came across the aptly named thief-takers. Men who, before the development of a detective police force, traced thieves and recovered stolen property. They seemed to be represented as a corrupt lot—men who were just as criminal as the thieves they were apprehending. And that set me thinking that there must have been some honest men among them. Dangerous men doing a dangerous job. Tough. Ruthless. Determined. The idea of my hero, Wolf, was born.

Wolf is a gritty Yorkshireman. A thief-taker, who's had to claw his way out of the gutter and get where he is off his own bat. But the recovery of his next thief is about to turn Wolf's world upside down and shake the very foundations on which he's built his life.

My heroine, Miss Rosalind Meadowfield, quiet, timid and skilled in blending in with the background, has spent a lifetime hiding her past. She appears to be the very antithesis of Wolf. But maybe Rosalind and Wolf have more in common than either of them realize, as each overcomes the barriers the other has built around their heart.

I had great fun being a part of the Regency Silk & Scandal series. Here is my humble offering—the story of Rosalind and Wolf and how they come to fall in love. I really do hope that you enjoy it.

Margaret

Look for these novels in the Regency miniseries

SILK & SCANDAL

The Lord and the Wayward Lady
by Louise Allen—June 2010

Paying the Virgin's Price
by Christine Merrill—July 2010

The Smuggler and the Society Bride
by Julia Justiss—August 2010

Claiming the Forbidden Bride
by Gayle Wilson—September 2010

The Viscount and the Virgin
by Annie Burrows—October 2010

Unlacing the Innocent Miss
by Margaret McPhee—November 2010

The Officer and the Proper Lady
by Louise Allen—December 2010

Taken by the Wicked Rake
by Christine Merrill—January 2011

Prologue

May 1815, London

Outside in the darkness of the night a dog was barking.

A necklace of diamonds lay within a nest of black silken rope coiled on Lord Evedon's desk. The diamonds glittered beneath the light of the candelabra as he picked up the necklace, letting it dangle and sway from his fingers, all the while watching the woman standing so quietly before him across the desk.

'Well?' he finally said, and his expression was cold. 'What have you to say for yourself, Miss Meadowfield?'

A look of confusion crossed Rosalind Meadowfield's face. The concern that she had felt at being summoned to attend Lord Evedon in his study had become fear. The hour was too late, and they were alone. His mood was not good, and it could be no coincidence that he was holding his mother's missing jewels.

'Lady Evedon's diamonds, they have been found?' She did not understand what else he expected her to say.

'Indeed they have.' He spoke quietly enough, politely even, but she could hear the anger that lay beneath. 'Do you know where they were found?'

Her puzzlement increased, along with her sense of foreboding. 'I do not.'

His eyes seemed to narrow and he glanced momentarily away as if in disgust. 'The crime is ill enough, Miss Meadowfield. Do not compound it by lying.'

The tempo of her heart increased. She eyed him warily. 'I am sorry, my lord, but I do not understand.'

'Then understand this,' he spoke abruptly. 'The diamonds were found hidden in your bedchamber, wrapped within your undergarments.'

'My undergarments?' She felt her stomach turn over. 'That is not possible.'

He did not answer, just stared at her with angry accusation. And in that small pregnant silence she knew precisely what he thought and why he had called her here.

'You cannot believe that I would steal from Lady Evedon?' Her words were faint, their pitch high with incredulity. 'I would not do such a thing. There must be some mistake.'

'There is no mistake. Graves himself was there when the diamonds were discovered within your chamber. Do you mean to call into question the propriety of the butler who has worked for the Evedon family for over forty years?'

'I do not, but neither do I know how the diamonds came to be hidden within my clothing.' She gripped her hands together, her palms sliding in their cold clamminess, and bit at her lower lip. 'I swear it is the truth, my lord.'

'And what is the significance of this?' From the surface of the desk he lifted the rope, and even in the subdued lighting from the candles and the fire, she could see its dark silken sheen. With one end of the rope secured tight within his fingers, he released the rest; as it dropped, Rosalind saw, to her horror, that it had been tied in the shape of a noose. She could not prevent the gasp escaping her lips.

'Well?' One movement of his fingers and the noose swung slightly.

'I have never seen that rope before. I know nothing of it.' Her heart was hammering so hard that she felt sick. All of her past was back in an instant—everything that she had fought so hard to hide—conjured by that one length of rope.

He made a sound of disbelief. 'I warned my mother against taking on a girl without a single name she could offer to provide her with a character. But Lady Evedon is too kind and trusting a spirit. What else have you been stealing these years that you have worked as her companion? Small items perhaps? Objects that would pass unnoticed? And now you become brave, taking advantage of a woman whose mind has grown fragile.'

'I deny it most fervently. I hav—'

But Evedon did not let her finish. 'I do not wish to hear it. You are a liar as well as a thief, Miss Meadowfield.'

She felt her face flood with heat, and her fingers were trembling so much that she gripped them all the tighter that he would not see it.

'The diamonds we have thankfully recovered; with the emeralds we have not been so fortunate. Will you at least have the decency to tell me where you have hidden them?'

She stared at him, her mind still reeling from shock, too slow and stilted to think coherently. 'I tell you, they are not within my possession.'

'Then you have sold them already?' The silken rope

slithered through his fingers to land in a dark pile upon the desk. He pocketed the diamond necklace. The clawed feet of his chair scraped loud, like talons gouging against the polished wooden floor, as he pushed the chair back and rose to his feet.

'Of course not.' Instinctively she stepped back, just a tiny pace, but enough to increase the distance between them. 'I have taken nothing belonging to her ladyship.'

'I doubt you have had time to rid yourself of the emeralds, and they are most assuredly not within your chamber. So where are they concealed?' He moved out from behind the barrier of the desk and walked round to stand before her, facing her directly.

Rosalind's throat dried. 'I am no thief,' she managed to whisper. 'There has been a terrible mistake here.'

He ignored her. 'Empty your pockets, Miss Meadowfield.'

She stared at him all the more, her heart beating a frenzied tattoo while her mind struggled to believe what he was saying, and she could not rid herself of the sensation that this nightmare into which she had walked could not really be happening.

'I said turn out your pockets.' He enunciated each word as if she were a simpleton.

Her hands were shaking and her cheeks burning as she removed a handkerchief from her pocket and pulled the interior out to show that it was empty.

'And the others.'

'I have no other pockets.'

'I do not believe you, Miss Meadowfield.' The logs crackled upon the fire. He stood there silent and still, before suddenly grabbing her arm and pulling her close enough to allow his hand to sweep a search over her bodice and skirts.

'Lord Evedon!' She struggled within his arms, trying to break free, but his grip tightened.

'I will not let the matter lie so lightly. You will tell me where they are.'

'I did not take them,' she cried and struggled all the harder.

The dog was still barking and, as if in harmony, came the sound of a woman's cries and shouts from upstairs within the house.

Rosalind ceased her resistance, knowing that it was the dowager that cried out.

Evedon knew it too, but he did not relinquish his hold upon her.

'Do not think to make a fool of me so easily, Miss Meadowfield. If you will not divulge the whereabouts of the emeralds to me, perhaps you will be more forthcoming to the constable in the morning.'

From other parts of the house came the sounds of voices and running. And of hurried footsteps approaching the study door.

'No,' she whispered, almost to herself, and in that moment, his grasp slackened so that she succeeded in wrenching herself free of him. But the force of the momentum carried her crashing backwards towards the desk. Her hands flailed wide seeking an anchor with which to save herself, and finding nothing but the pile of books stacked upon the desk. Her fingers gripped to them, clung to them, pulling them down with her. From the pale fan of their pages a single folded letter escaped to drift down. Rosalind landed in a heap alongside the books with the letter trapped flat beneath her fingertips.

Lord Evedon's face paled. She saw the sudden change in his expression—the undisguised horror, the fear—as he stared, not at her, but at the letter. He reached out and snatched it back, the violence of his action startling her.

A rap of knuckles sounded against the study door.

'Lord Evedon.' She recognized the voice as Mr Graves, the butler.

Evedon stuffed the letter hastily into his pocket. She saw the glimmer of sweat upon the skin of his upper lip and chin as she scrambled to her feet.

'Attend to your appearance,' he hissed in a whisper.

Only then did Rosalind realize that her chignon had unravelled, freeing her hair to uncoil down her back. She crouched and began searching for the missing hairpins.

'M'lord,' Graves called again. 'It is a matter of urgency.'

Lord Evedon quickly smoothed the front of his coat and waistcoat.

'Up.' And with a rough hand, he yanked her to her feet by the shoulder of her dress, ripping it slightly in the process. 'You will speak nothing of this to my mother. Do I make myself clear?'

She nodded.

At last he granted Graves admittance.

'Forgive me, m'lord, but it is Lady Evedon.'

'Another of her turns?'

Graves coughed delicately. 'I am afraid so, my lord. She requests Miss Meadowfield's presence.' The butler did not even glance in Rosalind's direction, and yet she could not help but remember what Lord Evedon had said about Graves overseeing the discovery of the diamonds. He had searched through her possessions, sparing nothing, not even her undergarments, and he thought her a thief. Her cheeks heated with the shame and injustice of it.

'Very well.' Lord Evedon's gaze moved from Graves

to Rosalind. 'You will attend her ladyship, and this other matter will be concluded upon the morning.'

She nodded, not trusting herself to speak, aware of her burning cheeks and her unkempt hair and of what Mr Graves and the small collection of maids and footmen gathered in the hallway all thought her. She could see the accusation in their eyes and the tightening of their lips in disapproval.

She wanted so much to deny the unjust accusation, to say that she was as shocked at what was unravelling as they, but all turned their faces from her. She had no option but to follow Mr Graves up the staircase, aware with every step that she took of Lord Evedon at her back and of what the morning would bring.

Lady Evedon was no longer crying by the time they reached the room. She lay there so small and exhausted and frail within the high four-poster bed, her face an unnatural shade of white.

'I saw his face,' she cried. 'He was there, right there.' She pointed to the window where she had pulled the curtain back.

'Who was there?' Rosalind followed the dowager's terrified gaze.

'The one that follows me always. The one that never leaves me,' she whispered. 'He was no gentleman. He lied…Robert lied and I believed him.'

Rosalind glanced nervously at Lord Evedon.

'There is no one there, mother. It is only you and me and Miss Meadowfield.'

'You are quite certain?' Lady Evedon asked.

'I am certain. It was another of your nightmares.' He pressed a hand to his mother's, his face filled with concern. 'I shall send for Dr Spentworth.'

'No.' Lady Evedon shook her head. 'There is no need. You are right. It was a nightmare, nothing more.'

'Then we will request the doctor's presence in the morning, to ensure that all is as it should be.'

'I understand well your implication, Charles; you think that I am going mad!'

'I was not suggesting any such thing. I am but concerned for your health.'

Lady Evedon nodded, but Rosalind could see in the lady's face that she was not convinced. 'Of course. I am merely tired, and the barking of that wretched animal outside woke me with a fright.' She seemed almost recovered. 'You may leave us now; Miss Meadowfield will read to me until I fall asleep. Her voice soothes my overly excited nerves.' She turned to Rosalind with a little smile. 'You look rather pale, my dear. Are you feeling unwell?'

'I—' Rosalind opened her mouth to speak and, feeling Lord Evedon's hard gaze upon her, quickly closed it again. With a sinking heart she realized that he had been right in his caution as they left the study. She could not tell Lady Evedon of the accusation of theft or any of the rest of it, not with the dowager's state of mind.

'I am quite well, thank you, my lady.'

'Your book.' Lord Evedon lifted a small book from the bedside table and handed it to his mother.

Lady Evedon smiled. 'Thank you, dear Charles.'

'I will leave Stevens outside the door to ensure that you two ladies are kept safe.' Lord Evedon's gaze met Rosalind's and she knew his words for the warning they were.

'I shall be glad to know that we are being so carefully protected.' Lady Evedon seemed reassured by the knowledge.

'Mama…Miss Meadowfield.' He bowed and left.

'Miss Meadowfield,' Lady Evedon held the copy of Wordsworth's poems out to her.

'My lady,' she said, and with only a slight tremor of her fingers she opened its leather cover.

She read aloud, keeping her voice calm and light. She read and read, and by the time that Lady Evedon finally fell asleep the candles on the bedside table had burned low.

She sat there, listening to Lady Evedon's quiet snores, her palms clammy even while her fingers were stiff with cold. Her mind raced with thoughts, with fears, with worried speculation. Once the constable arrived, it was only a matter of time before they discovered the truth: that Rosalind Meadowfield did not exist at all, that she had lied. Theft of this magnitude from an employer was a capital offence, and when they knew her real family name, there was no court in the land that would deal with her leniently. Prison. Transportation. Or even…hanging. Her hands balled to form fists, clutching so tightly that her fingernails cut into the flesh of her palms.

She remembered the anger on Lord Evedon's face, his rough search of her person and his cruel grip. He believed the worst of her. He thought she had betrayed the dowager's trust and stolen from her and that she was still hiding the emeralds. The accusation stung at her doubly, for not only was she innocent, but she had grown fond of Lady Evedon. From all she had come to learn of Charles Evedon over the years, she knew that he was a man who would not take what he believed to be a betrayal lightly. Not for Evedon a quiet dismissal. Already she knew he meant to call the constable. He wanted retribution, and he did not mean to be denied it. The guard outside the door was testament to that fact. Evedon would see her punished. And once he knew her true identity, he would see her hanged.

That knowledge had a cruel fatalism about it. She closed

her eyes, trying to suppress the dread, and thought again of
the black silken noose that had swung from Lord Evedon's
fingers. Did someone already know her secret? Or was it
just a warning of the fate that awaited a jewel thief?

She replaced the book on top of the copy of *The Times*
that lay upon Lady Evedon's bedside table, her eye catching
again the small advertisement she had read earlier on the
top right-hand corner of the front page. Oh, to be there on
the wild moorland of Scotland, so far from Lord Evedon
and the chaos that was unfolding around her. But such
dreams were without hope.

She rose to her feet and turned away from the bed
where the dowager lay sleeping, knowing she must return
to the small room that was her bedchamber even though its
humble privacy had been violated. The thought of Graves
and others of the servants raking through her undergarments, touching all that was personal to her, was deeply
humiliating.

The letter lay on the carpet behind the door. She saw
it immediately, lying pale and slightly crumpled upon the
deep rose and blue threads of silk, and she knew without
touching it, without even seeing it close up, that it was the
letter that Lord Evedon had stuffed into his pocket downstairs in his study. The same letter that he had snatched
away from her so angrily.

She walked towards it, lifted it, heard it crinkle with
her touch and felt the stiffness of the paper and the broken
sealing wax beneath her fingers. The large black spiky font
showed the letter to be addressed to Earl Evedon, Evedon
House, Cavendish Square, London. Normally, Rosalind
would not have dreamt of reading a letter addressed to
another, but there was nothing of normality about this evening. Beneath the low flickering light of Lady Evedon's
candles, Rosalind opened the letter and began to read.

The dowager's snores still sounded softly within the room, but Rosalind no longer heard them. She read the words and then read them again, and she understood the reason for Lord Evedon's anger—and his dread. A scrawl of words that Evedon would not want the world to know. A scrawl of words that could destroy him, just as he could destroy her.

She refolded the letter, knowing that fate had just dealt the final blow to her life as she knew it. She could not simply set the letter back on the carpet and pretend that she had not seen it. Once Lord Evedon realized that the letter was here in this room he would know that she had read it. And Stevens was standing guard outside the door so that she could not place it elsewhere. Besides, she would not wish another to chance upon it and read its words; Lady Evedon did not deserve that shame.

And the thought came to her that, if Evedon knew that she had this letter, he would not then call the constable. He would not call anyone. He would do nothing to risk the focus of attention upon the letter or the truth that it contained. For there could be no doubting that its words were the truth; she had seen the desperation on his face.

The realization was quiet in its dawning, a gentle waft of thought rather than a sudden inspired burst. She looked at the newspaper upon the bedside cabinet, weighing the thought in consideration for long minutes before she acted.

The newspaper ripped easily with little noise, and she read the small ragged square of words again before folding it neat and smaller still and slipping it within her pocket. She sat there for a while longer before finally folding the letter and pocketing it in just the same way.

She looked again at Lady Evedon sleeping so peacefully, all of the dowager's demons banished—for now. A final lingering glance around the room, then Rosalind rose and walked quietly to the door.

Stevens escorted her to her tiny bedchamber at the back of the house without a single word, and she was glad of his silence.

She did not know if he waited outside her chamber door, standing guard for fear that she would escape the justice Evedon meant to deal her. It made no difference if he waited there the whole night through, for the roof of the scullery was directly below her window. A strange calm had descended upon her, although her hands were trembling as she quietly packed her few possessions into the small bag and swung the cloak around her shoulders. She drew the window sash up as slowly and carefully as she could, cringing as the slide of wood seemed loud against the surrounding silence. The outside air was cold against her face as she breathed in its nocturnal dampness and the freedom that it promised.

She did not look around the bedchamber, at the mean narrow bed or its empty hearth, but kept her gaze fixed on the black sky in which the moon was hidden. A deep breath, and then another, before she climbed over the sill and carefully lowered herself to the slates below.

The dull yellow glow of the street lamps eased the night's darkness as she hurried over the cobblestones. She glanced back nervously at Evedon House. The dog had ceased its barking and the streets were so quiet and still, and she the only thing moving within them.

No footsteps followed, no breath sounded save for hers, yet her skin prickled with the sense that Evedon was there silently watching, so that she feared that he followed her.

Rosalind did not look back again. She began to run.

In a nearby alleyway, a man, dark as the shadows that surrounded him, waited until the woman had passed before stepping out from his hiding place to watch her. All around was hushed and sleeping, disturbed only by the echo of her hurried footsteps. Dressed in black, he stood where he was but his intent gaze followed the scurrying figure. He watched until she faded from sight, swallowed up by the darkness of the night. Only then, did he turn and walk away in the opposite direction, passing beneath the same street lamps under which she had fled. A small gold hoop in the lobe of one ear glinted against the ebony of his hair, and teeth that were white and straight were revealed by the smile that slid across his mouth.

'You might run, my dear Miss Rosalind Meadow-field, but you shall not escape the scandal. Justice will be done,' he whispered, and then setting his hat at a jaunty angle, he began to whistle an ancient Romany tune as he rounded the corner and sprang lightly up into the black coach that waited there. And then the stranger and his coach were gone, disappeared into the darkness of the sprawling metropolis beyond.

Chapter One

Munnoch Moor, Scotland, two weeks later

The night was dark and a chill wind howled through the forest. A solitary figure stood in silence, his presence concealed by the trees, watching the yard of the coaching inn. His focus never wavered from the mail coach that had stopped there, just stayed trained on the door while it opened and the steps were kicked into place. His pale silver gaze sharpened, like a hunter that sights its prey. As the lone woman alighted from the coach, Wolf smiled and knew that he had found his quarry.

The coach rumbled away into the night leaving Rosalind standing in the yard of the Blairadie coaching inn. No other passengers had disembarked; she was alone, save for the man who soon disappeared within the inn hauling the sack of letters that the coach had delivered. The lanterns swayed in the wind, creaking and sending their light dancing against the grey walls that encompassed the yard and the stonework of the stables. The hour was so late that there was no hum of voices from the inn, no blaze of lights or welcoming glow of fires. No chinks of light peeped through the curtains drawn across the windows. In the distance, a church clock struck twelve.

Rosalind glanced around the empty yard nervously, eyes searching through the dim lantern light to find the man her new employer had sent to collect her. She was unsure of what to do, whether to wait here outside alone, or follow the other man into the inn. A voice sounded, male, not Scottish like those she had grown accustomed to hearing for the past days in Edinburgh, but rather with an accent that had a strong Yorkshire vein.

'Miss Meadowfield?'

She started, and glanced round.

A tall man wearing a long dark riding coat stood by the yard's entrance. The brim of his hat kept his face shadowed and invisible. There was something about the figure, so dark and dangerous and predatory, that her heart seemed to cease beating and the breath caught in her throat. She thought in that moment that, despite all that she had done to escape him, Evedon had found her. And then, sense and reasoning kicked in and she told herself that, of course, he was Hunter's man sent to fetch her.

'You are from Mr Stewart of Benmore House?' she asked tentatively.

The man gave a nod. 'Come to collect the new house-keeper, ma'am.'

She smiled her relief and walked across the yard towards him. 'That is welcome news indeed, sir.' She was here at last. Only a few miles now lay between Rosalind and the start of her new life running the household of Mr Stewart at Benmore House on Munnoch Moor—far, far away from London and Lord Evedon.

He took the travelling bag from her hand. 'Allow me, ma'am.'

'Thank you.'

He turned and began to walk out of the inn's yard. 'We had best get a move on.'

'Of course.' She followed after him.

Outside the yard, the moonlight revealed the presence of a cart with a single horse parked at the road's side, a small inconsequential vehicle almost unnoticed against the dark edge of the trees. She wondered why he had travelled in a cart rather than a gig.

The man was tall, with long legs and a big stride. Rosalind quickened her pace to stay with him.

He dumped her bag in the back of the cart and climbed up to the seat at the front, before turning and reaching a hand down towards Rosalind.

The moon was behind him, rendering his face shadowed and the features invisible. Rosalind hesitated, an inexplicable shiver running down her spine. Overhead, the night sky hung like a canopy of rich black velvet studded with the brilliance of diamond stars. The moon was half full, a white opalescent semicircle that shone with an ethereal brilliance to light the road behind Mr Stewart's servant.

'Miss Meadowfield,' he urged in a tone that was hard and clipped.

And just for a moment she had the urge to turn where she was and run. She quelled the thought, telling herself not to be foolish, that what had happened at Evedon House was making her too fearful, too suspicious. London and Lord Evedon were close to five hundred miles away. She was safe here. She looked at the strong, long, blunt-tipped fingers extended towards her and, without further hesitation, reached her own hand to his.

His grasp was warm even through the fine leather of her glove, and strong. Again she was aware of that frisson of sensation that tingled through her. But she could think no more on it, for he was pulling her up to sit on the small wooden bench beside him.

He twitched the reins within his fingers and the cart began to roll forward, making Rosalind grab for the edge of the seat.

She felt, rather than saw, the way his head turned to look at her hands clutched so tightly and the uneasy way she sat forward, staring with trepidation at the horse before her. She could see the smoky condensation of the horse's breath against the darkness of the night, could hear its soft breathing and smell its strong scent. She inhaled deeply and slowly, releasing the breath even more slowly and loosening the tight grip of her fingers to something more reasonable.

He made no comment, yet even so, Rosalind felt the flush of warmth in her cheeks. Embarrassment made her seek something—anything—to say, desperately searching for a diversion from her awkwardness.

'It is a cold night for the time of year.' She looked round at him, and attempted to sit back more comfortably on the seat.

The man gave no response, just manipulated the reins, and made soft clicking noises to steer them round so that the horse and cart were ready to trot down a smaller road to the side. As they changed direction, the moon lit his face so that Rosalind saw him for the first time. He was not as old as she had expected; indeed, she estimated that he could not be so very much older than her own twenty-five years.

His were strong features, harsh and lean…and handsome. High cheekbones and a chiselled jawline, a straight manly nose and a hard uncompromising mouth that did not smile. A small pale scar slashed across the skin of his cheek beneath his right eye. And his face held a slightly mocking expression. But it was none of these things that caused the breath to catch in Rosalind's throat. Within the cool moonlight, the man's eyes seemed almost silver, and he was looking at her with an expression so cold as to freeze her.

The shock of it made her rapidly avert her gaze, and when she glanced again, his face was looking forward and in shadow once more. She wondered if she had been mistaken. And the thought occurred to her that perhaps he knew that she was lying to Mr Stewart and that she had come from Evedon House. Perhaps he even knew her real identity. It was impossible, of course. They had hanged her father twenty years ago. And as for the rest—Evedon and his accusations—she had been careful: writing her application from Louisa's in Edinburgh, lying about what she had been doing for the last years, erasing any hint of a connection with the dowager Lady Evedon.

The man was probably just irritated at being dragged from his bed in the middle of the night to fetch her. She was safe. She was going to Benmore House and everything would be fine. She took a deep breath and tried to convince herself of that.

'You have the advantage of me, sir. I do not know your name.' Small talk, something plucked from the air to break the uneasy silence that lay between them.

Within the quiet of the night, the horse's iron-shod hooves were loud against the compacted surface of the road. Rosalind deliberately kept her gaze averted from the horse, glancing round at Hunter's man instead. There was only the noise of the horse's hooves, and she thought that he would not answer her, but eventually he spoke.

'Wolversley, but they call me Wolf.' The silver eyes flicked down to meet hers once more.

Wolf. The skin on the nape of Rosalind's neck prickled, and not just at the name. There was an intensity in that single silver glance that shook her.

The reins twitched beneath his fingers and the horse began to pick up its pace. She could not help but grip again at the seat.

'Is the pace too fast for you, ma'am?' She thought she heard an edge of mockery in his words, but whether it was there in truth or was just a product of her own guilty imagination, she did not know.

'No, sir. The pace is perfectly fine.' Rosalind had no intention of admitting her fear to anyone at the Hunter residence. One more secret to be kept amidst many. 'Perhaps you could tell me something of Benmore House.'

'Best just to wait and see for yourself,' he replied. A moment's pause before he added, 'But happen you could tell me of Benmore's new housekeeper. We have been curious as to Miss Meadowfield.'

Not a question that Rosalind wished to answer, yet she knew that she would have to do so time and again within her new position, and she supposed that now was as good a time as any to start. 'There is little to tell, Mr Wolversley.'

'Wolf,' he corrected.

And again that strange sensation whispered down her spine. 'Where did you work prior to taking up this position? Mr Stewart said it was Edinburgh.'

'I did indeed work for a household in Edinburgh.'

'Anyone we would have heard of?'

'No one you would have heard of,' she replied quickly,

not wishing to drag her old school friend and her family into this any more than was necessary. It had been good of Louisa to take her in after her flight from London, especially given that she knew the truth of Rosalind's father. It had also been Louisa's idea to say that Rosalind had spent the last years as her housekeeper and to write her a glowing character in response to the advertisement that she had taken from Lady Evedon's chamber that terrible night. Even so, she had not told Louisa the truth of that night, just that there had been a disagreement and she wished to find paid employment.

'Where exactly did you work, ma'am, if you do not mind me asking?'

Rosalind's heart skipped a beat. 'Oh.' She forced a smile and tried to sound as if everything was perfectly normal. 'Ainslie Place. A fairly small household.'

'Ainslie Place?' Wolf turned his face to hers and she was struck anew at its strength and harsh handsomeness, and the cold cynical light in his eyes that he made no pretence of disguising. 'Interesting.'

And the thought that pulsed in her brain was that this Wolf might prove to be a very dangerous man to her, although in quite what way she did not know. 'I am glad that you think so,' she said with careful politeness and glanced away, desperate to think of some way of steering him on to a safer topic.

'What made you wish to leave?'

'I read Mr Stewart's advertisement in *The Times* and thought the position exactly suited to my purposes.' That much, at least, was true.

'You were not happy where you were?'

'I was very happy, but I am a little tired of the city. Benmore House's rural location attracted me greatly.' Indeed, it *was* Benmore's isolated location and distance from London as well as Mr Stewart's self-confessed hermit tendencies that had made it the perfect place for Rosalind. She could remain hidden in the safety of such obscurity and earn a living.

'What of you, sir?' she said, determined to draw him away from pursuing the matter any further. 'Yours does not sound to be a local accent.'

'I am a Yorkshire man.' There was a ruggedness to his voice.

'And have you worked at Benmore House for long?'

'Long enough,' he said and glanced round at her with that harsh unsmiling demeanour, and again she felt the faint shimmer of something ripple down her spine, something that she could not quite place. A warning—or excitement. More like foolishness and fatigue, she told herself firmly.

'Come straight over from Edinburgh have you?'

She gave a small nod of her head.

The man Wolf gave no comment, and Rosalind made no further attempt at conversation with a man who was more interested in asking his own questions rather than answering hers. Better an awkward silence than another awkward question, she thought. Perhaps this was going to be harder than she had anticipated. Perhaps her own lies would trip herself up in the first week. She closed her eyes against the thought. It was late and she was tired. Everything would be better once she reached Benmore House.

The horse's hooves clattered against the road's surface, the cart wheels rumbled as they turned, and all around was the whisper of the cool night breeze through the leaves of hedges and trees. They turned off the main road, taking first one country track before criss-crossing to another and another, until Rosalind lost all sense of direction. On and on, for what seemed like miles; Rosalind thought they would never reach their destination. Mr Stewart's advertisement had described Benmore House as a country house with a staff of twenty servants situated on the moorland some few miles from the Blairadie inn. To Rosalind, who was both nervous and weary, a few miles had never seemed so long.

Eventually he guided the horse and cart off the track, to follow a narrow path into some woodland. Through the trees to where they were heading, Rosalind saw a spiral of smoke curling pale against the darkness of the night sky. Benmore House, she thought, and a spurt of both relief and excitement surged through her. Soon she would be safe from Evedon. Soon she would start her new life. The horse rounded a corner, and she saw from where the smoke was coming.

A tiny woodsman's cottage stood in a clearing; two horses were tethered in its small lean-to stable.

Rosalind stared as the man brought the cart to a stop before it. She turned to him in confusion and looked up into his face.

'But this is not Benmore House.'

'No, it is not,' he said.

'I do not understand.'

'You will soon enough.' His lips curved ever so slightly emphasizing the mockery in his face.

Realization hit her hard, landing like a punch in her stomach. She reacted quickly, springing to her feet, ready to leap the distance to the ground, but a strong arm hooked around her, pulling her back against him.

'Oh, no, you do not,' he growled. He held her firm. 'Do not think to try to escape me, *Miss* Rosalind Meadowfield. I would fetch you back in the blink of an eye, and tan your backside, lady or not. Do I make myself clear?'

Her heart was thumping, fit to leap from within her ribcage.

'I did not hear your answer, miss,' he said in a voice that, for all its quietness, was unmistakable in its threat.

She swallowed hard and, not daring to look round at him, gave a small nod.

'I am glad we understand each other.'

Chapter Two

Rosalind's gaze moved to the cottage door as it creaked open. Two men, both dressed in jackets and loose working trousers, came out.

'You're back then?' said the bigger man of the two, in a broad Scottish accent.

From Wolf's knowledge of her name, Rosalind knew that this was no opportunistic spur of the moment abduction, but one that had been planned.

Her eyes flicked over the smaller man in the background and her stomach jolted. A planned abduction indeed, for Rosalind recognized the man as Pete Kempster, one of Lord Evedon's footmen.

Wolf lowered her from the edge of the cart. Even before her feet touched the ground, the big man was there before her, his hand firm around her elbow as he led her towards the cottage.

She tried to resist, pulling against the insistence of his

grip and kicking out at him, but the man laughed at her attempts and moved his hands to hold her by both arms.

'Quite the wee wildcat.' He was so big that he merely lifted her through the doorway that waited open to the interior of the cottage.

She was so frightened, so determined to escape, that she turned her face and tried to bite one the hands that restrained her.

The big man avoided her teeth and shouted at Wolf, 'I thought you said she was a lady.'

She heard Wolf laugh somewhere behind her. 'My mistake, Struan.'

The cottage comprised a single room. Wooden shutters were closed across the narrow windows, one in each of the front and back walls of the cottage. A fire burned on the hearth, casting dancing golden lights around the room and throwing out a warmth to chase away the night's dampness. Beneath the rear window, there was a small square wooden table under which were tucked three stools. In front of the fire were three large wooden spindle chairs with a wooden box in between that served as a table.

'You found her?' Kempster asked as the big man released her into the room. She heard the faint hint of surprise that edged his words.

'Is it her? Is she the lassie that we're after?' the man Wolf had called Struan said.

Kempster nodded.

Rosalind met his gaze across the room, knowing that the last time they had met, circumstances had been very different. He had been one of the servants gathered outside Lord Evedon's study that fateful night.

She did not know Pete Kempster well, even though she had seen him often enough around Evedon House. But his presence explained much. Wolf was not Hunter's man after all, he was Evedon's, and she cursed herself that she had not listened to the warning shiver that his presence elicited.

'Miss Meadowfield,' Kempster said formally, the expression on his handsome face unreadable.

'Mr Kempster,' she replied.

In the background, the big Scotsman picked up a tin mug from where it sat upon the small makeshift table and sipped from it, relaxing into one of the spindle chairs, while Wolf walked back into the room carrying his saddle.

She watched him place the saddle on the floor beside the others, before removing his hat and hanging it on one of the row of pegs fixed to the wall close by the door. His long dark leather greatcoat followed, to hang next to it, revealing a rather shabby brown jacket beneath. Her eyes moved down to take in the faded brown leather trousers that ran the long length of his legs and ended with a pair of scuffed boots covered in dried mud splashes.

He moved over to the fire and threw another log on to the blaze. 'Where's the food?'

Struan Campbell nodded towards the little table. 'Cooked ham, and cheese. We've already eaten. Bread's a bit stale but the ale's tolerable enough.'

Wolf helped himself to a plate of food and a bottle of ale. He worked in silence, not looking once at the woman although he was conscious of her attention fixed upon him. He did not need to look at her again to know every inch of her appearance. Wolf had both an eye and memory for detail. It had served him well during his time in the Army; it served him even better in his current occupation.

She looked nothing as he had expected. Her hair was escaping in long thick dark brown waves from the few pins that struggled to hold it in place. From his limited glimpses of her eyes through the moonlight or firelight, it was difficult to see their precise colour although he thought them to be brown. She appeared to be neither tall nor short, neither fat nor thin. Her features were not of outstanding beauty, yet she was not uncomely. Miss Rosalind Meadowfield was a woman who would easily blend unnoticed into whatever background she was placed—an ideal attribute for a ladies' companion…and a thief.

She stood at the other side of the room, totally silent and motionless as if she were hoping that they would forget about her.

'Sit down and eat,' Wolf directed.

She eyed the table dubiously and made no move. 'Who are you, sir, and why have you abducted me?'

'You already know the answers to both of those questions, Miss Meadowfield,' he said and did not even look up from his ale.

'You are from Lord Evedon.'

'You see, you do know, after all.' He looked at her and smiled cynically.

'I am surmising that, from Mr Kempster's presence.'

'Then you surmise correctly, miss.'

She met his gaze and he could see the suspicion and fear in her eyes. 'Why has he sent you?'

Wolf raised an eyebrow. 'Yet another question to which you already know the answer.'

She swallowed hard and gave a small shake of her head. 'I beg to differ, sir. What is his intention?'

She knew. He was sure of it, yet he told her bluntly. 'Unsurprisingly, his intention is the capture of the woman who stole his mother's jewels.'

She made a small sound that was something between a laugh and a sigh of disbelief. 'And he has sent you to fetch me back to him?'

'You did not think that he would let you go free after stealing from him, did you?' Wolf watched her closely.

She glanced away but not before he had seen the guilt in her eyes. 'Lord Evedon is mistaken. I am no thief.' Her hand fluttered nervously to her mouth.

She was lying, and Wolf knew all about lying and the ways in which people gave themselves away.

'Of course,' he said, 'and I suppose that is why he is paying such a generous sum for the recovery of you and the emeralds.'

'I have already told you sir, I did not steal the emeralds.'

'Just the diamonds that were found within your chamber.'

'I have no knowledge of how the diamonds came to be so hidden. Some other hand must have placed them there.'

'That is what they all say.'

'It is the truth.' She held her head high as if she were innocent, acting every inch a lady wronged. It irritated Wolf.

'Stealing from the dowager while you were acting as her companion.' He made a tut-tut sound. 'Such behaviour is to be expected from low-class riffraff such as myself, but better is expected of the likes of you. All your pa's money not enough for you, Miss Meadowfield, that you had to rob Evedon's old sick mam? No wonder he's mad at you.'

Normally by now they were trying to bargain with him, swearing their very souls to the devil and offering Wolf the world if they thought it would win their freedom. But Wolf had never retrieved a lady before. He wondered what Rosalind Meadowfield would offer him. Her rich father's money, or something else? He let his eyes range over the shapeless cloak that hid the figure beneath. Not that he would accept her offer, of course; he never did. Wolf hated the idea of being bought as much as he hated women like Miss Meadowfield.

'I am innocent.'

Wolf gave a dry humourless laugh. 'Of course, you are.' He placed a slice of ham upon a piece of bread and, watching her surreptitiously as if he had not the slightest interest, began to eat.

The colour had drained from the woman's face to render it pale as she leaned back against the whitewashed wall as though to merge into it and disappear, her eyes staring into the fire.

'Mr Stewart is expecting me. He shall enquire as to my absence.'

'Mr Stewart has been informed of your situation,' said Wolf coldly.

'What did you tell him?' Her expression was pained.

'I told him nothing.' Wolf chewed at his bread. 'Evedon has taken care of Hunter.'

She seemed to sag slightly against the wall. 'As he means to take care of me.' Her gaze was distant and her words were whispered so quietly that he only just heard them.

Wolf did not allow himself to soften. She had made her bed, and now she must lie in it, he thought. He had finished his food before she spoke again.

'How did you find me?'

'You left behind the newspaper. It was not difficult to discover which advertisement you had torn from it.'

She closed her eyes at that and was silent. When she opened them again she asked, 'Who are you Mr Wolversley? *What* are you? A Bow Street runner?'

'Nothing so official. Just a man that Evedon is paying to deliver you back to him.' He noticed how Kempster watched her.

Campbell sipped from the battered mug, an amused

expression upon his face. 'Ocht, he's just being modest. We're in the retrieval business, so to speak, and we're mighty good at retrieving. Some might call us thief-takers, Miss Meadowfield.'

'Do not take me back to him…please.' She spoke the words quietly.

The Scotsman gave her a contrite smile. 'I'm afraid that's our job, lassie.'

'Save your pleading for Evedon, Miss Meadowfield,' said Wolf. 'It is most assuredly wasted upon us.'

Campbell glanced away, an expression of awkwardness on his face.

Wolf took another sip of his ale. Her greed would cost her dear, he thought, but that was not his or Struan's problem to worry over, besides her type deserved to pay the price. He glanced round at the woman.

'Our journey starts at first light. You are returning to London come what may, Miss Meadowfield. I care not whether you eat, but be warned that starving yourself into a faint shall not delay our progress. I'll tie you across my saddle if I have to.'

Wolf said nothing more, just turned his attention to Campbell and Kempster, conversing with them in low tones, while the woman made her way hesitantly across the room to sit down upon a stool at the table and eat a little of the remaining bread, ham and cheese, all the while keeping a cautious eye on her captors.

Rosalind watched uneasily while the men made up makeshift blanket beds, rolling out four grey blankets side by side over the bare wooden floorboards before the fireplace. Her eyes measured the distance between her stool and the cottage door.

'Do not even think about it.' She heard the warning that edged Wolf's voice.

The pale eyes glanced up from where he had removed the chairs and was laying his coat out as a bed-cover in their place, and she wondered how he had known what she was thinking.

Rosalind did not move, just sat there, with a growing anxiety, watching their movements. She knew little about men. Her brother had long since disappeared, and with the disgrace of her father's execution and the lack of money, there had never been any question of a Season for either her or her sister. Her experience of men was limited to the few older gentlemen she met as Lady Evedon's companion, and Lord Evedon, of course. She bit at her lower lip.

'You need not concern yourself with me. I will sleep here on this stool.'

Wolf raised a sardonic brow and looked at her. 'You will sleep on the floor alongside the rest of us.'

'But…' she felt the heat of a blush flood her cheeks.

From across the room she heard Campbell chuckle, and from the corner of her eye she saw him shake his head.

'You need not worry, Mr Campbell and I not in the habit of *liasing* with the criminals that we're apprehending…no matter what they offer us in exchange for their freedom,' said Wolf.

She felt the blush deepen at his horrible insinuation.

The flicker of the flames lit golden highlights through his hair and emphasized the mocking tilt of his mouth. It was a hard face, a face which looked as if it felt no fear but knew well how to instil it. He made Kempster's pretty-boy looks appear weak and effeminate in comparison. And yet for all his harshness, there was something compelling about him, something darkly attractive. She shivered and wrapped the cloak more tightly around herself, trying to hide her vulnerability and anxiety.

Wolf walked towards her, and her eyes shifted to the coil of thin rope he held in his hand.

She rose slowly, warily, ready to flee.

'Come now, Miss Meadowfield. You do not think we mean to leave you free to run away again, do you?'

'You do not need to tie me. I will not run away, I give you my word.'

'Forgive me if I place little trust in your word, miss.'

Her eyes darted to the doorway and she tensed. His hand reached for her and she tried to rush past him, but he side-stepped, catching her to himself.

'No!' She struggled to pull free, but he held her, gently yet firmly, until at last she realized that her effort was in vain and she stilled. 'Please,' she whispered, unable to bear the thought of being trussed and completely at the mercy of these men.

He seemed to pause, and for a moment she thought he would heed her plea, but then he gestured Campbell over, and the two men bound her hands behind her back. It was Wolf who tied the knots, testing the tension of the rope before he did so, slipping his fingers between the coarse hemp and the skin of her wrists to ensure that it was not tied too tight.

He led her over to the blanket closest to the fire and farthest from the door, pushing her, not roughly, down to sit upon the grey wool. Then he bound her ankles, catching the rope over the soft leather of her boots before folding a second blanket for her pillow.

'You have no need of it as a cover; your fancy cloak is warm enough.' He stepped away and did not look back at her.

Rosalind lay there for a long time, just staring into the flames and listening to the men's breathing in the single room of the cottage. She was acutely aware of Wolf lying so close behind her back. It seemed that she could almost feel the heat of him across the small space that divided them. The floorboards pressed hard against her hip and shoulder bones, and her limbs were uncomfortable from the restriction of her bindings, but the fatigue that had weighed upon her earlier had disappeared. Her mind was wide awake, flitting with thoughts…and fears.

She had trusted in the letter, guarding it as a talisman, believing that its presence would prevent Evedon involving the law. And indeed it had done just that. But she had not banked on Evedon hiring a couple of ruffians to pursue her…and the letter. She berated her naivety. Of course Evedon would not just let her go free. She had been a fool to believe it. He wanted his letter back. And now all her plans and her hopes lay in ruins. The men would take her back to London. Evedon would have his letter and, once it was safe in his possession, he would send her to hang, not caring who she told of his secret. Without proof, her words would be taken as the rantings of a thief, nothing more. But he need not fear, she thought bitterly, for even then she would not tell. Regardless of what Lord Evedon did to her, she had no stomach to destroy his mother.

They would hang her. Her belly tightened with the dread of it. She knew all that would happen, had read the old newspaper report a hundred times over. And all because she had been caught by Wolf and the Scotsman.

In the quietness of the night, she could hear the catching snore of Campbell masking any sound the others might have made. She eased herself round on to her right-hand side and studied her captors.

Farthest away from the fire, Pete Kempster was curled facing the opposite wall, his body rising and falling in tiny motions with the shallow steady breaths of sleep. Next

came Campbell, lying on his back, mouth open, face slack.
And then there was Wolf. He lay facing her, eyes closed,
breath quiet and even. The flickering light of the flames
was warm and golden, softening his face, erasing all trace
of mockery and contempt, so that he was quite the most
handsome man she had ever seen, and she could not help
but stare. She studied the strong, lean angles of his face, the
dimpled cleft within the squareness of his chin, her gaze
moving to the pale skin of the scar that flicked across his
cheek, wondering as to the violence that had caused such
a wound. Her eyes slid back up to his.

The breath caught in her throat. She froze, her heart suddenly thudding with a fury, her face burning with embarrassment. For the silver eyes were looking right back at
her, filled with warning—and something else.

Her blood was rushing so loud she was sure that he must
hear it. And yet she could not look away, trapped as she
was in the moment, transfixed by his gaze.

He did not say a single word. He did not need to.

The moment stretched between them. Campbell's soft
snores went unnoticed. Everything seemed to fade to nothing so that there seemed only Wolf and the power of the
intensity that blazed in his gaze.

At last she managed to look away. She rolled to face the
fire and lay as before, eyes open, aware more than ever of
Wolf behind her: a man, dangerous and awake. The very
air seemed to vibrate with the tension that emanated from
him, and her skin tingled with it. This was the man who
would take her back to Evedon. This was the man with
whom she must travel the length of the country. And she
trembled at the thought. Lord save me, she pled a silent
prayer, from Evedon…and from Wolf.

Chapter Three

Wolf woke at dawn to the sweet scent of a woman. He smiled and, still drowsy with sleep, reached a hand out to curl her soft body into his. His fingers contacted the thick fur lining of a cloak, a covering, but no woman. He cracked his eyes open and all of it came flooding back, Evedon, the job, Rosalind Meadowfield.

She was lying with her back snug against the hearth, curled on her side facing him, and he could see that in sleep her face lost its suspicious frown so that she looked younger than the twenty-five years Evedon had told him, and extremely innocent. But Wolf was aware of how very deceptive looks could be. Her hair was long and mussed, framing her pale face with its dark tendrils. Her cloak had become unfastened in the night and covered more of the floor than the woman. His eyes travelled lower to what the cloak had previously hidden, to the plain blue dress, prim and somewhat old-fashioned and, although clearly expensive, hardly robust enough for the journey ahead.

Probably used to being ferried around in Lady Evedon's fine carriage. She'd learn how the other half travelled long before they reached London, he thought grimly.

His eyes lingered on the pale slim neck and the way that her bodice strained tight across her breasts where her arms were bound behind her back. He thought of Evedon's insistence on discretion. Just the same as the rest of the aristos, Evedon wanted his affairs kept quiet. Wolf supposed that it wouldn't do for it to get out that his mother's genteel companion had fleeced her and done a runner. He wondered fleetingly what Evedon would do once he had her. Arrange something between him and the woman's father… or perhaps even with the woman herself? The latter thought stirred an unease within him. Deliberately he thrust it away. What Evedon did was his own business and, besides, Miss Meadowfield had a rich papa to protect her well enough.

Evedon had told him that Miss Meadowfield was from a wealthy genteel family. That fact alone had been enough to convince Wolf to take the job. It did not hurt that Evedon had offered a considerable reward for the quiet return of the woman. Evedon must want her back badly. And just for a moment, Wolf could almost feel sorry for her. Almost. But then he reminded himself of what she was—a gentlewoman who had used those around her—and Wolf knew well from personal experience the damage such people could do. His lip curled at the memory from across the years. And when he looked again at Rosalind Meadowfield, any hint of compassion had vanished and his heart was hard.

The woman seemed to be in the depths of sleep with no sign of waking. The shadows beneath her eyes suggested that it had not been so the night through and he remembered the way she had studied him as she lay sleepless by the fireplace. Campbell and Kempster still slept soundly behind him. None of them stirred as he slipped outside into the chill.

The darkness of the night sky showed the first hint of lightening from the east, its deep blue colouration fading. Wolf knew that dawn would come quickly and that, in order to cover enough miles, they would have to be on the road heading south before day lit the sky fully. He turned back to the cottage.

The woman and Kempster still slept, but Campbell was up, yawning and rubbing his hands through his hair. Wolf gestured towards the door and the two men disappeared back outside, walking away from the cottage and into the cover of the trees before they spoke.

'What is the plan, then?' Campbell yawned again.

'We get on the road as soon as possible and start heading south. The woman will slow our speed a little, but we should still be able to cover about seventy miles a day. At that rate we'll be back in London in, say, a week's time.'

'And then we'll be in the money.' Campbell rubbed his hands together.

Wolf smiled. 'We will indeed.'

Campbell relieved himself behind the thick trunk of a tree. 'Do you think the lassie could be telling the truth when she said that she didnae thieve from Evedon?'

Wolf's lip curled with disdain. 'She's lying. The guilt was written all over her face. Some expensive clothes and a posh accent, and she's got your head turned.'

'You forgot the pretty face,' teased Campbell, 'expensive clothes, posh accent and a pretty face.'

Wolf gave a laugh and shook his head. 'We best get a move on. You see to the horses. I'll get Kempster and the woman moving.'

'Right you are, Lieutenant.'

Wolf peered round at the big Scotsman with a baleful expression.

'Sorry, it just slipped out.' Campbell's grin held nothing of contrition. 'Old habits die hard.'

Rosalind awoke with the sensation that someone had stroked her cheek. And then she remembered where she was and the nature of her predicament, and her heart began to hurry. Her eyes flicked open, fearing what she would find.

A man was half crouched, half kneeling by her side.

Sleep left her in an instant. Her gaze flew up to find his face.

'Awake at last, Miss Meadowfield?' said Kempster.

'What are you doing?' The words were a shocked whisper.

'What do you think? This is not Evedon House. You can't be lying abed half the day. I'm wakenin' you, sweetheart.'

His use of the endearment gave her a jolt of shock. She did not meet his gaze, just tried to sit up, wincing at the ache in her arms and shoulders as she moved. 'I am quite awake now, thank you, Mr Kempster.' Her voice was cold, offering the rebuke that her words had not.

'So I see,' he said, and, slipping a hand inside his jacket, produced a knife, its blade straight and wicked.

Rosalind's heart hammered harder. Her eyes slid slowly from the blade to Kempster's face, and such was the dryness in her throat that she could only stare at him and utter not a single word.

The clear blue eyes met hers. The knife raised in his hand.

Her breath held.

His mouth curved and with one swift strike, he severed the rope binding her ankles.

The gasp escaped her. She could not hold it back any more than she could stop the instinctive closing of her eyes or the way that she flinched at his motion.

He sliced the rope from her wrists and hauled her to her feet. 'That's better, ain't it, miss?' He smiled.

And when he moved away, she saw Wolf watching them from the doorway. 'We leave in five minutes,' Wolf said, and his gaze was cool and appraising.

Kempster's blanket was already rolled and stowed away in his bag. He carried the bag out to his horse.

Wolf scooped his and Campbell's blankets up.

'Is there somewhere I might be able to attend to my toilette?' Rosalind got to her feet, smoothing out the wrinkles in her skirt as she did so.

'See to your business outside behind a tree like the rest of us.'

'And water for washing?'

He raised an eyebrow and stared at her in mocking disbelief. 'Shall I fetch it warmed and ready for you, m'lady?'

She felt her cheeks grow heated at his tone and glanced away as she made her way towards the door.

He followed, the tread of his boots close behind.

She stopped in the doorway, rubbing the stiffness from her wrists, and looked up at him with as much courage as she could muster.

'Please grant me some little dignity, Mr Wolversley.' Her heart was racing with her own boldness, but she knew that what she did now would set a precedent for the rest of the journey.

His silver gaze was searing, stilling the movement of her hands, before it rose to meet her eyes. A moment passed, and then another, and her heart skittered all the faster, so that she remembered last night and the intensity of his gaze and the look of his face without its harsh mask of cynicism. And she thought from the look in his eyes that he remembered it too. Finally, he gave a small acknowledgement of his head.

'Play me for a fool, Miss Meadowfield, and I'll forget all about your dignity.'

She nodded her reply.

Over at the edge of the clearing, Kempster and Campbell were seeing to the horses. She walked in the opposite direction, glancing back at the cottage when she reached the trees. Wolf still stood within the door frame watching her.

Even across the distance that separated them, she could feel his gaze upon her, brooding and watchful. She shivered and disappeared into the trees.

Wolf packed up the rest of the bags, keeping one eye, through the open door, on the patch of woodland into which Miss Meadowfield had disappeared. If she did not appear in the next few minutes, he would go out there and fetch her back, and never mind her damned dignity. He remembered her lying sleepless by his side in the night, and the way she had looked at him; her eyes not brown as he had first thought, but a strange mix of green and brown and gold, and filled with shock and fear and such beguiling innocence as to persuade any man. But Wolf was not fooled. He did not trust her. He had learned a long time ago that those who appeared the most genteel, the most respectable, the very epitome of everything that gentility encompassed, were the most corrupt. Such ugly beautiful people. A golden gilding upon a rotten core, just as it was with Miss Meadowfield.

Such a proper gentle companion that she had exploited her employer's weakness. The prospect of a ruined reputation would drive her to desperation; she would attempt an escape before too long, of that he was sure. And he would be ready for her.

Her delivery to Evedon would earn Struan and him a nice fat fee, but his main reason for taking the job was for the satisfaction of ensuring that at least one of their kind would be brought to face the consequences of their actions. He smiled at the thought of that, and the hurt that was buried deep within him eased a little.

By the time that she appeared a few minutes later, the baggage had been strapped on to the horses and they were almost ready to leave. The worst of the wrinkles had been smoothed from her dress. He could see that she had tidied her hair; its long dark curls were caught and coiled into a severe knot at the nape of her neck beneath her mid-blue bonnet.

She stopped, then backed away and stared at the four horses. 'Where is the cart? I-I thought we would be travelling by cart.'

Kempster smiled ever so slightly. 'We travel by horseback—Mr Wolversley's orders.'

It seemed to Wolf that her face paled, and he wondered as to the reason. All women of her station could ride. Their parents bought them ponies as children, whereas in the streets of York, where Wolf had grown up, the children were lucky to have parents or food, never mind ponies.

He thought he saw something akin to terror flicker in her eyes. He frowned as the possibility struck him. 'You can ride, can you not?'

She gave no answer, just continued to stand stock-still and stare at the horses. It seemed to Wolf that she was holding her breath.

'Miss Meadowfield,' he prompted in a harsh voice.

Campbell and Kempster looked on in silence.

'I…I…' She did not drag her eyes from the horses to look at him.

'If you cannot ride, I shall take you up with me.'

She gave a slight shake of her head. Her cheeks were so white that he thought she might faint. 'I can ride,' she said so quietly that he had to strain to hear the words.

'Are you unwell, Miss Meadowfield?' he asked.

There was a pause before she answered in a calm voice that belied the rigid stance of her body. 'I am quite well, thank you, Mr Wolversley.'

Just a bloody ploy to delay us, he thought but he saw the way she leaned her weight back against the tree trunk behind her. In truth, Wolf conceded, the woman looked as if she were about to faint.

'Then what seems to be the problem?'

She hesitated again, before taking a deep breath and moving her gaze to meet his. 'There is no problem. I felt a little faint, that is all. The feeling has passed. I am better now.'

'There is some bread left from last night. Eat that. It will help,' said Wolf.

She shook her head. 'No thank you. As I said, I am feeling well enough now.'

'Then you will delay us no further.' Wolf turned away and swung himself up on to his horse.

Campbell and Kempster followed suit.

Wolf watched as the woman slowly pushed herself away from the tree and began to walk. There was a grim determination about her as she crossed the forest clearing. She stopped just short of the small bay mare that stood patiently waiting.

Wolf knew that she would be used to some servant

rushing to help her climb upon the horse's back. Even the sight of the sidesaddle irritated him. It was yet another sign of her status and all that she was. Common women rode astride the same as any man. She stood there, close by the horse's side, neither attempting to clamber up, nor asking for assistance.

'We'll be here all day at this rate,' muttered Kempster.

Wolf said nothing, knowing that Evedon's man only spoke what he himself was thinking. Yet he wanted her to know what it was like to survive without servants rushing to dance upon her every whim. He'd be damned if he'd climb down there and act like her lackey, so Wolf sat stubborn and silent, and waited, allowing the woman's discomfort to stretch.

It was Campbell who slipped down from his mount and moved to help her.

The big Scotsman stroked a hand against the mare's neck. 'She's a docile wee thing,' he said, and then bent and offered Miss Meadowfield his linked hands to use for her footing.

'Thank you,' she said quietly, and with a foot in Campbell's hands and a hand against his shoulder she mounted the small horse.

They moved off slowly.

Miss Meadowfield sat on her horse tensely, and although she looked ill at ease in the saddle, it was clear that she could indeed ride.

A delaying tactic, indeed, surmised Wolf sourly, and met Campbell's eye. They walked slowly and in silence through the trees and out on to the country road that lay beyond.

Wolf rode out in front, Campbell and Kempster at the rear. In between was Rosalind. She was managing quite admirably with the mare's gentle walk until they came out on to the narrow country road and Wolf kicked his horse first to a trot and then a canter.

Rosalind's horse came to a halt as her fingers tightened around the reins and she felt the panicked thudding of her heart. Her palms beneath the fine leather gloves were clammy. She wetted her dry lips and tried to swallow but her throat was so dry that its sides seemed to be in danger of sticking together.

Campbell and Kempster came abreast with her and she saw Wolf glance round, reining his mount in as he realized that her horse had stopped. He reeled around and drew up before her, his horse frisky with impatience.

'You are trying my patience, Miss Meadowfield. We've Gretna to reach by nightfall, so start riding.' Wolf's face was hard and uncompromising.

Rosalind made no move. Just the thought of galloping brought waves of nausea rolling up from her stomach. She swallowed them down, forced herself to breathe deeply, slowly. *I can do this,* she willed herself, fighting down the panic. The urge to slide down off the horse's back and run away was overwhelming. She glanced longingly down at the solidity of the road's rutted surface.

Wolf frowned and brought his horse in close by her side, scrutinizing her.

Rosalind averted her face, frightened of what he might see.

But Wolf leaned across, touched his fingers to her chin, forcing her face round to his.

His eyes were no longer silver but the same pale grey as the daylight. 'Any more delays and I'll lead the damn horse for you.' He released her and moved away.

She saw the cold dislike in his gaze and the bitter mocking tilt of his mouth and heard the promise in his voice. He would take her reins without a further thought and then the small mare's speed would be completely out of her control. Rosalind knew that she could not let that happen and she'd be damned if she'd give him the satisfaction of knowing of her fear. Deep within, she felt her temper ignite and flare. The anger welled up strong and fast, so that her breathing turned short and ragged. She glared at him with ferocity. Damn Wolf, she thought, Damn his arrogant, abrasive soul. And she did not care that she was cursing; she did not care about anything at all, except her fury at the man before her and her need to escape him.

'There would be no delay had my saddle been fitted properly,' she heard herself say in an imperious voice she barely recognized. 'It is slipping. And Lord Evedon wishes me to break my neck upon a scaffold, not for your incompetence to lead to me snapping it in a fall upon this road.' Courage, Rosalind, she thought, for once in your life, have courage.

Wolf scowled at her tone.

She forced herself to sit very still as Wolf and the others jumped down from horses. It was Wolf himself that came towards her.

Wait, she cautioned herself, *wait,* and her heart was thudding wildly with the audacity of what she was about to do. And she did wait, waited until he had almost reached her, until he was extending his hand towards her to lift her down.

Her fingers pulled gently at the leather of the reins, and the mare stepped round until she was facing the opposite direction of travel to the other three horses, as if she were nervous and eager to be moving once more.

'Keep her still,' Wolf snapped.

Rosalind felt a stab of satisfaction as her fingers tightened on the reins and she suddenly kicked the mare to a canter and careered off down the road.

'Hell!' she heard his grunted curse, and the men's shocked voices, but she was already leaving him behind as she sped off into the distance. Her heart was racing now in earnest and her mouth dry as a bone, but she knew that he was coming after her and that she would have to ride faster to outrun him.

Too soon she heard the rhythmic gallop of a single horse behind her. She glanced back to see Wolf on his great grey stallion storming after her.

'Faster!' she urged the little mare, her fear of the man pursuing her greater than her fear of the horse. She was galloping, clinging on for dear life, feeling precarious in the saddle as the road rushed by beneath her. She focused her mind and tried not to think about how fast she was going, tried not to think about the horse at all. A glance behind and she saw that Wolf was gaining on her. She kicked her heels by the mare's side, urging her to gallop faster, praying that he would not catch her.

But it was too late. A few seconds more and Wolf drew alongside.

She tried to veer away, but there was nowhere to go other than the ditch and the hedge at the side of the road.

The mare grew confused and started to panic, just as the horse had panicked all those years ago, edging towards the ditch despite all of Rosalind's efforts to guide her away. Rosalind tugged hard on the reins, knowing that she had to slow the horse's reckless pace. But the mare did not respond, just galloped even faster, her eyes wild with fear.

Rosalind felt her seat begin to slip in truth. It was the nightmare from across the years all over again. In her mind's eye, she saw Elizabeth's body slip from the saddle and she knew the terrible fate that would follow. She could not scream, could not make a single sound. And still the mare pounded on along the road, and still Rosalind pulled uselessly at the reins, until the leather made her fingers red and swollen. And then another pair of hands were beside hers, taking the reins from her. Wolf. And the mare seemed to respond to his touch, to his strong, calm voice.

'Whoa there, lass, whoa.'

The little horse began to slow.

He kept on talking. Rosalind could not hear the words, just his voice, low in timbre and reassuring, smoothing away the panic, loosening that terrible tight knot of fear. The mare finally came to a stop, standing still while Wolf's hands stroked smoothly at her neck.

'Poor lass,' he was saying softly, 'you're safe now.'

Rosalind felt something of her terror lift away, watching the mesmerizing movement of his hand and listening to the calming tone of his voice. She forgot that she had been trying to escape, forgot too that Wolf had just stopped her. Her only thought as she slipped from the saddle was that he had saved her. The relief was overwhelming, and, light-headed with it, her legs seemed to melt beneath her, and she stumbled, falling down on her knees. She was alive, alive and unhurt, and she reached forward and clutched at the road's dirt surface, revelling in the feel of its solid security. She was dimly aware of him guiding the mare away from the ditch, but she could not look to see, could do nothing other than cling to the road.

'What the hell do you think you're playing at?' A pair of dusty leather boots appeared on the dirt before her.

She raised her eyes to look up at him.

'You risked not only yourself, but a good horse, with

your foolishness.' The calm lilt of his voice was gone, only anger remained in its place. His eyes blazed with it, and appeared a deep dark grey as if all of the storm clouds had gathered ready to unleash their fury. He crouched low and looked into her eyes.

Rosalind felt the fear quiver deep within her.

'If you run, I will find you,' he said. 'As Campbell said, we are very good at retrieving. So do not waste your time or mine trying to escape.' He spoke quietly, softly almost, as if the anger was all reined in and the intensity of his words was all the greater for it.

His gaze held hers and she could not look away. 'Whatever foolish plans you may have in your head, Miss Meadowfield, the truth is that you shall not prevent me delivering you to Evedon. You do not wish to go, but you should have thought of the consequences before you stole from him.' He stood upright and reached his hand down towards hers to pull her up.

Rosalind stared at his hand, at the long strong fingers with their weathered tan. It was the first time since he had collected her in the cart from Blairadie Inn on Munnoch Moor that he had made any gesture of assistance. She turned her face away and, ignoring the dizziness in her head, rose rather unsteadily to her feet, alone.

'You know nothing of the truth,' she said and, because her eyes were blurring with tears, her voice was angry. 'Nothing at all.'

'I know a damn sight more of truth than you do, miss. I know of children who are starving as you sit at your fancy table laden with food. I know of soldiers, without eyes or limbs, who beg for a few coppers while you drive hurriedly by in your fancy carriage. I know of women who sell their bodies to any man that will have them so that their children might survive. And that men are hanged for stealing a loaf of bread to feed their families while you chat oblivious with Lady Evedon and her cronies over tea and cakes. This is the truth, Miss Meadowfield and what do you know of it?' His eyes were hard as flint. 'Nothing, I'll wager. So do not dare to lecture me.'

They stared at one another, the air thick with their animosity.

'Get back on your horse and try not to terrify the poor beast this time.'

Rosalind's stomach tightened. 'I would prefer to walk.' She looked away and forced her chin up, determined that he would not see her fear.

'We have not got all day, so mount the damn horse.'

Her heart was thudding fast and frenzied. Another wave of dizziness swept over her. She closed her eyes until it passed.

'Miss Meadowfield.'

His voice sounded closer and when she opened her eyes he had stepped towards her.

'I will not,' she said, rather shocked at her own blatant defiance.

'Get back on that horse or I'll sling you face down across its saddle like a bag of grain and tie you in place.'

She felt the blood drain from her face, felt her stomach clench hard at the prospect. 'You would not.'

He smiled his cold cynical smile. 'Oh, I would do so most gladly, Miss Meadowfield.'

Her legs were trembling and her mouth was so dry that she could no longer swallow. He would do it, she realized. She felt the nausea roll in her stomach and tried to halt the panic before it ran out of control. There was little choice, so she turned and forced herself to walk towards the horse. She took a deep breath and, hoisting her skirt up, let him help her up into the saddle. He took his own saddle and, with her reins secure in his hand, led her back to where Campbell and Kempster waited.

And all that Rosalind could think was that she had never met a more hateful man.

Chapter Four

The sky was beginning to darken by the time that Wolf led them into the yard of Gretna Hall. Her arms were aching, her backside was aching, her thighs were aching. Indeed, it seemed to Rosalind that there was not a bit of her that was not in pain. Her fear and anger had long since dwindled, and she was so tired that she did not think about being frightened of the little horse beneath her. So sore were certain areas of Rosalind's body that she slipped to the ground without looking for anyone to help her, and stood there in blessed relief that the saddle was no longer beneath her.

She felt Wolf's grip upon her arm escorting her with him across the yard and into the inn, but she was too tired to protest.

The inn was busy, most of the tables in the public room were filled, mainly with men. Men stood about the bar drinking their tankards of ale, turning curious eyes to the new arrivals. She heard the low tone of Wolf's voice to the landlord, and was aware of the exchange of money. She was aware, too, of the way that the landlord's gaze flicked over her before moving on to Kempster and Campbell and finally returning to Wolf, with unspoken speculation. But whatever the man saw in Wolf's face made him nod his acquiescence and turn to fetch the keys for the rooms. He showed them up a small narrow staircase to a narrow corridor along which several doors could be seen. The two furthest doors led to the rooms for which Wolf had paid.

They were still standing in the second room into which the landlord had shown them. Wolf scanned around, peered from the window then inspected the door.

'Dump the baggage and head downstairs. We'll eat first.' The bags were dropped on to the bare floorboards with a thud. He looked at Rosalind. 'I'll wait outside the door for you while you attend to your toilette.'

She nodded, knowing this was the best offer she was going to get, and watched the three men leave. As Wolf shut the door behind him, his eyes met hers in steely warning, and then he was gone.

Rosalind just stood there and stared at the closed door, hearing the other door open and close across the passage way, hearing the murmur of their voices. Her eyes shifted to the travelling bag on the floor just before her where Wolf had dropped it and she shifted it to lie across the door, as if she could block Wolf out with the bag. Hurriedly, she attended to her needs, washed her face and hands and tidied her hair.

He was leaning against the wall in the corridor when she opened the door, waiting as if patiently but it was not patience that she saw in his eyes when she looked at him. Not a word passed between them. A single movement of his head gestured towards the staircase. She began to walk along the dimly lit passage. There was the sound of a key turning in a lock before she heard his footsteps follow and sensed he was close. At the end of the landing she hesitated, and he passed her, taking the lead as they trod down the uneven staircase.

They were halfway down when he turned suddenly to her, surprising Rosalind so that she was too close to him. Standing on the stair above his, she found her eyes level with his for the first time. The light of the nearby flickering candles softened the angles of his face and made his eyes appear a smoky grey. He was so close that she could see the individual lashes, so close that it was all she could do to stifle a gasp.

She made to step back but her foot caught against the high-angled stair and only the sudden curve of his arm around her waist saved her from falling. He did not remove his hand, just left it where it was resting lightly against the small of her back. He stared at her, and she saw surprise in his eyes—and something else too, something that she could not name but that sent a quiver snaking throughout her body. He stared at her, and the moment stretched long so that she could feel the hard rapid thump of her heart and feel her blood coursing too fast.

The look of harsh cynicism had gone, leaving his expression unreadable. His breath was warm against her cheek, stirring the fine tendrils of hair that hung in spirals before her ears. The scent of soap and leather and masculinity filled her nose, and her heart tripped even faster so that she could hear the slight raggedness of her breath between them. His hold was so light that she could have easily broken free from it, yet she just stood there, as if entranced by the look in his eyes. It seemed to Rosalind that some strange force had come over her, enslaving her thinking, her body, so that she could do nothing other than stare at him. And the smoky eyes stared right back, and where his palm touched light against her back, her skin seemed to burn and pulse.

And as suddenly as it had arrived, it disappeared. She saw the moment that his eyes changed, reverting to a cool silver. He dropped his hand from her as if scalded, and she saw the flash of anger and loathing in his gaze. His expression was once more harsh and determined.

'Behave yourself down here, Miss Meadowfield,' he growled.

She was still reeling from the shock, not of his anger, but of what had gone before. 'I will not deign to reply to that, sir,' she managed.

She saw the slight curl of his lip. 'You do not deign to do much do you? Besides help yourself to other people's valuables.'

And then he turned and walked on, as if nothing at all had happened.

Rosalind stood stock still, trembling and shocked. What on earth had just happened? Why had she not moved away? Why had she let him stare at her in that…that inappropriate manner? Her heart was still beating too fast and her cheeks flushed with embarrassment.

He had reached the bottom of the staircase before he realized that she had not moved. The silver gaze met hers.

'Miss Meadowfield.' The words were uttered so softly that they barely carried up the stairs, yet the threat contained in them was louder than had he shouted at the top of his voice. The skin on the nape of her neck prickled and she hurried down after him, her hand gripping the banister rail.

Campbell and Kempster were seated over in a corner.

As she crossed the busy room with Wolf, she felt all eyes upon them.

'We ordered some mutton stew and chicken pies,' said Campbell in his gentle burr. 'Couldnae wait all night for yous to come down.' He grinned. 'We've a jug of ale for while we wait.'

A serving wench, with what looked to Rosalind to be an indecently revealing décolletage, brought cutlery and plates to the table.

'We are to eat…in here?' Rosalind had never eaten in the public room of an inn before. She glanced anxiously around.

'The food will be the same whether we eat here or waste our money paying for a private parlour,' said Wolf as he gestured for her to take the seat beside Campbell on the inside of the table.

She did as she bid, trying not to notice the less than subtle interest from the people seated around them. From the corner of her eye she saw the landlord make his way over.

'The rooms are to your liking, sir…' His eyes dropped to her hand, pausing just for a second or two on the bare fingers of her left hand. Rosalind held her head up defiantly, determined not to be shamed even though she knew what the man must think her. But the heat in her cheeks betrayed her.

Wolf gave a curt nod.

'And your lady?' The landlord persevered.

Wolf turned a glacial eye upon him.

The landlord paled. 'I'll see to your food, sir.'

Rosalind dropped her gaze, wishing that the ground would open up and swallow her. Was it her imagination or was there a lull in the surrounding buzz of conversation?

Only after the landlord had departed did she whisper furiously at Wolf, 'You should have told him I was not your lady.'

'So concerned for his good opinion, Miss Meadow-field?' He smiled a cold mocking smile.

Her cheeks burned all the hotter. 'No, but he will think the worst of me. My reputation—' She heard Kempster snigger, and broke off what she had been about to say, knowing how ridiculous her reaction was—for she had no reputation left to lose.

'Pray continue. Your reputation…?' Wolf raised an eyebrow.

She cast her gaze down, and spoke the words quietly, 'I meant only that I did not wish him to believe me something that I am not.'

'I see.'

She raised her eyes to his.

'You wished me to tell him that you are not my lady but a thief.' His words were spoken easily enough and in no hush.

'Ssh! People will hear.'

'Will they indeed?'

'They are beginning to stare,' she whispered in a panic.

'Let them,' he said. 'I am quite used to it.'

She heard the slight bitterness in his voice, and her eyes traced the scar that marked the honeyed skin of his cheek. Shame washed over her at her insensitivity and she bit at her lower lip. 'I did not mean…that is to say I was not referring to—'

His eyes met hers, and all of the words dried upon her tongue.

The awkwardness was broken by the arrival of the food. There was no more talk as the men devoured the stew and potatoes and cabbage and pie as if they had not eaten for a week, nor did the fact that it was scalding hot seem to slow them down any. The smell alone caused Rosalind's stomach to rumble; indeed the mutton stew was thick and tasty, and the pie hot and flavoursome. But she ate little of them, and merely toyed with the rest. In truth her stomach was too tense for food.

Wolf said nothing to her but she frequently felt his gaze on her throughout the meal, which seemed only to make her stomach flutter all the more, until at last they were done. Leaving Kempster and Campbell to another jug of ale, he rose and took her with him.

Within the small bedchamber Wolf felt a stab of annoyance at the wariness in the woman's eyes. As if he had no sense of honour as a man, as if he would force himself upon her like some kind of animal. Scarred or not, Wolf had no trouble finding willing women. And as for the forcing, she'd do better to look at her own class for that, he thought bitterly, and all of the memories were back again.

'Be ready to leave at first light,' he said, knowing that his voice was unnecessarily harsh. Indeed, all of his treatment of her had been too harsh. He knew that, but his heart was still hard, and more so because of his reaction to her upon the staircase earlier that evening.

She looked at him, and in the candlelight her eyes were as soft and dark as a woodland floor. He saw the flash of relief in them; she that had cared so much that people did not think her his woman. 'Good night, Mr Wolversley,' she said, and he had the sensation that she was dismissing him as if he were a servant. The thought irked him more than it should have. He would leave when he was damn well ready, and not at her say so. He stood where he was.

'Next time, eat your dinner rather than playing with it. People starve while you waste good food.'

'What I eat is none of your concern, sir.'

'On the contrary, Miss Meadowfield.' He walked up

right up to her, feeling a savage stab of satisfaction when she stepped back to maintain the distance between them. He saw the fear dart into her eyes, but she held his gaze. 'Until I hand you over to Evedon, you are mine and you will do as I say.'

She shivered. 'Evedon will see me hanged. Your threats mean nothing in comparison with that.'

He knew that Evedon would not have her hang. He doubted if the earl even meant to report her, not when he was so concerned with keeping the matter quiet. Evedon would probably be happy with the return of his emeralds, a word in Miss Meadowfield's father's ear and the removal of the lady herself from his house. Still, Wolf had no intention of enlightening Miss Meadowfield to those facts.

'There are worse things in life than death: things that you in your fine clothes, with your fine life, could not even begin to imagine. Sometimes the hangman's noose can be a blessed relief.' His voice was quiet. Wolf knew from bitter experience the truth in those words. 'Good night, Miss Meadowfield,' he said, and then turned and walked away.

As he closed the door behind him, she had not moved, just stood exactly as he had left her, staring after him. The look in her eyes made him want to call back the cruel words he had just uttered and made him think that he really was a bastard in every sense of the word.

Rosalind waited until she heard the key turn in the lock and the booted footsteps trace their path down the corridor before she allowed herself to sag against the wall, closing her eyes as she did so. Her legs trembled so much that she had been surprised that he did not hear her knees knocking together. She slid down the wall and crouched, wrapping her arms around her shins. And she wondered, really wondered, what on earth she was going to do. She had been so sure of her disappearance in Scotland. And now… Wolf's words played again in her mind. *There are worse things in life than death, things that you in your fine clothes, with your fine life, could not even begin to imagine.* Oh, her clothes were fine all right—chosen and paid for by Lady Evedon—but her life was not fine at all; it had not been fine for such a long time, not since she was four years old. And the irony of his words drew a cynical smile which Wolf himself would have been proud to own, even as her eyes swam with tears she could not allow herself to shed.

When he looked at her, she could see the contempt that he made no attempt to disguise. He seemed to resent her very existence. And yet tonight, on the staircase, there had been no hatred. He had looked at her in a way that made her heart beat too fast, and not because of fear. In those few moments there had been a strange compelling force between them; the memory of it made the butterflies flock in her stomach, so that in her mind's eye she saw again that handsome harsh face. She screwed her eyes shut to banish the image, but still it lingered and she knew that she had never met a man the like of Wolf. He was ill bred and bad mannered, a veritable rogue. But there was more to him than that: there was something in his eyes, something dark and dangerous…and strangely seductive. He possessed an underlying feral streak, an unpredictability that meant he did not act in the manner that she expected. She put her head down, resting her face upon her knee, feeling its hard press against her cheekbone.

He was a strong man—one prone to violence, if the scar on his face was anything to judge by—a man that no one would wish for their enemy, but that was exactly what he was to her, she thought dismally. And this man had roused in her such anger and pushed her from the reserve in which she normally held herself. This was the man that would take her to Evedon.

You are mine, he had said, and the thought of being completely under his control made her blood run cold. For she had only just begun to imagine what a man like Wolf could do to her. She remembered the way he had looked at her upon the staircase, and the warm press of his hand against the small of her back that seemed to scorch through all the layers of her clothing, and the clean enticing smell of him. She remembered, too, how she had been unable to move, unable to think, her own will seemingly sapped from her body, and how quickly the smoulder in his eyes had cooled and frozen back into hatred. Rosalind clutched a hand tight across her mouth to stop the whimper of shock that threatened to escape. He was both fascinating and frightening, and she did not understand the effect he had upon her. God help her, for he was harsh and ruthless and unstoppable. With Wolf as her enemy, she may as well flee back to Evedon and throw herself upon the earl's mercy.

Against her ribs, she felt the warmth of the linen package where she had hidden Evedon's letter, a reminder of what was at stake. Wolf might threaten her, but he would not kill her. Evedon would send her to the gallows. She squeezed her eyes tight, knowing what she was going to have to do. It had been difficult enough to escape Evedon; it was going to take a miracle to escape Wolf.

She clutched her knees tighter and began to pray.

Chapter Five

Wolf took a hearty swig of the ale in his tankard. 'I needed that.'

'Gave you a hard time, did she?' Campbell asked with a twinkle in his eye.

'Hardly,' said Wolf. 'She seems to be under the impression that Evedon will push to have her hanged.'

'And no doubt you did nothing to dissuade the lassie of that belief.' Campbell cocked an eyebrow.

'Why should I? Let her sweat a bit.' Wolf took another swig of his ale. 'This journey is likely to be the worst of her punishments.'

'What do you mean?' Kempster looked up from his beer. 'Evedon'll haul her through the courts. He'll not see her hang what with her being a lady, like, but she should get a spell in the gaol. Whatever he does, she'll be utterly ruined.'

'There will be no scandal.' Wolf gave a cynical laugh. 'Evedon wants the affair kept quiet. Why else do you think he's employed us? He wants her delivered back to him with the utmost of discretion. He has no intention of publicizing the fact she's done a runner with his mother's jewels.'

'But he cannot mean to let her off with stealing from the dowager?'

Wolf gave a hard mirthless smile at the outrage in Kempster's voice. 'You've much to learn of men like your employer, Mr Kempster.'

Kempster shook his head as if to deny Wolf's words.

'She's a pretty wee slip o' a lassie, Kempster,' said Campbell. 'Maybe Evedon has his own reasons for wanting her theft hushed up.'

But Kempster was not listening.

Campbell smiled.

'It doesn't matter what the hell she is, other than a thief,' said Wolf sourly. 'All we have to do is deliver her to Evedon. What he does with her then is none of our concern. And if we let her think the worst of it, then all the better. It is less than she deserves.'

'You're a hard man, Wolf,' said Campbell, 'a hard man indeed. Is that no' so, Mr Kempster?'

'Yeah.' Kempster brought his gaze back from the distance, and wiped the pensive expression from his face. He drained his glass. 'I'll fetch us another jug.' He gestured to the empty jug of beer standing in the middle of the table. 'Put it on Evedon's account as expenses.' He stood raising his hand to attract the serving wench's attention.

'Leave it,' said Wolf. 'We've an early start in the morning and a fair distance to travel. We'll need clear heads not beer-sopped groggy ones.'

'One more jug won't do no harm,' countered Kempster.

Wolf said nothing, but his hard gaze met the footman's and held.

'Now that I think about it, I might just go and stretch my legs before getting my head down.' Kempster went over and whispered into the serving wench's ear, before heading outside.

Two minutes later and Wolf and Campbell watched the girl follow Kempster.

'Young lust,' Campbell commented and set his tankard down on the table.

A vision of Rosalind Meadowfield flickered in Wolf's mind, of her clear hazel eyes and full pink lips and the dark curl of her hair swept back in its prim chignon. He swallowed hard, forcing the image away, and scowled at Campbell's quip.

'We should get some sleep,' he said and his voice was edged with the anger that he felt at himself for thinking of the woman.

Campbell drew Wolfe a quizzical glance but said nothing.

The two men retired for the night.

The next morning, Rosalind steeled herself not to flinch at the sight of the little mare in the yard. She could see that Wolf was watching her, his expression hard, his pale gaze cool and unyielding. And for all that her stomach was squirming with the prospect of riding, she knew that she would rather die than let Wolf know it. Kempster watched too, but there was no smirk upon his face today. She turned away from them, gathered her courage and, hiding her reluctance, let Campbell help her up into the mare's saddle.

She was careful to let nothing of her fear or apprehension show upon her features as they rode out of the inn's yard, following the same format as the previous day: Wolf riding in front of her, Campbell and Kempster behind. The road was in such a bad state that they could move no faster than a walk. But Rosalind was grateful for the pot holes and uneven surface, for fear held her tense in its grip and it was all she could do to mask it. They had ridden for almost an hour when Rosalind felt her horse react.

'Whoa, stop there, lassie,' she heard Campbell shouting behind her, before riding up and dismounting. She jumped down from the saddle while he examined one of the mare's rear legs. She watched how gentle and quiet his manner was for such a big strong man. And then Wolf was there, sliding down from his saddle to crouch at Campbell's side.

'We've got a problem: she's lame.' Campbell tipped his head towards the mare.

Wolf nodded. He did not look happy.

'We shouldn't be too far from the next village. Riderless and with a slow enough pace the mare should manage the distance. Campbell, you see to the beast; I'll see to Miss Meadowfield,' said Wolf and climbed back up into his saddle.

Campbell transferred her travelling bag from the mare to his own mount.

Rosalind did not like the sound of 'Wolf's seeing to Miss Meadowfield' one little bit. She looked at the great grey stallion by Wolf's side and a tremor of panic flitted through her. 'I can walk.'

'Really?' he said. 'I thought it was carriages and sedan chairs everywhere for ladies like you.'

She glared at him, wanting to tell him that he was more wrong than he could imagine, that he had no right to be here forcing her on to horseback; no right to be dragging her back to Evedon at all.

Wolf glared right back, the animosity crackling between them, his expression hard and uncompromising. Beneath him, his horse stared at her with an equally hard eye. She averted her gaze from the meanness contained in the beast's stare, and tried to ignore the horse's sheer size and the power and strength emanating from both horse and rider.

The proximity of his horse and the prospect of being taken up upon the massive beast was making her legs tremble and her stomach roil. She locked her knees and swallowed down the nausea. 'I would not wish to inconvenience you, sir.'

'I assure you that it is never an inconvenience bringing in a captive.' And when she looked again, his pale gaze was on hers. 'Miss Meadowfield.' He reached his hand down to her, ready to pull her up on to the saddle before him.

She stepped away, afraid of both the man and the horse, feeling the quickening thump of her heart and knowing that she must let nothing of her fears show. 'If the horse is lame, then we can travel no faster than her walk.'

'True. And?'

'I will walk,' she said too quickly. 'Do not fear that I would delay our pace, for I assure you I am quite capable of walking at an equivalent speed.'

'It is thirty miles to our destination this day.'

She gave a slight shrug of her shoulders as if what he said was of no great consequence. 'I said I will walk, sir.'

'Thirty miles?' He laughed, which served to stir her anger. 'Have you any idea of that distance?' The scepticism on his face made her all the more determined.

'I have walked further; thirty miles is no great matter,' she lied.

He looked at her as if he knew that she was lying. 'I think your memory is playing you false, Miss Meadowfield.'

'My memory is perfectly fine, Mr Wolversley,' she insisted.

He stepped his horse towards her.

She backed away in alarm, thinking he meant to snatch her up on to the beast.

He stopped where he was, and the cool silver gaze scrutinized her for a moment more. 'Very well then,' he said at last.

He glanced away. 'Campbell, you and Kempster ride in front with the mare. I'll stay behind with Miss Meadowfield.'

She sagged with the relief of not having to share Wolf's horse.

The small party moved off. Campbell led the mare, riding abreast with Kempster, then came Rosalind on foot, and finally Wolf.

There were no replacement horses in the next village. They left the little mare there and continued on.

Rosalind walked, and amidst the relief at having won this small battle was the awareness of the man that rode behind her. She could hear the steady rhythmic clop of his horse's hooves on the hard surface of the road. She tried to force her mind to turn away from him, to think other thoughts, to see anything but him, but all of her determination was useless. There was only the long road that stretched ahead and Wolf behind.

Miss Meadowfield had been walking for three hours when Wolf decided that he would have to intervene. Not one word of complaint had she uttered, nor one single glance back in his direction, not even when they had made a brief stop to let the horses and themselves drink had she looked at him. The thick fur cloak hung heavy over her arm, her cheeks were flushed prettily from fresh air and exertion, several dark tendrils of hair had escaped her bonnet to snake against her throat, and there was an undeniable weariness in her step.

He drew his horse alongside her.

'You've made your point, Miss Meadowfield. You can climb upon my horse without any injury to your pride.'

She did not turn her face to his, just kept on walking at the same steady pace. 'I prefer to walk, Mr Wolversley.'

'No doubt you do, but I've a mind to reach our next stop before nightfall.'

She glanced over at him then and he could see the wariness on her face. Her pace increased, her feet stepping out faster over the uneven surface of the road. 'I can walk faster.'

He edged his horse over to block her path. 'You have walked enough this day.'

'No.' She backed away from him, the pink of her cheeks draining to leave her face pale. The look in her eyes was one of terror. Had he been so hard on the woman as to cause such a response of dread?

'Miss Meadowfield,' he said more gently.

'No!' And this time he could hear the undertone of panic in the word. 'I wish to walk. I will not climb upon that horse. You cannot make me.'

Up ahead, Campbell and Kempster had stopped and were watching their exchange with interest. Wolf knew that, but his attention did not waver from the woman standing before him.

'We both know that I can,' he said softly.

'And do you mean to?' she breathed, and her gaze held his with an intensity that seemed to shake all of his convictions. She was trying desperately to hide her fear and failing miserably. His horse gave a whinny and turned his head in her direction.

Miss Meadowfield jumped, her face washed powder-white, and his suspicion was confirmed. It seemed that forcing her back on to the mare after her fright yesterday had not prevented her fear running out of hand. Forcing her on to horseback now would only make things worse.

A subtle shake of his head. 'No.'

'You will allow me to continue walking?' He could see the suspicion in her clear hazel eyes as if she did not quite believe him.

'For today,' he said.

She gave a cautious nod.

He slipped from his horse and walked towards her, seeing the way she tensed ready to run. 'Your cloak.' He stopped short of reaching her, and held out his hand.

And beneath the suspicion he saw surprise.

She hesitated, and her eyes raised to his as if in question as she handed him the cloak. 'Thank you.'

He rolled the cloak to a ball and fitted it into his saddlebags.

'Thank you,' she said again, and Wolf knew that her gratitude was not because of the cloak.

'Start walking,' he said in a harsh voice, lest she think that he was softening.

He took the horse's reins in his hand and leading the animal behind him, he began to walk by her side.

She stopped suddenly, stared at him with wide wary eyes. 'What are you doing?'

'Ensuring you keep to the pace,' he lied.

She looked uncertain, as if she was not sure whether to believe him or not. 'Can you not do so equally well on horseback?'

'No.' He did not elaborate the untruth.

She swallowed down what retort she would have given, and nodded cautiously.

They walked on in silence, side by side.

* * *

Rosalind was acutely conscious of Wolf's proximity, of his tall frame and long muscular legs. She knew without looking how easy his stride was, how relaxed and how unchallenged his breathing; clearly he was used to walking, unlike herself. She wondered why he was walking with her rather than riding behind. She should resent it, she thought, but she could not for she knew how easily he could have taken her up on his great grey stallion. Why he had chosen not to was a mystery.

She risked a subtle glance across at him. His face was just as hard and just as handsome in profile. He faced forward, his focus trained some distance ahead. Beneath the battered leather of his hat, feathers of fair hair fluttered in the breeze. She scanned the straight line of his nose, the angle of his cheekbone, and the scar that sat upon it. Her eyes traced the strong line of his jaw, up to his lips that for once were not pressed firm and hard together, and found herself wondering what he would look like if he were to smile, properly smile a smile of happiness instead of the cynical curve of his mouth she had seen.

Without warning, he turned his head and met her eyes, catching her quite unaware so that she blushed. She rapidly averted her gaze but not before she had felt the questioning intensity of his stare. She walked on—increasing her pace, not slowing it—and the whole right-hand side of her body, by which he walked, seemed to tingle with a strange awareness.

The hours passed slowly until the air had lost its warmth and the light was dimming as the clouds began to gather overhead. Miss Meadowfield was still walking. Wolf had not thought that she would last so long.

Her head was still held high, yet she was unable to hide

the slight droop of her shoulders or the slowing of her pace. He knew that she must be exhausted and her feet sore, for he was weary enough and he was used to walking and had walked a good number of hours less.

Wolf slipped back up into his saddle and rode past her to Campbell and Kempster. 'Penrith's a mile ahead. That's where we'll stop for the night.'

'You should have taken her up on your horse. We've lost too much time. Evedon'll be getting jumpy if we're delayed.'

Wolf turned a hard eye on Kempster. 'Evedon will have her in plenty of time. You need not concern yourself with our schedule, Mr Kempster.'

'Just sayin'' said Kempster with a shrug.

'Best to say nothing, laddie.' Campbell smiled but the smile did not touch his eyes.

'Ride on ahead to the Crown Inn and secure us a couple of rooms. Here.' Wolf drew a leather purse from his pocket and threw it to Kempster.

The other man gave a nod, and manoeuvred his horse out to the middle of the road.

'And Kempster,' called Wolf.

He looked back.

'It's counted.'

Kempster's mouth tightened, but he said nothing, just kicked his heels into his horse's flanks and rode off.

Campbell waited until Kempster was out of earshot before speaking. 'He's right you know.'

'He is that.' Wolf's horse kept on walking. He glanced behind at where Miss Meadowfield followed.

Her face was pale and covered in dust, but her eyes met his and held before she averted her gaze.

'You've punished her enough, Wolf, I doubt she'll try another escape after this.'

'This is nothing of punishment, Struan. What the hell kind of man do you think me?'

'One that hates everything that Miss Meadowfield represents.'

He gave a sigh. 'I cannot argue with that, but the greater punishment would have been to take her up with me.'

Campbell's brow knitted. 'You're makin' no sense. Come the morn' she'll be begging for you to take her up.'

'On the contrary, Struan, Miss Meadowfield would rather crawl on all fours than climb up beside me.'

'Taken a bit o' a dislike to you has she? Cannae think why.' Campbell raised an eyebrow in an expression of irony.

'The mare bolted when she was trying to make a run for it yesterday. She lost control of the horse and it gave her one hell of a fright, not that she'd admit as much. She's a poor horsewoman; you saw how uneasy she was around horses even before yesterday's episode. The woman's terrified of riding again.'

'That explains why she had a face white as chalk when you brought her back. But she was riding the mare then.'

'Aye, she was that, but only because I forced her back in the saddle straight off. Best thing after an incident like that. Usually conquers the fear.'

'Except it doesnae seem to have worked in Miss Meadowfield's case.'

'No, Struan, it does not.'

'The lassie's dead on her feet. Maybe this day of walking will make her change her mind.'

'Somehow I do not think so,' said Wolf grimly. Her discomfort served her right, he told himself, but he did not believe it. She had been so damned insistent on walking. It was not anything that the poor did not do every day of their lives. But Rosalind Meadowfield was not poor. She had not walked to collect water, walked to rummage in midden heaps to find food, walked the streets because there was nowhere else to go. She knew nothing of survival, and what was so wrong in letting her taste a little of how the other half lived? Yet still he dropped his horse back until he was level with her, and swung himself down to walk once more by her side.

She briefly glanced in his direction before turning her face forward once more, but not before he saw how pale she was and the unmistakable fatigue that shadowed her eyes. He felt the hand of guilt squeeze at his innards.

'One more mile,' he said to her.

She nodded. He doubted she had energy enough left to speak.

They continued on, the silence only broken by their footsteps and the clop of his horse's hooves behind. He did not look at her, not once, and yet he was aware of her every breath, of the slight awkwardness in the light tread of her boots through the dust of the road, and of every tired nuance in her frame. And although she still represented everything that he had been raised to hate, he found perversely that there was a part of him that was willing her on, step by step of that last mile.

A mile had never seemed so long, yet Rosalind gritted her teeth against the pain and kept going. Only when they had finally reached their destination and she was alone within the bedchamber of the Crown Inn did she give in to it. She was so tired she could not think straight, so tired that she could not stop the flow of silent tears that leaked down her cheeks. And she did not even understand why she wept, only that she felt so small and weak in comparison to the task that lay ahead.

He would come for her in a minute, to take her down to

the public room. She thought of how he had walked by her side, and there had been nothing of mockery and anger in him then. Indeed, she had the feeling he was supporting her, buoying her up, willing her on. And then there was the way that he had not taken her by force upon his horse, allowing her to walk, almost as if he understood her fear. A ridiculous notion for sure. Wolf was harsh and cruel. He hated her. He was taking her to Evedon. Wasn't he? But his actions today ran contrary to all she thought of him. This day had not been as she expected. *He* had not been as she expected.

She felt numb from exhaustion, numb, and yet she still she wept. Her cheeks were hot, even though the bedchamber was cool and the grate empty. No candles had been lit and there was a sense of comfort in the dusky shadowed grey light. She sat down upon the bed, wiping the tears from her face with dust-stained fingers, knowing she could not let him see her like this. The bed was narrow, its covers coarse and worn. Yet she lay her length upon it as if it were a silken luxury, easing the weight from the throbbing ache in her legs. Two minutes. Just to rest for two minutes. The pillow was soft as down beneath her head. She closed her eyelids against the hot grittiness of her eyes and welcomed the darkness.

Wolf was feeling uneasy about the day as he knocked upon Miss Meadowfield's door. The woman had surprised him this day. He had seen the fear that she tried to hide and he recognized the dogged determination that sprung from it. Thirty miles, and not one word of complaint. The incident with the little mare must have scared her more than he had realized. Only once had she looked at him, and he thought again of the faint colour that had warmed her pale cheeks as he had caught her.

* * *

No reply came from within the room, but Wolf waited where he was without a word just the same. The minutes passed. He knocked again and called her name. No response. No sound of movement of any kind. What game was she playing now? Had she sneaked away in those few moments alone, or was she blatantly ignoring him in an attempt to put him back in his place where he belonged? He felt the flare of his temper, and without further ado thrust the door open.

Rosalind Meadowfield lay on the bed, limp and motionless, her bonnet askew and crushed upon her head, her clothes still thick with the road's dust. Dread twisted in Wolf's chest, and all of his anger was gone in a second. He did not remember how he got there, just that he was by her side, leaning over her, examining, listening. Only when he heard her breath did he release his own in a gush. He saw then the tracks her tears had made through the dirt on her cheeks; something tightened in his stomach and he knew it was guilt.

Beneath the filth her cheeks were flushed. His hand moved to gently cup her heated skin.

She stirred in her sleep, opened her eyes to look at him. 'Wolf,' she murmured, forgoing her usual 'Mr Wolversley' for the first time, and there was such exhaustion in that one word that he felt it pierce his soul.

'Forgive me, I—' she said, and tried to sit up.

But he slid his hand down to gently still her.

'Nay, lass. Rest a while. I'll have a tray sent up to you. See that you eat before you sleep.'

She nodded and her eyes clung to his and what he could see in her gaze was pain and hurt and loneliness to rival his own. And for the first time since leaving London, a shadow of doubt moved over his heart.

* * *

Rosalind woke the next morning to a hand touching her shoulder.

'Miss Meadowfield.' A man's voice, and one that she recognized. 'Miss Meadowfield,' he said again.

Sleep was heavy upon her and she forced herself to struggle out from beneath it and prise her eyes open. It felt as if she had only closed her eyes a few minutes ago. And for a moment, she thought she was back in her bed-chamber in Evedon House, just for a moment, before she remembered and with memory came the fear twisting again in her stomach. She raised her eyes and found herself looking up into Wolf's pale grey ones.

'Wolf…?' Her voice was hoarse and dry with sleep, her head still thick with it.

'There is warm water upon the dresser. When you are ready, come down to the public room for breakfast. We shall wait for you there.'

There was nothing of mockery or contempt in his face this morning, and the harsh tone had gone from his voice. And she remembered her dream from the night of Wolf, of kindness and a touch so tender that soothed her hurt. But she was not dreaming now, and she wondered at this change in him.

'Thank you,' she murmured and her eyes held his, scared to look away lest when she looked again all of his resentment was back.

He gave a gruff nod. 'I am trusting you, Miss Meadowfield.' And then he rose and left.

She lay there listening to the sound of his boots receding along the passageway and down the staircase. His words whispered again through her mind, *I am trusting you, Miss Meadowfield,* and as her eyes swivelled towards the door she realized what he had meant. No key had sounded within the lock. She slipped from the bed, wincing as her feet touched the floor. And when she bent to examine them, she saw the clotted, weeping, bloodied mess where the leather of her boots had chafed the skin of her feet to rawness. Her feet had been sore yesterday, but nothing to compare with the pain of this morning.

She hobbled to the door. The knob turned within her hand, and the door swung open towards her. She heard the hurried thud of heavy footsteps upon the stairs and, quickly and quietly, closed the door again, leaning against its panelled wood while she waited, holding her breath in case it was Wolf returning. Only when the footsteps disappeared into one of the other rooms did she breathe again. But it did not prevent the small shiver that rippled down her spine at the thought of him. The door was open, but she could not run…yet.

Outside, crows were calling, their cawing loud and sinister in the morning air. Rosalind glanced around the small shabby room, her eyes stopping on a small table. It was not too heavy as she lifted it and positioned it to barricade the door, building herself a modicum of security.

The water within the cream china pitcher was warm, just as he had said. She stripped off her clothes. Chilled and vulnerable in her nakedness, she began to wash yesterday's dust and sweat from her body.

Down in the public room was the smell of breakfast, of coffee and freshly baked bread, frying ham and eggs. But beneath it, last night's beer, stale and uninviting, lingered faintly. The three men sat at the table, drinking their coffee, and did not speak.

The minutes ticked by and Wolf's eyes shifted again to the door, wedged open in the corner of the public room, showing a clear view of the lower half of the staircase.

'Forty-five minutes and still she is not down. Miss Meadowfield is slow in her appearance this morning,' said Kempster.

Campbell murmured a caution beneath his breath and sipped at his coffee.

The footman chose not to heed Campbell's words. 'But then she is not used to dressing without the help of a maid.'

Campbell gave a slight wince at this and glanced at Wolf who was already getting to his feet. 'Leave it, Wolf. The lassie will be here any minute.'

Wolf's gaze met his friend's. 'She's mocking us, Struan.' He did not wait for a reply, just moved across the public room towards the staircase.

By the time he reached Miss Meadowfield's bedroom, the slow burning fuse of his anger was already well ignited. He had trusted her and she had shown him that he was a fool to have done so. He strode along the corridor, his booted footsteps ringing loud. One glance from those hazel eyes and already he was forgetting what this was about. There he was feeling sorry for her plight! She, who was of the gentry, a woman who cared only for her own selfish gain, with no regard for who she trampled upon to obtain it. What compassion had she for those beneath her?

She was wrapped up in the pettiness of her reputation and Society's opinion. A gentlewoman with nothing of gentleness, all of it a pretence to mask what lay below. Wolf hated the gentility and nobility with every fibre of his being. And just because she was a woman, with eyes to haunt a man, she thought she could play him, blind him to what she really was. And he, like a fool, had fallen for it, his heart softening, when in reality she deserved everything that she got, and more. His anger was simmering such that, upon reaching her bedchamber, he did not even knock.

The handle of the door turned easily but the door did not open; he felt it contact something hard and heavy, and he knew that she had barricaded the door against him. He had trusted her, leaving the door unlocked, and this was how she repaid him. And all of that molten anger erupted in a blaze of fury both at her and his own stupidity.

'Who is there?' he heard her call.

He gave no reply, just leaned his shoulder on the door and pushed his weight against it. There was a sound of scraping wood and the door moved quickly.

'Please wait!' Miss Meadowfield's voice sounded from the other side of the room.

He did not stop. Something wooden and heavy fell over, hitting the floor with a loud thud and the door swung open.

She was standing fully clothed by the bed. He heard her gasp as he walked slowly across the threshold and carefully shut the door behind him.

Chapter Six

Any gentleness, any sense of reason had gone. Rosalind saw the hard set of Wolf's jaw. She saw too that his eyes had changed from a cool silver to a stormy dark grey. Even the air around him seemed tense. He was wearing the leather trousers, worn and scuffed as his boots, the lace threading the outer seams running the length of his long legs. Beneath his jacket she could see no waistcoat, only a white shirt and neckcloth. He stood there, the door behind him, tall and powerful, his legs slightly apart as if he were balanced, poised, ready to strike. A man about to do battle, a man whose anger was unmistakable. Everything about him seemed to scream a warning of danger. She stepped back, feeling the urge to run, knowing that there was nowhere to run to; that Wolf stood between her and the room's only exit.

'What merits this behaviour, sir?' She cleared her throat and braced her shoulders. 'You did not need to resort to such violence.' She glanced towards the table that now lay on its side upon the floor. 'Had you knocked upon the door, I would have answered.'

Still he said nothing, just stood there looking at her, silent, unmoving, and his very calm made her more nervous of the storm that she was sure he was about to unleash. Her stomach somersaulted, and she felt her throat grow dry. 'You have damaged the floorboards.' She gestured towards the marks that the table legs had scraped. 'The landlord will be angry and…' Her words petered out as her eyes came back once more to Wolf. He was not looking at the table or the scraped floorboards. His gaze was fixed quite firmly upon Rosalind, and the look in his eyes made her begin to tremble. She gripped her hands together that he would not see her nervousness.

'Mr…Wolversley,' she started, trying to ignore the tight feeling around the base of her throat.

He moved then, so fast that she had little time to react. Crossing the room, closing the distance between them until there was none.

She tried to back away, but his hands were on her pulling her close, holding her secure so that she had no hope of evading him.

'Three-quarters of an hour,' he whispered softly, his very breath suffused with danger and threat. 'Forty-five minutes.'

Her breathing was ragged and loud. 'I am almost ready,' and her voice trembled.

'Almost?' He raised his eyebrows as if he found her incredulous. 'Perhaps you think my words are not worth heeding.' He leaned closer until his breath tickled against her cheek. 'That they are uttered so idly that you seek to try me over this most trivial of matters.'

She shook her head in denial. 'I assure you that is not the case.'

'And yet you do try me most sorely, Miss Meadow-field.'

There was nothing she could say to that. Her heart skittered in her chest. She waited for what he meant to do.

'Kempster tells us that you cannot ready yourself in forty-five minutes for you cannot dress without a maid. Is it true?' he demanded, still in that same softly spoken voice.

'Of course not.'

'But you did use a maid to help you at Evedon House.'

She swallowed hard, knowing that it would be pointless to deny the truth, and gave a small nod.

She saw the curl of his top lip, as if his contempt was so great that this one small betrayal slipped out when all of the rest of him was so still and so controlled.

'Should I then act as your maid, Miss Meadowfield?'

The shock jolted right through her. 'No!' She tried to pull away from him, but there was no yielding in the grip he had upon her.

'Forty-five minutes,' he said, 'and still you tell me that you are not ready.'

'I am ready, sir,' she countered.

'Almost, you said but a minute since.'

'I was mistaken. I am ready now.'

The silver eyes bored into hers. 'Maybe it's about time that someone taught you how to dress yourself.'

'I know full well how to dress. I need neither a maid nor a lesson.' She stared up into his eyes, seeing the danger that lurked so shallow beneath his surface.

'Then pray tell me, Miss Meadowfield, what exactly took you so long that my breakfast is no doubt growing cold downstairs while I am up here fetching you?'

She shook her head feeling the slight warmth in her cheeks.

'Miss Meadowfield,' he said with such loaded warning in those soft quiet words. 'Do not make me ask you a second time.'

She shut her eyes then, closing herself against his scrutiny, knowing that she would bear his wrath rather than tell him the truth.

'I had to wash, put some semblance of order to my hair and brush my clothes,' she said steadily. 'A lady's toilette takes time.'

'Indeed?' His eyes narrowed. 'Perhaps you do not realize the fragility of your position, Miss Meadowfield, to bait me so sorely.'

And even though she was quaking inside, she met his gaze. 'On the contrary. sir, I understand exactly my predicament and to where it will lead.'

'I do not think that you do, miss.' He stepped closer and his eyes were dark and deadly.

Her heart gave a somersault. She gathered her courage. 'I took too long to ready myself this morning. Do you intend to beat me over it?'

'Never in my life have I raised a hand to a woman.' But he did not release her.

'Then what do you wish? That I beg your forgiveness?'

'It would be a start,' he said coolly.

She stared at him, the flare of her own anger tempting her to defy him, yet the small voice of reason urged her to finish the matter.

He stared right back, the smoulder of his anger rendering hers small and inconsequential in comparison.

'I beg your pardon, sir,' she said without a shred of sincerity, 'I am sorry for the delay in my toilette.'

He looked unconvinced, yet even so he gave a small nod of acknowledgement.

She turned her face away from his.

But she had reckoned without Wolf. Keeping one hand around her arm, he removed the other to place his fingers on her chin and turn her face back to his, keeping his fingers there so that she could not look away. 'It is not nice being made to eat humble pie, is it, Miss Meadowfield? Remember that for the future when you're making some poor housemaid grovel.'

She gasped her disbelief. What kind of woman did he think her? 'You are much mistaken in your assessment of me, Mr Wolversley.'

'No, miss, I know your type very well indeed. I know the way you treat those that are beneath you. Your kind are all the same.'

She stared at him, the injustice of his accusation wounding her. 'You do not know me at all, sir,' she snapped.

'I know you better than you think.' She heard the chill in the softness of his voice. 'Now put your boots on and get moving. We should be on the road by now.' He released her so suddenly that she staggered before he put out a hand to steady her.

She withdrew as if his touch burned her.

Wolf let his hand drop, but stood where he was without the slightest sign of moving.

The boots sat in a neat pair by the bedside table, her stockings and ribbons folded in a pile upon them. Beneath her skirts, the makeshift bandages were complete on one foot but only partially covered the other. She had no desire for Wolf to see either.

'If you would be so kind as to avert your eyes, sir. My stockings…' She bit at her lips and felt the blush warm her cheeks. She dared to raise her eyes to his.

The steady grey gaze was unwavering. 'Put them on, Miss Meadowfield or I will do it for you.'

There was little choice. She sat herself down on the bed, careful to keep her feet tucked beneath the length of her skirt, and pulled the stockings and boots close to its hem. Beneath the cold blast of Wolf's scrutiny she tried to slip one stocking on to her foot beneath the cover of her skirt, steeling herself not to wince.

Wolf caught a glimpse of a white material strip dangling from Rosalind Meadowfield's foot and knew instantly what it was. He bent and caught hold of her left ankle and, pushing back the curtain of skirt, revealed the truth. He knew then why she had taken so long to ready herself. The loose winding of the makeshift bandage only partially covered her foot, the rest that had yet to be wound lay long and limp, its edges ragged. The ball of her foot and toes were still exposed, and what he saw there made his chest tighten. The skin was rubbed raw, its cleansed blisters weeping afresh. He lifted the hem of her skirt, saw the torn petticoat and her right foot fully bound.

'You should have told me,' he said, and the knowledge that he had misread her made his voice too harsh.

She pulled her foot from his grasp and fixed her skirts back down into place. 'It is none of your concern, sir.' Indignation blazed in her eyes before she looked away. Her movements were jerky, her hands trembling as she grabbed a boot and started to pull it roughly on to her foot using the strength of her defiance against the pain.

His hands moved to possess hers, stilling their action.

She gasped. 'How dare you? You have no right to touch me!'

The pale gaze slid to hers. 'We have already been through this, but I'll remind you, as you seem to have forgotten. Until we reach London, you are under my control—completely and absolutely.'

She glared at him. Her heart was racing, and it seemed

that the skin on her ankles still tingled where his fingers had touched.

'Your feet are cut to ribbons.' He grabbed up one of her boots and, turning it over, looked at the thin sole with its holes and tears, before throwing it back down.

'As I have already said, sir, it is none of your concern.'

'You still do not realize, do you? What do I have to do to make you understand?'

Rosalind's heart was beating fit to burst, and her stomach was a small tight ball of fear. She could feel the warm press of his fingers around hers as he took her hands again.

'Mr Wolversley.' His name sounded hoarse in the aridity of her throat.

'You will tell me the next time that you are injured or hurt.' It was not a question, but an assertion.

'What does it matter? You are taking me to Evedon. Why would you care about a few cuts on my feet?'

He did not reply at once, so that the tension that lay between them seemed to Rosalind to wind unbearably tight. 'Evedon wants you in one piece,' he said finally. *Why else indeed,* he thought grimly, yet the sight of her wounded feet tore at him.

Her hands fluttered and struggled within his, seeking an escape, but he firmed his grip slightly, holding her until the movement ceased. 'Miss Meadowfield,' he said more softly. His eyes met hers. And he saw that she was embarrassed and angry and afraid.

'Two thin dressings placed over the raw patches will give better protection, and keep the binding thin and firm. Too thick and they will make your boots press all the tighter; too loose and they will chafe the skin all the more.' He spoke calmly, matter of factly, as if he were not kneeling on the floor with her hands within his and her feet and ankles bare before him.

She watched him with the wariness of a trapped animal.

He released her hands then, took hold of her left foot and began to unwind the binding.

'Sir! What on earth do you think you are doing?' Her eyes were wide with shock, their colour a gold-flecked green in the daylight.

'I'm binding your feet so that you will make it through this day with some degree of comfort.'

'But…!' Her cheeks were scalded pink, and she pulled her foot away.

'Do you wish to be unable to walk by the end of this day?' he demanded. 'It is of little concern to me, for, whether it is Campbell or Kempster or myself that must carry you, our journey shall not be delayed.'

'You cannot carry me,' she whispered in a scandalized tone.

'Can I not?'

The silence stretched between them.

'So what is it to be, Miss Meadowfield? Shall I bind your feet or not?'

He saw the hard swallow, the deep in-breath to her lungs. She raised her head and focused her gaze upon the corner of the room. 'Very well, sir.'

Wolf's touch was gentle for so fierce a man. His hand moved with a confident assurance, undoing that which had taken her so long to put in place. And when he inspected her feet, bare and sore, it was all she could do not to pull them from his gaze and hide them once more beneath her skirts. Yet he laid the dressings and bound them in place so expertly that she found his touch both calming and compulsive. She knew it was wrong to feel like that. She should be wishing for the mortification to end. Instead, it was as if something else had taken over her body. His touch was soothing and pleasurable. She knew she should not look, but she could not help herself. Her eyes moved to the strong hands that worked upon her feet.

His fingers were tanned beside the pallor of her ankles, his skin roughened in contrast to her smoothness and, for all their days on the road, his nails were short and clean. He worked deftly and when he touched her, where he touched her, her skin tingled. She watched those hands first on one foot and then the other, and everything in his movement was gentle yet with a strength and competence that were undeniable. He knew what he was doing. At last he tucked the end of the binding in and she thought he was finished, but he was not. He lifted her stocking.

Rosalind's heart gave a somersault. She knew she should draw her foot back, but it was as if she were entranced. She just sat there, with her foot within his hand, and waited, waited, her breath holding tight in her lungs, her blood thrumming with anticipation. Slowly, carefully, he eased her foot into the silken case of her stocking, so that the binding was not dislodged. The silk pooled around her ankle, his fingers resting above it on the nakedness of her skin. And still she sat, unable to move, as if cast as a statue, her lower leg exposed before him.

He hesitated.

A breath in, and out.

Her skin burned beneath the touch of his fingers. She moved her eyes to his, but his focus was fixed upon her ankle, at where his hands cupped around her leg.

He was still, unnaturally so, and tense; she could feel it even through the feather-light touch of his hands. Slowly, as if against his will, he raised his gaze to hers.

His eyes smouldered a deep smoky grey, and they were filled not with anger or loathing or mockery, but with something that she had never seen in any man's eyes.

She looked and could not look away. Something in her seemed to open, some need that she did not understand. She felt his thumb flicker against her skin, an infinitesimal movement—so small as to barely exist at all, and yet a caress all the same. And still their gazes held, locked, caught in some strange new world in which only the two of them existed. She could not move, could not breathe. The pulse in her throat throbbed, her heart thumping wildly, her blood rushing madly. She was acutely conscious of where his hand lingered and of his very proximity. Her skin burned beneath his touch.

She gasped as she felt the caress of his fingers against the skin of her calf.

His face came nearer.

Rosalind leaned towards him, the tiniest motion, but enough.

His mouth moved closer so that she could feel the warmth of his breath upon her cheek.

'Wolf,' she whispered, and not once did the intensity of their gaze waver.

His lips parted.

She closed her eyes.

A knock sounded on the door.

She started with fright, gasping, the spell shattered in an instant.

The doorknob turned and Pete Kempster appeared in the doorway. But Wolf was already on his feet, facing Kempster, standing so that he partially blocked Rosalind from the footman's view.

'Everything all right, Mr Wolversley?' His dark gaze slid from Wolf to Rosalind. 'Breakfasts are ready and on the table. Mr Campbell sent me to fetch you.'

'We'll be down directly,' Wolf said to him. An effective

dismissal, yet the footman lingered, his gaze turned towards her, so that she could see the surprise within it.

'Kempster,' said Wolf in low warning.

She could not see Wolf's face but Kempster could, and what he saw there made him give a grudging nod of acknowledgement before turning on his heel and beating a hasty retreat.

Rosalind and Wolf were alone again. The footsteps died away and there was only silence.

She did not know what to do, what to say, what to think even. What had just happened, what they had come so close to doing…The incredulity of it lay thick and awkward between them.

Wolf turned then, and she saw that the shock in his eyes mirrored that in her heart, before he masked it with a tight controlled expression. 'Fit your stockings and your boots, Miss Meadowfield.' He waited by the door, his gaze not on her but on the wall opposite.

She did as he bid and came to stand before him, her cheeks burning, her gaze averted. She followed him along the passageway and down the stairs into the public room. They did not speak or even look at one another, as if pretending that nothing had happened, that everything was as it had been before. But nothing was the same; they both knew that.

She did not think of the tenderness of her feet, or the slowed pace of his walking as they made their way down to the public room. She did not think of anything at all, except for Wolf and the power of what had just passed between them.

Wolf did not sit down at their table in the public room.

'I'll ready the horses. See if the landlord has any bread and cheese to spare that we may purchase to take with us. We have wasted enough damn time this morning.' He strode out of the inn towards the stables without so much as a backward glance, slamming the door behind him.

He did not stop until he was out in the stable, standing by the stall in which his great grey stallion was housed.

What the hell had just happened in there? He had gone up to her chamber intent on delivering her a warning, of ensuring that she knew he would not stand for her to play him a fool. And he had ended up on his knees, caressing her bare legs. Had not Kempster arrived when he did, Wolf knew that the footman would have interrupted something even worse. Wolf would have kissed her, and God only knew what else. He clasped a hand to his head, unable to believe it.

What in damnation had he been thinking? She was everything that he despised. She led a privileged pampered life. She was from the sort of genteel social-climbing family that he loathed. Money and the *ton's* opinion were everything to her, so much so that she thought she could skin her employer and get away with it. Because that's what people of her station did, they took what they wanted without a single consideration for the outcome. They never saw the effects of their actions, never faced the consequences. And Wolf hated them for it…and he hated Miss Meadowfield just the same, for she was one of them.

He hated her, and yet in those moments in that room, he had wanted her. Too damned long without a woman. There could be nothing more to it than that. She was young and attractive. He was just a man, after all. A man that should find the likes of Rosalind Meadowfield the least attractive of all women. Bloody fool, he chastised himself.

'You all right?' Campbell stood in the stable entrance.

'I'm fine,' Wolf said curtly and opened the stall gate.

'You didnae eat your breakfast.'

Wolf finished buckling up the leather straps around the horse's girth. 'I'm not hungry.'

Campbell looked unconvinced. 'Did you tell her there are no horses for hire?'

'Didn't get round to that.'

A single eyebrow arched on Campbell's face. 'What did she say of her wee attempt at escape?'

'Nothing.' Wolf concentrated on finishing off fastening the tack.

'Then you were discussing her thirty-mile walk?'

'Something like that.' He did not look round at Campbell.

'And will the lassie be walking the day?'

'Not likely; her feet are cut to ribbons.'

'Told you that did she?' Campbell probed.

Wolf ignored the question. 'She'll ride pillion as she's told to.'

'I'll take your baggage upon my horse. Give you a bit more room for Miss Meadowfield.'

'I'll carry the baggage; the woman can ride with you or Kempster.' What had just happened in her room was warning enough, and Wolf was no fool.

There was a silent pause before Campbell moved to see to his own horse. 'As you will, Lieutenant,' and the fleeting gaze that met Wolf's was too knowing. He lifted the saddle and sat it upon the horse's back. 'You were up in her room quite some time…' He let the words trail off suggestively.

Wolf recognized that tone. He turned a baleful eye on his friend. 'What the hell is Kempster doing in there? We need to get moving. The sooner we are rid of Rosalind Meadowfield to Evedon, the better.' And then he turned back to his horse.

Campbell watched him with a thoughtful expression upon his face.

* * *

Rosalind sipped at her coffee, but could not bring herself to eat the fried food that lay on the plate before her. The cup was hot beneath her fingers, yet she was almost glad of its scald for it gave her something else upon which to focus. Although her gaze was lowered, she was aware of Kempster's ill-tempered mood and the way that he was watching her.

Wolf had touched the bare calf of her leg. And the way that he had looked at her, the feel of his touch…In those moments, there had been nothing of mockery, nothing of anger, and she had forgotten that he hated her, forgotten that he was dragging her back to Evedon. She should have thrust his hands aside and slapped his face and told him in no uncertain terms that she was not that sort of a woman. Instead, Rosalind Meadowfield had behaved like the worst of wantons, letting him touch her, encouraging him, waiting like a Jezebel for his kiss. She thanked God for Kempster's interruption, that she had not made a worse fool of herself.

Her face glowed hot at the memory of it, and she could have wept from the shame. And she did not know why she had behaved in such a ridiculous way. It did not make any sense. She did not even like Wolf. She hated him, hated him for destroying her chance of freedom, for his anger and for the way he made her feel. More than that, she thought, she hated herself for what she had just done. Wolf regretted it too; she had seen it in the way he had stormed past, his breakfast untouched upon the table, and in the angry slam of the door in his wake.

Another sip of coffee, and she calmed herself, forcing herself to see the sense of the situation. She was far from home, far from friends, surrounded by enemies. Her feet were a sore mess and Wolf had been right: without binding, they would only get worse. And she had no wish to be carried as he had threatened. She had had little choice but to let him bind her feet. And as for the rest of it, she had been overcome by the softening in his harsh demeanour. The days of worry and fear over Evedon had taken their toll on her so that her thinking was confused.

In a few moments, she must go out there and climb upon a horse and ride in Wolf's wake all of the day. The thought of facing him again was anathema, but it had to be done. There could be no running away from it. She placed the cup down upon its saucer, marvelling at the steadiness of her hands. There were more important things at stake than Wolf's or her own sensibilities. Quite simply, if she did not escape, she was a dead woman. It was the truth in all its starkness.

Her thoughts were interrupted by Kempster getting to his feet. 'After you, Miss Meadowfield.' There was a sarcastic edge to his voice as he gestured her towards the door.

She took a deep breath and walked, out of the public room, out of the inn, to the yard…and Wolf.

Chapter Seven

By the time they were standing in the inn's stables with only the same three large horses before them there was a definite dread in Rosalind's belly.

'We have yet to collect the little mare's replacement?' she asked and saw the look that Campbell shot at Wolf. Something was wrong, and Rosalind had a horrible idea what that something might be.

'There is no replacement,' said Wolf harshly and fitted the battered leather hat back on to his head. 'No horses for hire in this town.'

'What of carriages? We could hire a carriage.' The words were out before she could stop them.

'Round this place?' Kempster gave a laugh. 'You must be joking!'

'Then we are to wait here until a horse becomes available?' She looked across at Wolf's horse and saw her bag strapped beside his and knew her answer. And for all that she had been so calm and determined, she felt the stirrings of panic at the thought of riding up on one of the large horses with any of the men.

'No,' said Wolf succinctly.

She began to back away.

His cool gaze met hers. 'You cannot walk,' he said and swung himself up on to his horse.

She shook her head in denial, feeling the dread gripping at her. 'I *can* walk. My feet are not so bad.' And even as she said it, she knew that it was not true.

'You ride with Kempster.' Wolf's eyes were grey and implacable, his voice hard and resolute. There was not one hint of gentleness—nothing of the man who had bound her feet.

From the corner of her eye, she saw a small smile play about Kempster's mouth.

A wave of panic threatened to rise. She damped it down, squaring her shoulders and facing Wolf defiantly. She damn well would not beg him. And the thought of her letting such a man touch her, of almost letting him kiss her, swept a blaze of anger through her, and the anger lent her courage. He would not have her dignity; he would not take her pride. With her head held high she walked over to Kempster and let him lift her up on to his saddle.

Wolf watched as Rosalind sat stiffly on Kempster's horse, her focus fixed rigidly on some distant point ahead. The colour had gone from her cheeks, the darkness of her hair rendering her face all the paler. For all that she was trying to hide it, he knew that she was afraid and, God help him, in that moment he was seized with the desire to take her up before him, to hold her there safe and secure, her body hard against his own. He thought of her legs bare within his hands, of his mouth moving to take hers, and something tightened within him. She was of the gentry, a social climber, a thief; a woman who thought she was above justice. He turned his gaze away and led out so that he need not look upon her. Behind him was only the clatter of horses' hooves, no other sound. And against all logic, Wolf felt a sense of guilt.

Sunshine warmed the chill from the air, birds were singing and the day promised to be fine, but Rosalind was oblivious to it all. It took all her concentration to stay balanced on Kempster's horse without touching him. There was little enough room in the saddle and, no matter how far away she edged, Kempster's leg seemed to brush against hers. Her left hip was hard against the pommel which she gripped tightly with both hands.

When the horse began to trot, it was all she could do not to hold on to Kempster. Up ahead, Campbell rode beside Wolf; the burr of their quiet chatter drifted back to her.

Impulse made her glance round at Kempster, and she saw that he was watching her. He smiled as her gaze met his, but it did not set her mind at rest.

In Evedon House all of the women thought Pete Kempster handsome, with his dark hair and pale skin, his straight regular features, and perhaps most striking of all, eyes that were of such bright blue as to quite take a woman's breath away. He had a cheeky charm that won him many conquests. Even Lady Evedon had a soft spot for the footman.

'You work quick, Miss Meadowfield. I'll give you that much.' His voice sounded close above her right ear.

'I do not know to what you are referring, Mr Kempster.'

'Don't you?' he asked, and she could hear the smile in his voice. 'You and Wolf. Do you think that if you bed with him he'll release you?'

'Bed with him!' She stared round at him aghast. 'How could you think such a thing?'

'How, indeed?' He smiled again, that lazy smile of his, as if he had not just insulted her. 'You seem to be forgettin' that I saw what the two of you were up to this morning in your chamber.'

'What you saw,' she said coolly, 'was Mr Wolversley binding my feet. Yesterday's walking has blistered them. He was helping me, nothing more.'

'*Helping you?* That's a good one.'

Her face flamed. She turned away, determined to ignore his crudity.

But Kempster was not to be silenced. 'I'm acting as a friend, so to speak, Miss Meadowfield.'

She glanced back at him. 'You say such things to me under the pretence of friendship?'

'Why else?' he answered and looked at her with such sincerity in his eyes that she almost believed him.

'I'm just trying to warn you. Whatever he tells you, Miss Meadowfield, he'll still take you back to Evedon. The sum of money his lordship has placed upon your head will insure that. And if you let him, Wolf will have his cake and eat it, if you catch my meaning.'

'You are mistaken in thinking that there is anything between Mr Wolversley and me.'

'You're a thief, Miss Meadowfield,' said Kempster soberly, 'and he's a thief-taker. And nothing that you do will change that in Wolf's view.' He shook his head, as if she were a simpleton believing it would be otherwise.

'I am well aware of that, thank you, Mr Kempster.'

'I'm not at all sure that you are, miss. You don't seem to know who's your friend and who's your enemy.' He paused. 'Like back in Evedon House, keeping yourself apart from the rest of us. Ignoring them that would have offered friendship. Some, not me I hasten to add, saw it as you thinking that you were too good for the rest of us.'

'It was not like that. I was Lady Evedon's companion. I could not—' She stopped. A man like Kempster would never understand what it was like to be caught between two worlds. She was neither like the other servants nor a member of the family. She belonged nowhere. Always an outsider, always looking in on where she did not belong. Besides, how could she strike a friendship with anyone when she had so much to hide? If the truth of her father was to have come out, she would have lost her position. Not that any of that mattered any more.

'Could not what?'

'It is of no matter.'

He paused, watching her. 'No, I suppose it ain't, not now that you're a thief.'

His words hit home, and it hurt knowing that she could not refute them. She looked away.

Time passed, until they reached the main road and Kempster geed the horse to a canter. Her hand swung to grab at the lapel of his jacket, gripping it hard to secure her seat. Her heart was pounding, her stomach clenching with the sudden spurt of fear.

She felt Kempster's arm snake around her waist, his fingers splaying over her left hip. 'Best keep you safe, Miss Meadowfield. We don't want you falling off, do we?'

She said nothing, just swallowed down the memory that his words threatened to conjure.

'Don't be shy, miss. You can hold on to me; I don't mind.'

She felt him pull her closer. He was holding her so tight that she felt his fingers bite into her hip.

'Mr Kempster!' And despite the canter of the horse

she struggled to keep some distance between her body and his.

'No need to be shy, Miss Meadowfield. I know all about your little secret.'

Even in the midst of her fear her heart missed a beat, and she felt her stomach plummet. Did he know of her father? Did he know who she was? 'What do you mean, *little secret?*'

'Why, your fear of horses, of course. What other secrets are you keeping?'

Relief, in part. 'I have no secrets,' she lied with a bravado that she did not feel. 'And you are quite mistaken in thinking that I am afraid of horses.' She turned her face from his lest he see the truth in it.

Kempster suddenly removed his arm from where it anchored her in place, letting it drop in a leisurely fashion to rest against his thigh.

She felt herself sway at the sudden freedom and instinctively reached for security, wrapping her arm around his back, unmindful of the close proximity of their bodies.

'Am I?' His face was so close to hers that she could feel his breath upon her cheek, smell the scent of him, see every detail of that vibrant blue gaze.

She closed her eyes, blocking out the sight of him, but she could not release where she held to him, no matter how much she willed it.

'Shall we race Wolf and Campbell?' She felt his whisper against her ear, the honeyed tone of his voice so contrary to the cruelty of his words. 'Urge this gelding to a gallop? He's a fast one, frisky too. Who knows what might happen if I—'

'No!' She clung all the tighter, wedging herself against him.

'Then you admit you are afraid of horses?' His words were soft as a caress.

Even now she was determined not to make the admission. 'I…'

Kempster's heels brushed against the gelding's flank, urging him faster.

Rosalind could bear it no more. 'No! Please!'

'Why not?'

She shook her head, ashamed to admit the words.

The horse responded to Kempster's spur, accelerating to a gallop, overtaking Wolf and Campbell to leave the two men in the distance.

His lips touched to her ear. 'Tell me.'

'I am afraid of horses!' she cried, and she could hear the thump of hooves directly behind them, and a shouted command.

'Kempster!' the angry voice roared. Wolf. 'Pull up!'

The footman slowed the horse in an instant.

'I am afraid of horses,' Rosalind said again, quietly this time, and she did not know whether she was saying the words to herself, or to Kempster or to Wolf. She was aware of nothing save the humiliation of the admission and the pain of memory it brought with it.

'That wasn't so hard, was it?' he said softly, as if nothing had just happened.

'Kempster!' Wolf barked again, and this time the horse stopped.

She looked neither at Wolf or Kempster, nor did she loose where she held to the footman so tightly. The knuckles of her left hand gripping the saddle's edge shone white and bloodless. 'I think that I am going to be sick.' She swallowed hard, forced herself to breathe, trying to still the rebellion in her stomach. She could not even look round at Kempster.

Still she could not release where she gripped so tightly. She was not even aware of Wolf dismounting, just that he was there, lifting her down to the ground. Her stomach heaved. Unmindful of her sore feet, she ran towards the hawthorn trees that bordered the road, seeking some privacy. She was barely into the wood when she wretched and wretched, stooping to rid herself of a sickness that did not come. She heard Wolf's voice and stumbled further into the wood, collapsing against the side of a tree, holding on to its overhanging branches to steady the swaying inside her head.

And after a small while, there was the sound of a man's tread through the undergrowth, following the path she had taken. She did not need to look round to know that it was Wolf.

She was kneeling by the time he reached her. She did not look up, but she recognized the scuffed leather of the boots that stopped close by.

He set a silver hip flask down beside her, not saying anything. Even then, she did not look at him. She did not want him to see her like this: weak and disadvantaged, with no strength left in her to fight him.

'Drink a little,' he said, 'and rest for a while, until you feel better. There's a stream down there if you want to wash your face and hands.'

And then he was gone, the sound of his boots swathing a path back through the grass and bluebells.

She could hear the chirp of sparrows and from somewhere in the distance, the call of a wren. A breeze stirred the leaves in the trees all around, and she looked up to see the early blossom of the creamy white flowers upon their branches. The sun was shining in earnest, and the sky was the palest of blues. It was so peaceful. So calm and healing. The scent of spring with all its new growth surrounded

her. She got to her feet, lifting the silver hip flask as she
did so, and followed down the slope strewn with the bluebells with their broad deep green leaves and pretty violet-
blue flowers. At the bottom of the slope was the stream
of which Wolf had spoken. The water ran clear and clean.
She crouched by its bank, sitting the hip flask by her side,
and rinsed her hands. The water was cold and refreshing
as she splashed it upon her face, dabbing herself dry with
her handkerchief. The terrible nausea had gone, yet just the
thought of climbing back up beside Kempster on his horse
threatened to bring it right back again; Rosalind knew that,
so she turned her mind away from the prospect.

The hip flask was still by her side. She lifted it and,
noticing the engraved words, examined it more closely—
Lieutenant Will Wolversley, 26th Regiment of Foot. So
he had been a lieutenant in the Army. The revelation was
surprising, given that she had him pegged as some kind
of semi-criminal ruffian. Even so, she could imagine that
Wolf would make a very good lieutenant. He was a natural
leader: hard and ruthless and utterly determined, with an
undoubted ability to kill. That thought made her shiver.
With England still at war with Napoleon, she wondered
why Wolf was no longer within the Army.

It was brandy in the flask, not gin as she had first expected. She sipped only a little and felt the spirit burn a path
down her throat into her stomach. Wolf had been right; it
did make her feel better.

The stream flowed smooth and quiet over its bed of
stones. She was still alone, no sign of Wolf or the others,
and she realized in that moment that this was her chance to
escape, the best opportunity that she would get. A glance
behind to where she had come from—nothing and no one.
She thought of Wolf touching her bare ankles with such
intimacy, and of the smoulder in his eye. She thought too of

his face leaning in towards hers, and admitted for the first time that she had wanted him to kiss her—Rosalind who had never before desired any man's kiss. It was shocking and ridiculous and an absolute absurdity. And because of it, she knew that she most definitely had to go. That he was taking her to Evedon was almost an afterthought.

She set the flask down where he would find it and winced as she got to her feet. One more glance behind and then she picked her way over the few stepping-stones to the other side of the stream. Ignoring the pain in her damaged feet, Rosalind broke into a run.

Kempster was standing by his horse, adjusting the strap of his stirrup when Wolf strode up to him.

'What the hell did you think you were doing? I told you to ride easy with her.'

'I was just muckin' about.' Kempster held his hands up in an innocent gesture. 'No harm done.'

'Stupid sod, couldn't you see that you were terrifying her?'

'What's to terrify?' he asked, so that Wolf had the urge to land his fist in the footman's face. 'We were just riding.'

Wolf scowled at him. 'Ride like that again with her and I'll plant my foot up your arse.'

'Keep your hair on, gov'nor. I didn't realize you had such a concern for Miss Meadowfield's welfare.'

Wolf's dislike of the footman was fast escalating. 'My only concern is delivering Miss Meadowfield to Lord Evedon—in one piece. Now go and fetch her back.' Wolf made to turn away, and then stopped. 'On second thoughts, you go in his place, Campbell. She's down by the stream.'

Campbell drew Kempster a foul look, before disappearing into the wood.

Wolf waited by his own horse, and in his mind he saw again the fear in Miss Meadowfield's face as she sat frozen upon Kempster's horse. The woman had been genuinely terrified. The sight of her distress caused a clenching in his own stomach so that he wanted to punch Kempster's idiot face for what the footman had done. And he knew none of this would have happened had he only taken her upon his mount instead of passing her off to Kempster. Maybe Wolf had misjudged this whole thing. Maybe he was making her suffer for another's crime, avenging his own bitterness at her expense.

Two minutes later and Wolf had revised his opinion.

Campbell appeared, running, out of breath, and alone. 'There's no sign of Miss Meadowfield. This is the only thing by the stream.' He threw something into Wolf's hands.

The hip flask.

'She's done a runner,' Campbell added.

Kempster could barely keep the smile from his face. 'The sickness must have been feigned. She's played you good and proper, Mr Wolversley.' And there was a smugness in his tone that made Wolf's fist itch again to hit him. 'Made fools of us all.'

Wolf's mouth hardened. She had made a fool of him all right. He felt the flicker of an anger that was searing in its heat. He slipped the flask back into the inner pocket of his coat. 'Go on ahead to the Angel Inn in Catterick. I'll meet you there by nightfall.'

'Shouldn't we help you find her?' asked Kempster.

'No need.'

'But—' started Kempster, and stopped when he saw Campbell's warning shake of the head.

'Get on your horse, Mr Kempster,' said Campbell, and as Kempster did as he was bid, Campbell turned to Wolf.

His eyes met Wolf's. 'Have a care how you do this,' he said quietly, 'for both your sake and the lassie's.'

'I'll have a care, all right,' said Wolf with quiet promise. 'More care than you can imagine.' He watched Campbell and Kempster ride off before leading his horse into the wood, tethering him by the stream, and crouching low to view the surrounding ground. From where he squatted, he could see quite clearly the path Rosalind Meadowfield's feet had taken through the mass of bluebells on the opposite bank. Wolf smiled and the smile was small and hard and cold. He rose and moved to follow her trail.

Chapter Eight

The soles of Rosalind's feet felt like they were on fire yet still she kept on running. Her breathing was ragged and so loud that she feared that it would mask the sound of her pursuers. They would come after her, of course; Wolf would not let her go so easily, and it would not take him long to discover her disappearance. She wondered if he was on her trail yet, scouring the wood, hunting her. That thought made her shiver and kept her legs running even though they were heavy and aching to stop. It was not fear of Wolf that drove her on, for she knew now that for all his harshness he would not hurt her, nor did she think of Evedon. She remembered too well the tantalising caress of those long tanned fingers and her own shameful response. Lord help her but she did not understand why she had behaved in such a way.

She pushed on harder, until there was a sharp stitch pain in her side and her lungs were gasping in air as if they were fit to burst. Her feet, raw and aching, stumbled over clumps of grass and fallen logs and rocks, yet she kept on going, ignoring the whip and scratch of branches against her face, clearing a path through their barrier with her hands. She felt the snag of her skirts upon something solid and sharp, and wrenched the material free, knowing that every second counted in her bid to escape.

She ran for as long as she could before slowing to a walk, looking behind her every few steps, listening beyond her own breathing. Walking and walking, and then half running again. The birds were singing and the wood stretched on ahead a vivid carpet of bluebells with the occasional patch of pale yellow primroses. The scent of bluebells filled her nose from the flower-heads crushed beneath her feet.

She was glancing back more often, hurrying on, hopeful now that she really could evade him, that perhaps he had not yet noticed her absence. But there was nothing save the trees and the sway of their branches in the wind. She kept on trotting, and after a while, she noticed that the birds no longer sang, that everything was quiet, and even the wind seemed to have died away to leave only the sound of her own tread through the undergrowth and the panting of her breath. The surrounding stillness was unnatural and unnerving; she could not rid herself of the conviction that someone or something was following her, stalking her. And even though she was flushed pink with warmth and sweat, she shivered.

Again and again, she looked behind, her eyes scanning through the trees, and each time, she saw nothing that should not have been there. Maybe she truly was free; maybe he would never find her. She wondered whether she dare find her way to the nearest inn and stay there for the night or whether Wolf would search all inns in the locality. It was what she would do were she him, she thought. Maybe she should just find shelter out here, but then she had left her cloak behind, and the night would be cold and filled with unknown predators. She was just worrying over this quandary, glancing back once more when a large figure suddenly stepped out before her.

The scream was piercing and short, escaping her lips before she even had time to think. Her heart was hammering against her ribs, her blood pounding so hard that she thought she would faint. She stared at him with incredulity, disbelieving that he could really be there standing so perfectly motionless and silent before her.

'Wolf!' His name was a whisper upon her tongue.

'Feeling better, Miss Meadowfield?' he asked, and although his words were harmless enough, his tone was not. Everything about him was still and waiting and watchful. She could see the ferocity of his mood in the deep grey of his eyes, a torrent of anger held in check, ready to be released.

She took one small step back, and then another. 'I—I—' The words seemed to freeze beneath the darkness of his stare.

'You…?' He raised a sardonic eyebrow and waited, like a cat that waits before striking at the mouse captured within its claws.

She whirled and tried to run but he caught her, his hands firm against her arms, hauling her back in, until her spine was tight against his chest. She could feel the heat that emanated from him and smell the scent of him surrounding her: leather and soap and masculinity. With one hand he held her, with the other he untied the ribbons of her bonnet beneath her chin and, freeing the bonnet from her head, threw it carelessly aside. An arm clasped firm around her waist.

He bent his head and she could feel his breath warm

against the side of her face, whispering over her cheekbone, her eyelid, her forehead. His stubbled chin was rough as it slid against her hair, until his mouth found her ear.

'Tut, tut, Miss Meadowfield. I did warn you not to run.'

His lips were so close that their vibration set up a tingle in her ear that emanated from that one point to suffuse throughout her body. Goose pimples raised on her skin. His forearm was against her stomach, touching lightly against the lower part of her breasts, so that her body tingled and her nipples felt strangely tight and sensitive. It was so close, so intimate as to have almost been a lover's embrace. She trembled with the audacity of it.

'Mr Wolversley!' she gasped, trying to hide the shock in her voice beneath indignation. He held her so firm that she could not look round at him.

'I do not like thieves that try to make a fool of me.' Even though she could not see his face, his voice was hard with dislike.

'I did not…Kempster and his horse…I was unwell.' She could hear the quiet steadiness of his breathing so different from the raggedness of her own.

'So unwell that you could run away,' he said.

'You cannot blame me for trying. You are taking me to Evedon, for pity's sake. He will see me hang.'

'Then you should not have stolen his mother's jewels.' His voice was harsh, without anything of compassion.

She shook her head, feeling her chignon loosen slightly as she did so. 'I know you do not believe me, Mr Wolversley, but I did not steal anything belonging to Lady Evedon.'

'You are right, I do not believe you, Miss Meadowfield.' Without releasing her, he turned her in his arms, so that his face loomed just above hers.

She shivered at the intensity of the look in his eyes.

'We have yet to talk of what you have done with the emeralds.'

She shot him a glare.

'Do not worry,' he said, 'I'm saving that for later. For now, I want to know why you did not tell me of your fear of horses.'

There was no more point in denials. He had witnessed her response to Kempster's actions. 'It was not your business to know, sir.' She stared at him defiantly.

'Had you told me, Miss Meadowfield, I would have hired a coach and four for the journey. You could have travelled in some small degree of comfort.'

His words swept away all that she would have said. Lies, of course. He was saying it only to torment her further. 'I do not believe you.'

'Why not?' he asked, and his eyes were as cold as ever.

'Because you are a cruel man, Mr Wolversley,' she taunted.

'You think me cruel, Miss Meadowfield, because I am a thief-catcher and you are the thief that I have caught.'

She said nothing, just stood where he held her.

'Am I cruel because I will not let you escape me?' His voice was harsh. 'Or because of what I will do to prevent you from trying again?'

Her heart flip-flopped.

'Should I beat you, Miss Meadowfield?'

He had said that he had never raised his hand to a woman in his life and she believed him, yet still she bit at her lip to prevent its tremble.

'Bind and gag you and strap you over my saddle for the rest of the journey?' he demanded.

She felt the blood rush from her head and her legs grow weak just at the thought.

'Or maybe I can think of something even better.'

'You would not,' she said, and, for all its determination, her voice was barely more than a whisper.

'But such are the actions of a cruel man,' he said with a deadly softness, and he released one hand to stroke his thumb against her cheek.

The action shocked her more than his words.

She wrenched her face away from his touch—both incensed at his audacity and shocked at the flare of excitement that his caress elicited—and heard his quiet laugh.

Keeping hold of one of her arms, he began to walk back through the woodland through which she had run. 'Do not try anything foolish, or I will bind your hands behind you and put a rope around your neck.'

'Savage!' she muttered beneath her breath, but Wolf heard her.

'Aye,' he growled, 'I'm that all right, and you best not forget it.'

Rosalind forced her gaze away from the contempt in his eyes. She was acutely conscious of the overwhelming strength of the man, of the extent of his anger. He was all tall and lean and hard, broad-shouldered and long-legged. She glanced at the light yet unbreakable grip of his long tanned fingers surrounding her arm.

'My bonnet,' she tried to pull free. 'We must go back.'

His grip did not slacken beneath her pressure. 'Forget the bonnet,' and he frogmarched her back through the wood through which she had fled with such hope, back down the slope and across the stream.

His horse was tethered to the nearby hawthorn trees.

Rosalind could see the big stallion and the way that his

eye stared with undisguised ill temper at her. She started to fight against Wolf's progress, digging in her heels, trying to pull away from him. 'No!' she cried, 'I will not let you do this!'

He dragged her round to face him, holding her still. All of the fierceness had gone from his eyes, and in its place was a calm confidence that stilled her struggle.

He would take her up on the horse and make him gallop, just as Kempster had done. And in her mind, she saw again that terrible scene again from across the years and Elizabeth's poor bloodied body. 'No,' she whispered, pushing the memory away. 'I will not,' she said, no longer caring if he heard the desperation in her voice.

In the silence that followed, there was only the trickle of the nearby stream.

'We must reach the inn by nightfall. It is too far for us to walk.'

Her stomach clenched, she knew what was coming. She would not beg. She looked into his eyes and waited.

'I will ride him at a trot, nothing faster. You shall be quite safe; I will not let you fall.' His voice was calm and reassuring, all of the harshness stripped away; it reminded her of how he had spoken to the little mare.

She wanted to believe him, but after Kempster, the fear was back stronger than ever.

'I give you my word, Miss Meadowfield.' He released his hold upon her and looked at her with eyes as silver as that first night they had met. But this time, there was a gentleness in them that surprised her.

There was little choice. To run again was pointless; he would only fetch her back once more. She glanced across at Wolf's horse; it was bigger and looked meaner by far than the beast Kempster rode, as mean as Wolf himself when he was angry. But his anger seemed to have dropped away, she reasoned.

She swallowed hard and gave a small nod.

Only then did he untie the reins, and swing himself up into the saddle.

Rosalind stood where she was, feeling the tremor shimmer through her body.

He reached down for her, and she let him lift her with one arm into place, sitting, as before, as if on a sidesaddle. His other arm fastened her into place, securing her to both the saddle and the warm hardness of his chest.

She gripped at the pommel with her left hand and hesitantly wrapped her right arm around him. The intimacy of their position brought a blush to her pale cheeks.

His eyes met hers once more, and there was nothing of the storminess that she had seen in them before. He seemed almost concerned. 'Ready?'

'Ready,' she answered quietly, aware that sitting snug against Wolf was nothing like sitting near Kempster. Ashamed though she was to admit it, she liked the smell of Wolf, the feel of him. Her whole body seemed to hum with an inexplicable awareness of him—this man who had just thwarted her escape, again; this man who would take her back to Evedon.

A twitch of the reins between his fingers and the horse began to walk.

The stallion walked until it reached the road and then Wolf urged it to a trot. And that is the way it stayed, just as he had said, trotting for hour after hour, in silence, while she sat safe in Wolf's arms.

The sun was setting by the time that they reached the Angel Inn, a glorious red ball sinking towards the horizon and washing the fading blue sky a vibrant pink. A promise of a cold night and fine morrow. His horse's hooves, clad with their iron shoes, clattered loud within the inn's yard.

Wolf slid the woman down on to the cobblestones before dismounting and handing his horse to an ostler who waited by the lantern-lit stable. He dropped some money into the ostler's palm that the man would attend to the horse.

Miss Meadowfield stood where she was, bareheaded, her dark hair escaping the chignon at the nape of her neck, its long thick strands curling over her shoulders and glowing red where the setting sun touched upon it. She touched a hand self-consciously against it, trying to poke the loose tendrils back up, but only succeeding in making things worse. Several hairpins dropped to the ground with a tinkle and she stooped to gather them.

Wolf saw the small beggar boy dart from his position by the gate, his outstretched grubby palm at the ready at the possibility of a coin or two from the new arrivals. The boy's clothes were ragged and dirty, his frame small and undernourished. He pulled the filthy cap from his head, revealing dingy fair hair that framed a gaunt little face that seemed too old for the child. Wolf felt that same stab of kinship and recognition that he always felt on seeing such children. Twenty years earlier and it might have been Wolf himself that stood there begging, cap in hand. His eyes slid to Miss Meadowfield, ready to see the revulsion and distaste upon it but there was nothing of any such emotions as she crouched down by the child. Wolf watched in amazement as she touched a hand gently to the child's cheek.

She smiled, and it was a smile filled with such tenderness and sadness that Wolf felt as if a hand had reached into his chest to squeeze upon his heart. He stared, unable to believe what he was seeing. And as he stared, he saw her slip her hand into the pocket of her dress and remove a small purse. She unlaced it and dropped a few coins into the boy's hand. And then she leaned forward to kiss his cheek. The child ducked away, staring at Miss Meadowfield with shocked suspicion, an expression that mirrored what Wolf was feeling. Having got what he came for, the boy disappeared as quickly as he had appeared.

Wolf saw the blush rise in her cheeks as she realized that he was staring at her. She got to her feet and stood somewhat awkwardly.

'Thank you, Mr Wolversley, for the horse…for understanding.' Her voice was quiet. She glanced up into his eyes, and he could see the sincerity in hers.

Wolf found he could not look away. She had nothing for which to thank him. He was taking her to Evedon. Forcing her on a hard journey the length of the country on horseback, when she was clearly terrified of horses. He had prevented her escape. Yet she thanked him. There was a tightness in his chest. He felt a brute. And when he spoke, there was a hoarseness to his words.

'I thought it was what had happened with the mare the other day that made you afraid of the horse, but it was not, was it?'

She shook her head, and the dark curls danced against her breast. 'It is from many years ago, when I was much younger.'

'Whatever happened must have frightened you very badly.' He wanted her to tell him, wanted her to share what had happened, yet Wolf knew that he of all people had no right to ask.

'Yes,' she said so quietly that he had to strain to hear it. She looked away, to where the sky was red and streaked, and in a halting voice began to tell him. 'I was riding out in the park one day with a friend. A carriage suddenly appeared. We did not see him until it was too late. He drove too close, too fast. A young gentleman racing another. My friend's horse took fright. It bolted. Elizabeth fell from the saddle, and her foot caught in the stirrup. I tried to stop her horse, as did those who came to help, but he galloped for more than a mile. It was too late by then. They said that she died quickly, but I know, Mr Wolversley, that she did not.' She looked up into his eyes then. 'I did not ride again after that day.'

Wolf felt her pain as clearly as if it was his own. He reached out to her without realizing that he did so, the touch of his hand to her arm offering some small measure of comfort.

She did not draw back, just looked at him, and her eyes were dark with the misery of the memory, and down her cheek he saw the glittering trail of a single tear. He stepped closer and wiped it away with his thumb.

She stared up at him as if mesmerized, and the same magnetic sensation that had flowed between them before was there again.

Slowly, he pulled her into his arms, holding her gently against him, his hand stroking her hair, so that the last of her pins were lost and it spilled long and curling down her back.

'I'm sorry, lass,' he whispered against the top of her head, and the faint scent of roses drifted up from her hair. 'It was no sight for a girl to see.'

He felt her take a deep stuttering breath as if she suppressed a sob, and she pressed her face against his chest. And when after a few minutes, she tilted her face up to his and looked into his eyes, it seemed the most natural thing in the world to kiss her.

She tasted of all that was sweet and good and he kissed

her softly, tenderly as if he would salve the hurt she had been dealt all those years ago.

The stable door opened and the ostler returned. Wolf pulled back, realizing just what he was doing.

Miss Meadowfield turned quickly away, but not before he had seen the lost expression upon her face.

'We must go inside,' he said.

'We must,' she agreed, but her voice was breathless.

The last of the red orb disappeared beneath the horizon as he led her into the inn.

Only when Rosalind Meadowfield was safely locked in a bedchamber upstairs in the Angel Inn did Wolf return to Campbell and Kempster in the taproom.

'You found her then?' Campbell glanced up from the tankard of ale before him and met Wolf's eye.

'Did you doubt that I would?' Wolf kept his face impartial, unwilling to reveal in any way what had just happened outside with the woman.

Campbell shook his head and laughed. 'On the contrary, you just won me two shillings.' He thrust an open hand to Kempster. 'Pay up, laddie.'

Kempster grumbled and dropped two silver shillings into Campbell's waiting palm.

'Back before dinner with the lassie in hand,' said Campbell with a smile. 'Watch and learn, laddie, watch and learn.'

'Where was she?' asked Kempster.

'That does not matter, now that she's back where she should be, under lock and key.' Wolf gestured a serving wench over and ordered some ale before sitting down. 'I'll speak to the landlord later, and see if we can arrange a post-chaise for our travel tomorrow.'

'For Miss Meadowfield?' Kempster looked surprised.

Even Campbell raised his brow.

'We need a decent pace of travel to reach London in a reasonable time, and that's not what we're going to get with Miss Meadowfield on horseback.'

'Giving in to the lady's demands?' asked Kempster wryly.

The comment touched a sore point in Wolf, yet he knew that he was unjustified in feeling it. 'Hardly.' Wolf's ale arrived and he took a long drink from it.

'Post-chaise will cost a pretty penny,' said Kempster.

'Evedon's paying.'

They ordered food, including a tray for Miss Meadowfield. 'Not taking any chances, Mr Wolversley?' asked Kempster with a cheeky grin. 'Scared you might lose her again if you loose her from that room?'

Wolf forced a smile at the lad's teasing. 'No fear of that.'

'Take the tray up to her, shall I? And maybe apologize for what happened earlier with the horse. I didn't realize the situation between her and horses.'

Wolf wanted to take the tray up to her, but he could not very well insist on doing so. It would look as if he had an interest in the woman, which he did not. He threw the key over to the footman. 'Go on then, but be quick about it.'

Kempster nodded. 'Of course. Don't want my dinner gettin' cold.' And then with a smile, he rose from the table and left, following the serving maid who was carrying Miss Meadowfield's tray across the room.

Wolf waited until they reached the stairs before he spoke. 'There's something not right about this, Struan.'

Campbell darted a surprised glance at him. 'You think that the lassie's innocent after all?'

'She's guilty of something, but whether it's of what Evedon's accuses her, I'm not sure.' He thought of her kindness to the little beggar lad. 'She doesn't fit the picture that Evedon painted of her.'

'She's no' quite the pampered miss he said.' Campbell looked serious. 'So what's Evedon up to?'

'I don't know, Struan, but I mean to find out. Kempster should be able to tell us about Evedon and Miss Meadowfield.'

Wolf waited until the dinner was eaten, the plates cleared and a few jugs of ale had been emptied, before starting to question the footman. 'You've worked for Evedon for a fair time, have you not?'

Kempster smiled. 'Nigh on three years. Don't know why I've stayed so long when he's such a stingy bugger. Pays pennies, he does.'

'And you were there the night of the theft. You saw what happened.'

'I did. Evedon had the whole house searched for the dowager's missing jewels. As you already know, the diamonds turned up in Miss Meadowfield's room. But as to the whereabouts of the emeralds…' A sly expression came over his face. 'You'll have to ask Miss Meadowfield about that.'

'So you think her guilty?'

Kempster laughed. 'Course she's bleedin' guilty. The diamonds were hidden within her shift, weren't they?'

'It does not mean that she put them there,' said Wolf.

Kempster looked at him strangely, then laughed again as if Wolf's words were ridiculous. 'You think someone else thieved the stones and hid them in Miss Meadowfield's underwear?' He shook his head. 'Well, I've heard some ideas in my time, but that one takes the biscuit. She's guilty as sin, Mr Wolversley.'

'Tell me about Miss Meadowfield.'

Kempster smiled in a knowing way that Wolf did not care for. 'She's a looker all right. I'd give her one myself if you weren't already in there.' He nudged Wolf's elbow and grinned.

Wolf's expression hardened. 'What the hell are you insinuating, Kempster?'

One look at Wolf, and Kempster tried to backtrack. 'Just kidding, just a jest, Mr Wolversley.'

'Do you see me laughing?' snarled Wolf.

The footman glanced away awkwardly.

'Why would she steal the old lady's jewels when she's the daughter of a rich gentleman? Does her father not send her an allowance?'

'Her father's dead.'

'And the rest of her family?'

'Never heard her speak of no family at all. What ever became of the rest of them I don't know, save that they left her with no money to speak of.'

Wolf's eyes narrowed. 'You mean she's penniless?'

Kempster nodded. 'It's Lady Evedon that clothes her and Lady Evedon that pays for all else. Miss Meadowfield herself ain't got two farthings to rub together. Suppose that's motive enough for her to steal from the old dame, ain't it?'

Wolf looked thoughtfully towards the stairs that led to Miss Meadowfield's room, aware that he had done the woman a greater disservice than he had realized.

'What of Evedon and the woman? Was there anything between them?'

'Was he doin' her, you mean?' Kempster smiled and raised an eyebrow. 'I fancy he was. Maybe he was dumping her and she stole the stones to get back at him.'

'And maybe she did not steal the stones at all.' Wolf rose

from the table and held out his expectant palm to Kempster. 'The key for her room.'

Kempster glanced up in surprise, the smile falling from his face. 'I'll fetch her empty tray if you like.'

'I'm not collecting her bloody tray.' Wolf's face was hard and determined.

The footman fumbled in his pocket before dropping the key on to Wolf's hand. 'What are you goin' to do?'

Wolf's eyes met the footman's. 'Discover the truth about Miss Meadowfield.' His fingers closed around the key to her room and he was gone.

'But we already know the truth.' Kempster wiped a hand across his mouth as he watched Wolf making his way across the taproom to the stairs.

'Do we?' said Campbell softly, his eyes, too, trained on the retreating back of his friend. 'By the time he comes down, we will.'

Chapter Nine

Rosalind was standing by the window looking out at the yard and the landscape beyond, trying to make sense of her reaction to Wolf. He had kissed her, and she had kissed him back. Logic told her that she should hate him, but her heart was saying something quite different. When he touched her, when he looked at her with that smoulder in his eyes, all rational thought seemed to flee and she wanted him to hold her in his arms, to take her mouth with his. Her heart skipped faster just at the thought, and there was the same whir of excitement within her stomach that she always felt in response to him.

He was taking her to Evedon, she reminded herself, and that fact made her response to him even more of a madness. He was taking her to Evedon and she revelled in his kiss. Rosalind had never felt this way before. She shook her head, not understanding what was happening to her, and the thick fur-lined cloak hanging around her shoulders swayed gently with the motion.

The candle on the small bedstand had expired leaving only the moon as her light, and the fireplace was empty of coal and logs. From the taproom below came the sound of men's voices, their laughter and shouts. She pulled the cloak more tightly around her to ward off the night's chill.

She started when she heard the lock tumble, then chastised herself, for it would only be Kempster come back to collect her dinner tray. She moved to face him. It was not Kempster that stepped into the room but Wolf. She caught her breath, backed away, recoiling at the shock of finding him there, and to her great shame, all she could think of was how he had kissed her and the warmth of his lips upon hers.

'Miss Meadowfield,' he closed the door quietly behind him.

She saw the way he locked it before turning to her. Her heart began to beat too fast…and not from fear. The strange tension flowed strong between them. She shivered with an unbidden anticipation.

His eyes flitted from the heavy cloak around her shoulders to the empty fireplace and back to her face. 'I'll have the landlord send someone to make up a fire, but first there are matters of which we must speak.'

'Which matters?' she asked slowly. She knew that she must make it clear to him that her outrageous behaviour had been an aberration and that it most definitely would not happen again. She knew that she had represented herself very badly. Rosalind Meadowfield did not kiss men. And she certainly did not allow them to touch her bare legs. She was gently and properly raised. Her mama had taught her right from wrong. And yet all her resolve, all her best intentions, fell away with him standing there before her with his hard, handsome face and his hidden darkness that seemed to call out to her.

'I want you to tell me the truth, Miss Meadowfield.'

He was here to talk about the theft, nothing more. She allowed herself to relax a little, feeling both relief and disappointment. She blushed at the realization and was angry with herself. Anger was good; it made her strong. She faced him with a measure of confidence. 'I've already done so on more than one occasion. You did not believe me then, why would you do so now?'

'Tell me of matters between you and Lord Evedon.'

She felt her stomach flip over. What did he know? 'What bearing can such a thing have on the crime of which I stand accused?'

'Let me be the judge of that.'

She gave a hiccup of a laugh. 'I did not steal the jewels. Is that not enough?'

'Nowhere near enough,' he replied. His eyes were silver in the moonlight as he stood and watched her. 'The diamonds were found hidden wrapped in your shift.'

'Then someone else placed them there.'

'And why would anyone have done that?'

'I do not know.' She shook her head. 'Perhaps they sought a place to hide them that they thought would not be searched.'

'Or to frame you for a theft you did not commit?'

'Perhaps,' she agreed, wondering what had brought on this sudden questioning and whether he was beginning to believe her. 'Although I do not know who would wish to do such a thing.'

'Who are your enemies, Miss Meadowfield?'

'I have none,' she answered, and her eyes were without a trace of guile.

Had it ever been so for himself, he thought, and knew the answer to that. There had never been a time he had not known there were people who would hurt him.

'Except perhaps…' She hesitated and glanced nervously away, so that he knew what she would have said.

'Evedon,' he finished for her.

'Yes.'

There was a short pause before he asked, 'Are you Evedon's mistress, Miss Meadowfield?'

Her eyes widened with indignation. 'No! Most certainly not.'

'Usually in my employment, I am paid not only to retrieve the guilty party but any items stolen. Yet in your case, Evedon was most adamant that I do not search you or your baggage. I am permitted only to question you lightly to discover what you might have done with them. Indeed, he seemed more interested in retrieving you than his mother's emeralds. I wonder why that might be.'

'I do not know the workings of Lord Evedon's mind.'

'Yet you seem to be very sure that he will see you hanged. What is there between the two of you?'

She did not answer him, just stood there in silence.

'Perhaps he has made inappropriate advances? Perhaps he wishes to—'

'No!' She prevented what he would have said. 'Nothing of that nature.'

'He says that you are a thief, Miss Meadowfield. Are you?'

She felt the traitorous heat rise in her cheeks. She should have been shouting her denial, but the words dried upon her tongue. For all that she knew she should, she could not lie to him. The seconds ticked by.

'No denials?'

'I did not steal the jewels,' she said hurriedly.

'Then what did you steal?' he asked softly.

She felt her eyes widen at his words, felt the breath catch

in her throat. She shook her head. 'Nothing,' but the word was cracked and hollow.

'I know that you are lying,' he said. 'Admit it is so.'

'I have stolen nothing,' she said; this time her voice was stronger and she was glad of it.

The silver gaze seemed to pinion her. 'I do not believe you.'

She held her courage in both hands, knowing she could not afford to betray the existence of the letter. 'Then it seems that we are at an impasse, Mr Wolversley,' she said coolly.

The angles in his face seemed to harden at that. 'Believe me, Miss Meadowfield, this is no impasse.' And he began to walk across the room towards her.

She felt her heart give a flutter and her stomach suddenly tighten. She backed away from him.

But Wolf was not to be thwarted. He closed the distance between them.

She tried to step back farther but she felt the heavy material of the curtains framing the edge of the window and the firmness of the wall behind her.

His fingers closed around her left wrist, effectively binding her to him. 'Tell me of your parents, your background.'

She caught her breath at his question coming so unexpectedly. Her heart was hammering within her chest and her blood rushing in her ears. 'Of what interest can that be to you, sir?'

'Of extreme interest, I assure you.' The moonlight flooding the window lit his face well, showing every aspect of the features she had come to know, and revealing the scar that sat across the top of his cheek in clear detail. His jawline was square, hard and determined below a mouth that was sculpted and kissable. She remembered the feel of it pressed against her own. She swallowed hard at the sudden heat that shot low in her belly. Quickly her gaze moved on, taking in his straight manly nose, his nostrils slightly flared with the dark anger that simmered always so close beneath his surface. High angular cheekbones and those silver eyes whose gaze seemed to rake Rosalind's soul.

For a moment she was lost in his eyes, entranced so that she could not think straight, and then in the corner of her mind she remembered all she had to lose, and she gathered every last bit of her resolve and managed to break his gaze. And when she looked at him again she was stronger to resist.

'There is nothing to say.' She looked at him steadily, knowing that she needed every last ounce of determination to keep her nerve.

'Why will you not tell me?' he said softly.

She swallowed and her throat was so dry that the sides of it seemed to stick together. 'I have already told you the truth.'

'Of what?'

She glanced away, scared that he would see what she was trying to hide.

He pulled her marginally closer, staring down at her with eyes that seemed to see her very core. 'Kempster says that your father is dead. Is it true?'

She jumped at his words, afraid that he was touching too close to her secret. Please make him stop questioning her. She did not want him to know of her real identity and of her father. 'My family is none of your concern, sir.'

'Have we not already been through the matter of what is my concern when it comes to you?' His voice was soft as a caress, the words delivered as from one lover to another.

Her eyes shuttered momentarily. He was standing so

close that she could feel the warmth of his breath upon her forehead. She felt herself weakening.

'Miss Meadowfield,' he said gently and she opened her eyes to find the silver gaze fixed on hers. He released her wrist and moved to hold her hand. His fingers were warm as they encompassed hers, and she felt her skin tingle beneath his touch. 'Will you not trust me?'

Lord help her, but she wanted to. She wanted to tell him and for him to take her in his arms and hold her, just hold her. She wanted so much to be free of the burden she had carried for so long. Her steadfastness wavered.

'Wolf,' she whispered, and gently rubbed her thumb against his, where their hands embraced. 'I...'

And then the hint of smoke reached her nose, and instinctively she turned her face to the window and the cold moonlit yard.

They both saw it, just as the hammering started at the bedchamber door, with Campbell's voice yelling loud, and from below they could hear other shouts and the scrape and bang of chairs and stools against the wooden floor. Down in the inn's stables was the flicker of flames.

By the time Wolf reached the yard, the smoke was billowing thick and the flames had spread. From within the stables came the scream of panicked horses. Men were already leading some of the terrified animals out, taking them on to the road beyond, struggling to control their frantic responses. Women were screaming, men were shouting, running, drawing water from the pump, carrying buckets from which more water spilled than remained to be poured upon the flames.

'Hell,' Wolf swore softly beneath his breath, not wanting to be involved in any of this, but knowing he was all the same. He organized the rabble of men into a chain along which the buckets of water could be passed, minimizing spillage, allaying confusion, dowsing the fire. Wolf knew it was too late to save the stables, but there was still a chance to prevent the flames from reaching the inn building. There was chaos all around. The fire roared louder than the men's shouts. Wolf ran into the stable to save the last of the horses.

The heat and the smoke within the yard were bad enough; inside the stable, they were almost unbearable. He moved quickly, knowing that they did not have much time left before the whole place would be engulfed. He found the last remaining occupied stall, slipped the bolt on its door, and, grabbing the terrified gelding by the mane, led him towards the stable's big open doors, towards fresh air and freedom. Campbell was running at the other side of the horse, coaxing the beast on, reassuring him with quiet words. They were nearly there when they passed Rosalind Meadowfield, still wearing her great long cloak, running the opposite way.

Wolf's gaze spun round after, unable to believe what he thought he was seeing, but then Campbell was shouting her name, and he knew that he had not been mistaken.

'Get yourself and the horse out,' he yelled at Campbell 'I'll fetch her.'

'Be quick, Wolf, or the whole damn place will be down on both your heads.'

But Wolf was already running, clutching his handkerchief to his mouth and nose, trying to stave off the worst of the thick acrid smoke.

She was running towards the ladder that led up to the hayloft, and he sprinted across to head her off. He grabbed her round the waist just as she set foot on the bottom rung, hauled her off and began to carry her towards the door.

But she fought him, just as strongly as she had done in the woods earlier that day.

'No!' she screamed and struggled all the more to get back to the ladder.

'What the hell are you doing? We'll both die in here if you do not move!' He lifted her body and moved to swing her over his shoulder.

'The boy,' she yelled. 'The little beggar boy is in here. I saw him come in earlier this evening.'

'He'll be gone.'

'No!' she wriggled so hard that he almost dropped her, and had to clasp her firm in place as he began to stride away.

'Please, Wolf! Do not leave him to burn!' She was still struggling against him, and then he heard the weak cry from above and, glanced back to see the small terrified face staring down from the hayloft.

'Mister!' the boy shouted; his voice was wavering with fear.

Wolf set Miss Meadowfield down on her feet. 'Get out of here fast,' he instructed. 'I'll fetch the lad.' He gave her a push towards the door, and turned back towards the ladder. The heat was unbearable as he climbed its rungs as fast as he could, the wood sliding beneath the sweat where his fingers gripped. He grabbed the boy just as part of the hayloft collapsed and the flames began to lick around the ladder. He looked over the edge, gauging the distance to the ground, and unbelievably, saw Miss Meadowfield standing there, staring right back up at him.

'You will have to drop him over. I will try to catch him,' she shouted up at him.

She was right, he realized. There was not time for anything else. He shouted a warning and then dropped the boy towards her. He saw her reach for the small body, and catch him, the impact sending her sprawling on to her back. But Wolf had already jumped and was lifting the boy and dragging Miss Meadowfield up. With the boy in his arms and Miss Meadowfield by his side, he ran for the door, as behind him the last of the hayloft disintegrated and the fire roared with a raging intensity at being deprived of its victims.

He carried the boy out on to the road before laying him down.

The child lay there still and unmoving, his little face all blackened by smoke.

Wolf slapped gently at the boy's cheeks, muttering soft words. 'Come on, lad. Speak to me.'

And then he saw Miss Meadowfield unfasten her cloak and crouch down by the boy's body to put the thick fur-lined material over him. 'Is he…' Her eyes met Wolf's in the moonlight, and in them he could see the dread that he heard in her voice. Her gaze moved to the boy, and she reached a hand down to tenderly stroke his face.

The boy moaned and then began to cough a terrible hacking cough, coughing and coughing until he rolled on his side and was sick.

'He'll live,' said Wolf, and saw her shoulders slump with the relief of it.

'Thank God,' she whispered.

'How did you know he was still in there? He might have left since you saw him go in.'

She shook her head. 'I was by the window for most of the evening and I did not see him again. I followed you down and checked round all of the crowd; the boy was not amongst them. Then one of the ostlers told me that the child sometimes slept in the hayloft.'

'You could have been killed,' said Wolf harshly .

'No more so than you,' she uttered defiantly. 'I could not leave him to burn.'

'Aye, happen you could not,' and his voice was less hard this time and she saw the understanding in his eyes.

It was his gentleness that was her undoing. She stared at Wolf and could no longer hide her anguish. 'He must be all of five years old and he sleeps alone in a hayloft.' Her voice broke and she began to weep.

Wolf began to reach for her but then Campbell was there and Kempster and more people, including a doctor, and Rosalind Meadowfield was swallowed up by the crowd.

Rosalind felt a hand close around her elbow, and she looked up into the face of Pete Kempster. He helped her up, as people closed in all around her hiding Wolf and the child. She felt Kempster take her arm, and guide her through the crowd.

'Come on,' he said as they reached the edge where the density of people thinned.

She shook her head and tried to pull free from his grip. 'I should help Wolf with the boy.'

'Ain't nothing more you can do for him. Get moving.'

She started to walk towards the inn.

'Not that way.'

He caught her back, then pushed her in quite the opposite direction.

She looked at him in bewilderment. 'What are you doing?'

'You want to escape, don't you?'

'Yes, but—'

'Then get going before it's too late. I'll take you to the next mail stop.'

She stared at him, unable to believe what he was saying. 'Why would you help me?'

'Maybe I don't like the thought of Evedon hanging you after all.'

'But they will know that you helped me.'

'I'll be back before they even notice that I've gone.'

'But the fire…the boy… I cannot leave now. In the morning—'

'It'll be too late by the morning. We go now, or not at all.' Kempster was still holding her arm. His face was flushed and dirty with black smudges smeared across his cheeks. 'Make your choice, Miss Meadowfield: escape, or will you let Wolf cart you back to swing from a Newgate scaffold?'

He was right. There was nothing more she could do to help the boy. Tomorrow there would be Wolf to face once more, and his questions and this thing that was growing between them. She did not think that she had the strength to resist him. And for all that was happening to them both, he would still take her to Evedon.

Kempster was right: she had to go now. It was her last chance, her only chance. But the decision sat uneasy with her, for she wanted to know of the little boy's health, of where he would stay and who would care for him. She wanted to thank Wolf for saving him. Wanted to look into those silver eyes one more time. She caught back the thought, knowing that her mind must truly be befuddled. Survival was her priority. She must go now while she still had the chance.

She turned to Kempster. 'I must fetch my bag first.'

'Forget your bag.'

'If I am to survive alone, I will need it,' she insisted.

'Then be quick about it, or your chance will be lost.'

She gave a nod, and with his hand still around her arm he steered her towards the inn. One last glance back and the crowd parted momentarily so that she was granted a final glimpse of Wolf. And then Rosalind was hurrying alongside Kempster, feeling every inch a rat deserting a sinking ship.

Wolf carried the boy to a nearby cottage and saw that he was settled, before returning to fight what was left of the fire. Men were still passing buckets of water along their human chain, throwing water upon the flames. The stable building had all but collapsed and the ferocity of the fire was waning, but Wolf knew the danger to the inn itself was still there. He organized a second chain of men working parallel with the first to increase the water being thrown at the fire, hefting the buckets alongside Campbell, sweat soaking his body, his muscles aching from the relentless toil. His eyes were still stinging from the smoke, and the skin on his face and the backs of his hands felt as if they had been singed by the flames. Yet Wolf knew there was still much work to be done to ensure the safety of the inn.

They worked without rest, for hour after hour, all the men of the village, all the men of the inn, locals and guests alike. It was the early hours of the morning before the flames were finally dead and the remains of the stables stood as a black smouldering heap. Only then did the men wash the filth from themselves in buckets and troughs, drying themselves on towels supplied by the innkeeper's wife, before heading back to their homes and their beds.

Wolf slipped away to check on the boy before returning to the inn.

Campbell was sitting at the bar when he came in, a half-full tankard of ale before him. His face was pale even beneath the light of the candles and the layer of smoky grime that still clung to it. His eyes were red and sore from both fatigue and smoke.

'You all right, Struan?'

'Aye, I'm all right, Wolf, but I'm gonnae kick that Kempster's arse when I find him, the lazy wee turd's done a runner.'

'I'm going to do a sight more than that to the little bastard,' muttered Wolf. 'Have you checked on Miss Meadowfield?'

'Her door's locked. You have the key. And I didnae want to wake her. The lassie looked wrung out the last time I saw her.'

Wolf looked at him. 'I left the key in the door.'

'She must have locked it from the inside.'

But Wolf's instinct was telling him otherwise. He muttered a curse beneath his breath.

'Wolf—'

But Wolf was already moving, crossing the taproom floor to the stairs that would take him to Rosalind Meadowfield's bedchamber.

Campbell smiled at the landlord who was sitting on a nearby stool. 'There's no stopping a man wi' the bit between his teeth.' One last swig from the tankard and he was off and following in Wolf's wake.

Wolf ran up the stairs and barrelled down the corridor, only stopping when he reached the last room on the left. He knocked loud and long against the door. 'Miss Meadowfield.'

'Ssh!' hushed Campbell from behind. 'You'll have everyone up.'

'Miss Meadowfield!' Wolf's voice raised in volume.

No sound from within.

He tried the handle. It rattled uselessly within his fingers.

'Feeling strong?' he asked Campbell.

Campbell smiled and then drew back as he and Wolf kicked the door open.

The room was empty, of course, just as he had known that it would be. Of Miss Meadowfield and her bag there was no sign.

'Where the hell is she?' said Campbell from over his shoulder.

'Run away with Kempster,' said Wolf.

'In the name of all that's holy! She cannae have—'

'Believe me, she has,' said Wolf grimly, feeling like the biggest fool on earth.

'They must have left hours ago. They could be anywhere.'

'Not anywhere,' said Wolf. 'We know they're not travelling on horseback, and with the fire there are no gigs, carts or carriages to be spared. They're walking, Struan, and, because of Miss Meadowfield's feet, their progress will be slow.'

'Aye, maybe, but we've no idea of the direction they've taken.'

'Where would you go?'

A frown marred Campbell's brows. 'That would depend on why I was helping the lassie escape in the first place.'

Wolf's mouth curved to a mirthless smile. 'I doubt he wants to save her. Kempster's not the compassionate type.'

'Maybe he's sweet on her. Maybe there was something going on between them in London.'

Wolf shook his head. 'There's nought of affection in the way that he looks at her.'

'So why is he helping her then?'

'You've known lads like Kempster. What do they want?'

'An easy ride. A quick coin with least effort.'

'Exactly. So maybe he's not helping her; maybe he's

helping himself. Maybe he's taking her back to Evedon thinking to earn the fee for himself.'

'The lassie wouldnae have gone with him were that the case.'

'I doubt he'll have told her his plan.'

'Bastard,' said Campbell, 'I'll wring his conniving neck.'

'He'll be looking to travel fast.'

'The London mail then,' said Campbell. 'But they could-nae wait around here to catch it.'

'The landlord will be able to tell us its next stop.'

Campbell gave a nod.

The two men's eyes met.

'I hope you're right about this, Wolf. How can you be sure that she went with him of her own accord?'

'Had Kempster abducted her, he would not have come back for her bag,' said Wolf. 'Besides, I saw her walking away with him and she looked willing enough.'

There was a silence.

'Why was she in the stables tonight?' asked Campbell. 'If she's so frightened of horses, what the hell was she doing running in there when it was ablaze?'

Wolf leaned back against the door frame, tilting his head back to look up to the ceiling. 'She went into the stables to save the boy.'

'Hell!' said Campbell and Wolf could see the way that Campbell looked at him.

Another silence.

'We'd best be away after her then,' Campbell finally said.

Wolf looked at him a moment longer. 'There's something else you should know, Struan.'

Campbell tensed.

'The lad saw who started the fire.'

'It was deliberate?' He saw the shock register on Campbell's face.

'Aye, it was deliberate, all right,' said Wolf quietly.

'And who was it that the wee yin saw?'

Wolf's eyes met Campbell's. 'Pete Kempster.'

Chapter Ten

Rosalind was trudging along the road after Kempster. The dawn was grey and dismal, with a coolness in the air.

'Not much longer now,' Kempster said.

Rosalind nodded. Their hurried walk through the darkness of the night had ruptured the blisters again on her feet. The sole on one of her boots had finally worn right through, and her stocking and binding was damp from the dew on the grass. Her head was pounding, her throat and top of her chest were aching, and her eyes felt red-raw. Yet she knew that it was imperative that they push on to put a big enough distance between themselves and Wolf.

Wolf. Just his name sent a tremor through her. She knew that he must have discovered their absence by now and she could only guess at the level of his anger. He would come after them—she had no doubt of that—enraged and ruthless and determined to find them.

She thought of him carrying the little beggar boy from the burning stables, of his gentleness as he had tried to rouse the boy. *Come on, lad. Speak to me.* She thought of him walking those long miles by her side. One thought led to another, and she was reliving the touch of his lips against hers, the tenderness of his kiss. *Will you not trust me?* he had asked. She closed her eyes to block out the memories. He was being paid by Evedon to catch her. He was a common rogue, a man filled with anger and bitterness whom she had known but a few days. It was only sense not to trust him. It was the right thing to run from him, to take her chance of escape.

She knew all of these things, had told herself them again and again during her long march through the night. She was doing the right thing. So why did it feel so wrong? She seemed to hear the whisper of his words again: *Will you not trust me?* Rosalind had not trusted him. Instead she had accepted Kempster's offer of help, choosing to trust the footman, who had taken such delight in frightening her, rather than Wolf. And her heart was heavy with the knowledge.

Rosalind forced herself on with a determination that she had not known she possessed. Wolf would take her back to Evedon. The little boy's near death in the fire, and exhaustion were making her thoughts foolish. She resolved to think no more, and beneath the layers of her clothes, the press of the letter against her skin reminded her that Evedon would show no mercy. Rosalind kept on walking.

Wolf urged his horse on. They were covering ground fast, heading towards Leeming Lane seven miles to the south, where the mail coach to London stopped. They stuck to the main road, but scanned the surrounding countryside as they rode.

Wolf knew that there could only be one reason for Kempster to have started the fire—and that was so that no one was looking when he slipped away with Rosalind Meadowfield. The memory of Miss Meadowfield following Kempster into the inn while Wolf knelt by the boy's side flashed in his mind. There had been nothing of force there, nothing of coercion; she had followed quite willingly, more than willingly if her glance back had been anything to go by. He had seen the guilt as her gaze touched to his. He had not understood that look at the time; he understood it now. There had been every reason for guilt when she was running away, and with Kempster of all people. Had his taunting her upon the horse been all of an act to set up her miserable attempt at escape yesterday? Somehow he doubted it. But there could be no doubt over today.

When had they planned it? It must have been when Kempster had taken up her tray of food last night. But to burn the stable…And the horrible thought was there again in the back of his mind, niggling at him, just as it had been since the lad had named Kempster as the fire starter and he had discovered Miss Meadowfield and the footman gone. Had she known what Kempster meant to do? Is that why she had stood by the window in her room looking down over the stables, still wearing her cloak—waiting for him to start the blaze?

Was she complicit in the deed? Is that why she had cared so much for the life of a small beggar boy? The memory of her within that burning stable was one that would not leave him, and neither would the expression upon her face when she had looked upon the boy and wept. None of that had been feigned; he would stake his life on it.

He had spent the past days believing the very worst of Rosalind Meadowfield. Indeed, he had been prejudiced against her before he had even set his eyes upon her. It was enough to hear from Evedon that she was the daughter of a rich gentleman—that fact alone had seen Wolf judge her.

He had disliked her at first, despised her even, but the days since had changed that, those hauntingly beautiful eyes making him question all that Evedon had told him.

Damn his own weakness. His attraction to her was blinding him to the truth. He could believe that she had gone willingly with Kempster, even after she had stood in that moonlit room, and he had felt the small stroke of her thumb against his. Such a minuscule action and yet, to him, it had meant so much. But what Wolf did not want to believe was that Rosalind Meadowfield had had any role in the fire. The irony of it struck him hard. He felt the bitterness rise in his throat, and a sense of betrayal. She was everything that he had initially thought, so why did he feel that he had just been punched in the stomach?

He thought of the attraction he felt for her, of the lust—for it could be nothing else. She represented everything that he had been raised to hate. She was the very antithesis of him, and yet he wanted her, wanted her with a desire that he had not previously been willing to admit to himself. He admitted it now. And the knowledge filled him with self-loathing.

He thought of Kempster and of all the women that the footman had tumbled since setting out from London. Kempster, with his tongue so silvered that he could seduce the very birds from the trees. He told women what they wanted to hear, words of love that meant nothing, words that, coupled with his dark pretty-boy looks, had the women hitching up their skirts and splaying their legs. Two chamber maids, three serving wenches, a landlord's wife, a rich widow and the widow's daughter. Wolf had seen Kempster at work, and he did not suppose that the footman would make an exception for Miss Meadowfield. And maybe Miss Meadowfield would not want him to. Maybe she would want what all those other women had wanted. Maybe she would want Kempster.

He thought of Kempster's perfect face, and charming words. He thought of him lighting the fire that could have killed the little lad in the stables. He thought too of him seducing Miss Meadowfield, of the footman kissing her, touching her, bedding her. And deep within Wolf, a cold determined rage flared. In his mind, he saw himself smashing his fist into Kempster's jaw again and again and again, and the feeling was good.

He glanced over at Campbell and spurred his horse on faster.

Rosalind waited outside while Kempster took the last of her money into the Royal Oak Inn. It was still early in the morning, and they had some time to wait before the mail coach's arrival. Stable boys went about their business cleaning out the stables of the post-horses, sweeping and shovelling and forking, until the stalls were clean and sweet smelling.

Rosalind stood close to the inn's door, trying hard to merge with the wall behind her. She knew that she must present a dismal sight with her head uncovered, her red-rimmed eyes and the remnants of grime that still clung to her face and hands. Her dress was dirty and snagged, her boots scraped and worn. A strand of hair that had escaped her pins curved against her throat, while several others wisped against her cheeks and forehead. Self-consciously she tried to tuck them back into place, seeing the curious glances that the stable boys were sending her way. She was a far cry from the Miss Meadowfield that had stepped from the coach on Munnoch Moor to find the tall silver-eyed man waiting for her. Wolf. She glanced towards the road outside, feeling the beat of a thousand tiny wings rise within her stomach. Was he searching for her even now? Part of her dreaded it, and part wished it was so.

The door opened and Kempster reappeared, stuffing something into his pocket. 'London mail is in one hour.'

'London?' She stared at him, feeling the shock jolt her. 'But I thought to go north.'

'Wolf would catch you again too easily there. London's a big place, big enough for a lady to disappear in, never to be found.' He smiled reassuringly.

'I am not so convinced.'

'You worry too much, Miss Meadowfield. Trust me when I tell you that London is a far safer bet than the wilds of Scotland.'

She bit at her lower lip, reticent to go anywhere near Evedon House ever again.

'Besides I've already bought the tickets.'

'Tickets?' She stared at him, her heart beating suddenly too fast. 'Have I need of more than one?'

'It ain't safe for a lady travelling on her own these days. Should anything happen to you, I could not live with myself. It's safer if I escort you.'

'But if you do not go back to the inn, then Mr Wolversley will know that you are helping me, and Evedon will learn of it too. I thought—'

'Don't worry so, miss. I'll find a way round it, but for now, speak no more on the matter, for my mind is quite decided.'

Yet she was worried, and her underlying unease with Kempster was growing by the minute. Everything had seemed clear last night, but now with his insistence on accompanying her, it all looked very different.

'How do I know that you will not take me to Evedon yourself?'

Kempster's eyes widened as if he was wounded by the

very suggestion. 'If I wanted to see you hang, then I'd have left you with Wolf—not risked my neck to help you.' His gaze was filled with such sincerity that her suspicion seemed unreasonable.

'Mr Kempster, I am sorry but I cannot let you travel with me. I thank you for all that you have done for me but, please, go back to Mr Wolversley. Leave me here to make my own way.'

Kempster turned the blueness of his gaze upon her. 'You know that I cannot do that, Miss Meadowfield.'

'I will be safe enough on my own, and I have no wish to cause you trouble with Mr Wolversley or Lord Evedon. Indeed, I insist upon travelling alone.'

There was only the sound of the stable boys sweeping. And when Rosalind glanced round, she could see that the boy closest to them was listening.

'We should continue this discussion somewhere more private.' Kempster took hold of her arm.

Little bells of warning began to sound in Rosalind's head. She stopped where she was.

'Unless you want the whole yard to hear your business, miss, and somehow I don't think that that's such a good idea, do you?'

He was right of course. She nodded and let him lead her out into the street and down a nearby alleyway. Only when they were within the narrow shady alleyway did he stop.

'Your concern for my welfare is touchin', Miss Meadowfield, but I assure you that I have no intention of allowing you to travel alone.' His voice was still deep and charming, but Rosalind thought she could detect an undertone of irritation.

'No, Mr Kempster—' she began, but he did not let her finish.

'You travel with me, or not at all, Miss Meadowfield,' he said, and there was a distinct chill in his gaze.

The hand of fear stroked the nape of her neck so that she felt her skin prickle with foreboding. 'Then take me back.'

He looked at her strangely for a second, as if he could not believe what she had just said. 'I'm offering you freedom and you choose to go back?'

'You wish to take me to London, Mr Kempster. Forgive me if it does not much seem like an offer of escape. I have made a mistake. I wish you to take me back to the inn.'

'To Wolf?' There was an element of ridicule in his words.

'Yes, to Wolf.'

His eyes narrowed and their blueness seemed to intensify. 'You're right, Miss Meadowfield, you have made a mistake,' he said softly. All the charm had gone, and when she looked at him, there was an unmistakable cruelty about his handsome features.

She tried to turn away, to leave the isolation of this dank alleyway filled with shadows, but Kempster stepped closer, trapping her where she was.

'You're travellin' to London with me, miss, if I have to knock you unconscious and carry you on to that mail coach myself.'

She felt the dread constrict her chest and the shock of his threat ripple through her. 'You *are* taking me to Evedon!' She stared at him aghast.

'Dear lady.' He smiled a small sly smile. 'Where else would I be taking you?'

'I do not understand why you should do such a thing, and neither will Lord Evedon.'

'Evedon will not care, as long as he has you. Besides, I

find I have a need to get back to London in a hurry: Wolf's asking too many questions.'

'What sort of questions?'

'Questions about you; questions that make me think he's havin' doubts over your guilt.'

'He believes me innocent?' Kempster's revelation came as a surprise. She knew that she had been wrong to accept his offer of escape.

'Did you persuade him while he was binding your feet?' His chuckle had an unpleasant ring to it. He leaned his face down to hers, his arms snaking around her body. She shrank back, but her head and spine hit against cold stonework.

'No need for such pretence,' he murmured. 'You were not so coy with Wolf, or with Evedon for that matter.'

'I do not know what you mean.'

Kempster smiled with a leering insolence that made Rosalind more afraid than ever. 'I saw you with Wolf, remember, having your feet bound, and I saw you with Evedon too. I was there the night the jewels were found, when Graves fetched you both from the study. I saw your hair all long and wanton. I saw your rosy flushed cheeks and the way your dress gaped from your shoulder. One look and I knew what you'd been up to. Quite the little whore, ain't you, Miss Meadowfield?'

'You have run mad!'

'Oh, cease your game, miss, I'm better looking than the two of them. I've had my share of noble ladies— countesses, duchesses even.' He leaned in and licked the length of her cheek.

She yanked her face away. 'Stand away from me, Mr Kempster. I want none of this.'

'You cannot possibly prefer that scar-faced bastard to

me. He *is* a bastard, you know. Did he not tell you that little detail when he was binding your feet?'

'How dare you?' she gasped.

But his mouth closed over hers and he was kissing her, forcing his tongue between her lips. He was pressing his body too close to hers, sliding his hands over her, one hand groping at her buttocks while the other closed around her breast.

She struggled against him, pushing him off, all of her anger and indignation and fear lending her a strength that she did not know she had. 'Unhand me!' she cried. 'Leave me alone.'

But he did not. He pulled her closer, trying to kiss her, his hand fondling her breast. 'Which petticoats are you wearing, Miss Meadowfield, which shift? The one with the lace, I hope.'

She pushed hard against him, but he did not budge. 'Cease this!' she yelled.

'It was such a pretty match for that black silken rope. Do you know that some women like to be tied up while they are ridden by a man? Maybe I should bind you with some rope,' he whispered against her ear and pressed his crotch into her hips.

Within those vulgar horrible words Rosalind heard the truth. She stopped struggling then, and looked at him. 'It was you,' she whispered, her face aghast. 'You stole the jewels and hid them in my chamber.'

'Now you know why I am eager to return to London—before Wolf works it out.'

'Then you admit your guilt?'

'Gladly.' He smiled. 'No one will believe you, Miss Meadowfield. You'll be a desperate woman trying to save her reputation. Besides it was Graves that found the diamonds in your shift, not me. He's a butler beyond reproach. Surely you know that?'

'Why do you hate me so much? Because I would not walk out with you?'

'I do not hate you, Miss Meadowfield.'

'Then why do such a thing?'

'Money,' he said simply. 'Someone offered me a lot of money to set you up as a thief. I found the offer too good to refuse.'

Her blood ran cold. 'Who?' she whispered.

'He did not exactly introduce himself. A gentleman, a stranger, dark, mysterious, a bit of a foreigner, I think. Asked all sorts of questions about you, Miss Meadowfield. He did not like you too much. Oh, and the rope was at his instruction. Tied it like a noose himself. Said you would understand its meaning all too well.'

She shook her head, unwilling to believe that it was a reference to her father and his execution. She had changed her name, severed contact with her mother, with Nell, all so that the Evedons would not discover her real identity. And yet a dark stranger had known that a silken noose would have a significance for her.

'Whomever is behind this, Mr Kempster, wishes me to hang for a crime I did not commit. If you return me to Evedon, you may as well place the noose around my neck with your own hands.'

Kempster laughed. 'They'll not hang you, Miss Meadowfield, we all know that. You're a lady, a gentlewoman; they do not hang the likes of you. The gentleman just wants to see you ruined, so he said. Shame about Evedon wantin' it all kept quiet. And just so you know, I've already sent the gent warning that Evedon means to hush up the scandal.' He smiled and stroked her cheek. 'I'm sure that he'd want to know of it. Very generous gentleman he is, very generous indeed.'

'You are a monster beyond imagination, Mr Kempster!'

'Spread your legs, darlin' and I'll show you a monster.'
He pushed her back hard against the wall, and his mouth closed over hers suffocating her with its hard demand, while his hands wrenched her dress from her shoulders.

She pushed and kicked, but Kempster just thrust his body hard against hers to still her legs and he held her arms in a cruel imprisonment. She tried to scream, but she could barely breathe with his lips effectively a gag against hers. She bit him, tasting blood before he started back.

He stared at her as if he could not believe what she had just done, dabbing his fingers gingerly to his lip. 'You little bitch!' He looked down at the glistening crimson smear that stained his fingers. 'You've marked me!' His eyes were dark with malice and anger.

She tried to run then, pushing past him, but he caught her back, his hand like a vice around her arm.

'You're going to pay for that, missy,' and then quick as lightning, he lashed out with a smack of his hand across her face.

The force of the blow sent Rosalind reeling. She hit against the wall, and then stumbled, falling on to her knees.

He reached for her and Rosalind tried to scrabble away, but not fast enough. His hand grabbed at her hair, yanking her back. 'Now, I am goin' to have you, Miss Rosalind Meadowfield, and you're goin' to stand there and let me. And when the mail coach arrives you will climb upon it with me. Fight me, and I'll do all of these things having rendered you senseless.'

'You are the very devil,' she whispered.

He smiled, and then pressed his mouth against hers with

a savagery that could not be called a kiss, while his fingers clawed their way through the layers of her clothing to find the nakedness of her breasts.

She had not trusted Wolf, she thought. And now she would pay the price.

Chapter Eleven

'Kempster, you little rat,' a voice suddenly rang out in the alleyway, a voice that Rosalind recognized. Her heart leapt in hope.

There was the tall figure of Wolf standing as he had stood the night she had first seen him in his long brown leather coat and brown leather hat with its wide brim. And for a moment, she wondered whether he was really there, in this stinking alley with Kempster, or whether it was her wishful mind playing cruel tricks upon her. The silver gaze met hers momentarily before passing on to fix itself upon Kempster, and she knew from the shiver that rippled right through her body that he was no apparition.

'It's not what you think.' Kempster released his grip on her. 'I saw her making a run for it, and followed her here. I was bringing her back to you, Mr Wolversley, honest I was. But she was not making it easy. I had to restrain her somehow.' He held his hands out towards Wolf, palms up.

Wolf said nothing, and yet the threat emanating from him was overwhelming without the need for a single word. His expression was utterly ruthless. There was a hard line to his jaw that hinted at barely suppressed violence, and his eyes…Rosalind trembled just to look at them, for Wolf's eyes held the promise of death. Kempster must have seen it too. She saw him pale and begin to back away.

He was like some victim trapped in the stare of his predator.

Wolf's gaze flicked to the alley beyond Kempster's shoulder before coming back to his victim once more, and Kempster could not help himself from turning his head to glance in the same direction.

The huge figure of Struan Campbell stood not so very far away behind him. 'Good morning, Mr Kempster,' the Scotsman said, and there was a dark dangerous intensity about his face that matched Wolf's.

Rosalind began to edge away from Kempster, towards Wolf.

Wolf moved then, seizing hold of her, pulling her to safety behind him. And not once, as he did it, did his eyes leave the footman's.

He heard Kempster mumble a curse. 'You've got this all wrong,' he said, backing away.

'You're the one that's got it wrong, Kempster.' Wolf's voice was quiet and deadly.

He struck then, his fist hitting hard against Kempster's face, sending him staggering back towards Campbell. From the corner of his eye, he saw Miss Meadowfield start.

Campbell pushed Kempster forward again to where Wolf stood waiting.

Kempster put his head down and ran at Wolf swinging his fists, but Wolf had fought men like Kempster before, in York and London, Walcheren and the Peninsula, and he knew what to do. He dodged back, ducking left then right, Kempster's enraged blows missing him.

Let him waste his energy, lose his control, think he had a chance of winning, Wolf might get some answers then. He jabbed at Kempster's left cheek, then at his right, dropping his guard just low enough to let a blow land. Kempster accepted the invitation, and Wolf felt the footman's fist contact his mouth. The metallic taste of blood was warm against his tongue. He heard Miss Meadowfield gasp loudly and he gave a step and then another, allowing Kempster to come forward, to take the lead. He saw the smile that curved upon Kempster's face, exposing teeth that were washed red with blood, and knew that he had him.

'Evedon wouldn't have paid you for her you know. You're his servant. He thinks he owns you already.'

'It's not about Evedon.' Kempster smiled. 'She begged me to help her escape you.'

'I did no such thing!' The denial burst from Rosalind Meadowfield's lips.

Wolf glanced across at where she stood. Her face was pale and there was a smear of blood in the corner of her lips. Her eyes met his, and he could see the indignation there.

He looked back at Kempster. 'And I suppose you felt obliged to help her out of the goodness of you heart?'

'That and the money she offered.'

Wolf's eyes narrowed.

'There was no money. He is lying.' Miss Meadowfield stared from Wolf to Kempster and back again.

'Lying am I?' Kempster looked at her in a desultory manner. 'Are you claiming that I abducted you? Do you deny that you came with me willingly?'

'You said you would take me to catch the mail, that you would help me escape,' she said, shaking her head.

Kempster smiled, knowing that her words confirmed his story. He turned to Wolf, brave now that he thought he had a chance of besting him. 'I see the way you look at her, Wolf. You say that you hate her kind, but you want Miss Rosalind Meadowfield all the same.'

Wolf said nothing but his expression was dark as thunder.

'Did you really think that she would choose a scar-faced bastard like you, over me?' Kempster taunted.

Wolf forced himself not to rise to the bait; he breathed slow and even, until the rage was controlled.

'She was paying me to get her away from you, Wolf,' he said and laughed.

It was all Wolf could do not to land the blow right then and there. He held back.

'Did she pay you to start the fire too?' Wolf asked.

For once Kempster was lost for words, as if he had not expected Wolf to know what he had done.

'Or did you forget to tell her that you started the fire as a distraction so that you both might make your getaway?' Wolf felt something tighten in his gut in anticipation of Kempster's answer.

Rosalind Meadowfield moved forward to stand by Wolf's side. She was staring at Kempster with a look of horror on her face. 'You started the fire?'

'I did not know that the boy was in there, did I? I thought everyone had gone home.'

She shook her head in disbelief. 'You could have killed that child, and the horses too.'

'But I did not,' said Kempster smugly. 'Besides, what do you care about horses, or a beggar boy for that matter?'

There was a silence.

Wolf did not take his eyes off Kempster, but he could

sense the sudden stillness in Miss Meadowfield by his side.

'You are a fiend,' she whispered, and Wolf could hear the break in her voice. 'A damnable fiend.'

And then, against all that Wolf was expecting, she launched herself at Kempster, hitting and slapping at him and crying as she did so.

Wolf stared, stunned for a second, before catching her round the waist and dragging her off.

'No!' The tears were spilling down her cheeks. 'Leave me be, he deserves it!' She struggled against him.

'Aye, he does that,' said Wolf against her ear. 'But leave him to me.' He pushed her towards Campbell. 'See to Miss Meadowfield, Struan.'

'Little bitch!' Kempster snapped, dabbing a finger at the bite mark on his lip that was now bleeding again. 'Look what she's done to me. I'll kill her.'

'No, you will not,' said Wolf grimly, and saw Kempster's eyes look up to meet his. Wolf took off his hat and coat, and threw them to Campbell. He slipped off his waistcoat and rolled up his shirt sleeves.

'You think you're a man, Kempster, when you're not even fit to be called a dog.' He landed Kempster a single almighty punch into which all of his strength had been focused.

The younger man staggered back beneath the force to slump against the wall behind, before slithering down to land in a limp pile on the filth of the alley's soil.

Miss Meadowfield walked slowly to stand by Wolf's side and all the while she was staring at Kempster's crumpled body. Just staring and staring.

She reached a hand blindly to clutch at Wolf's arm. 'Is he dead? Have we killed him?' Her voice was flat, the volume barely above a whisper. He noticed her use of the word 'we', as if she took as much responsibility for Kempster's state as Wolf himself.

'He is very much alive, more is the pity.'

And she stood there motionless, her eyes still fixed on Kempster, and Wolf could feel the tremble in her fingers that clung to him. She had probably never witnessed a fight before, let alone been involved in one.

'Miss Meadowfield.'

No response.

'Miss Meadowfield,' he said again.

She seemed to hear him then and, glancing round, saw that she was gripping for dear life to his arm. Her hand dropped away. 'I am sorry,' she said, and looked up at him.

Her face was dirty and tear-stained, her cheeks devoid of colour save for the blood that trickled from the corner of her mouth. There were dark shadows beneath her red-rimmed eyes. Her hair hung long and curling and wild around her shoulders, her dress was torn, and the stench of smoke still clung to her. Yet she met his gaze and he saw in it bewilderment and shock and pain. She was lost, set adrift from everything that she knew and had known, the security of her own small world shattered.

'I know, lass,' he said gently.

She said nothing, just stared at him with a need that was as raw and aching as his own and her face seemed to grow whiter by the minute.

He retrieved his coat and draped it around her, while he spoke his instructions quietly to Campbell, not wanting to frighten her. And when he took her hand in his and led her out of the alley, she went with him as trusting as a child.

Rosalind sat on the edge of the bed in a bedchamber of the Royal Oak Inn in Leeming Lane. She had scoured

Kempster's touch from her body, and changed into a fresh dress. Her hair was in some semblance of order, raked by her fingers and fastened tidily with a ribbon. Her lips had been scrubbed, her face was washed and the dust wiped from her boots, but Rosalind still felt unclean.

She sat there, unmoving. Despite the mildness of the day, her hands and feet were ice cold. Her mind was filled with the images of Wolf and Kempster fighting, of the terrible ferocity of the blows, of the sound of fist contacting flesh and the smell of the blood that splattered the walls of the alley and the soil beneath. She thought too of Kempster's lies. The footman had lied to them all, to Evedon and Wolf and herself. He had stolen the jewels and framed Rosalind. He had been prepared to see her hang, and all for money from some stranger.

Kempster had lied to her from the start, and Rosalind had been too blind and too stupid to see it. She knew now that he had never intended to help her at all. He was 'stealing' her from Wolf, taking her back to Evedon. She had been a fool a hundred times over, trusting a villain's lies instead of trusting Wolf.

Wolf. She thought of him appearing there in that alleyway—the man from whom she had run, the man she had told herself that she hated—standing there so tall and strong and resolute. And she had known then, in that single moment, that she was safe, that Wolf would save her from Kempster. She did not remember that he was a thief-taker or that Evedon had employed him to capture her. She just saw Wolf and his rugged severity and the silver blaze of danger in his eyes and the simmering fury that he focused upon the footman. Her relief had been such that she could have run to him and thrown herself into his arms were it not for Kempster.

She thought of the warm strength of Wolf's grip as he

had pulled her to him, thrusting her behind him, protecting her with his body. It was true that he was unlike any man she had ever met. His appearance, his manner, his voice—all of them were harsh, hard, threatening almost. But when these were stripped away, what was left beneath? A man who had walked miles by her side because he knew she was afraid of horses, a man who had bound the wounds on her feet, a man who had risked his life to rescue a child from a fire. He had not ceased in his effort to prevent the blaze's spread. He had worked all night to douse the fire, while Rosalind had run…with Kempster. She closed her eyes at the thought, ashamed of her decision.

She had listened to logic, to sense and rationale; Wolf was her captor and she had run from him, but her heart knew the truth of him, she could no longer deny it. She had judged Wolf a villain and a rogue but it was herself and Kempster that owned those names, choosing to run when they should have stood firm to help and all because of Kempster's lies and her own misjudgement.

And what of the lies that Kempster had told of her? She did not think that Wolf would be fool enough to believe them. Today, in that alleyway, she had run to him instinctively—wanting him, needing him. She did not understand it. She was reeling, confused, emotional, no longer knowing what was right and what was wrong, no longer knowing what to feel. She put her head in her hands, and did not know what to do.

Wolf and Campbell stood in the yard of the inn and watched Kempster ride away.

'No bloody evidence,' said Campbell. Sunshine washed the darkness of his hair mahogany.

'The likes of beggar boys do not make credible enough witnesses for magistrates.' Wolf's expression was bitter.

Campbell's glance gestured towards the fold of bank notes that Wolf still held in his hand. 'Thirty pounds is a lot of money for a footman to have in his purse.'

'He says that it came from Miss Meadowfield, a bribe for his assistance. A considerable sum for a poor ladies' companion to offer.' Wolf's voice dripped with cynicism.

'You think that it's the money from the emeralds, that she sold them before she left London?'

'I do not know what to think any more, Struan.'

Campbell gave a grunt of agreement. There was a small pause before he asked, 'What of Miss Meadowfield?'

'What of her?' Wolf kept his gaze trained on the retreating figure of Kempster.

'Is she hurt?'

'Bruised and shaken. Nothing more as far as I could see.'

'Then he hadnae…?' Campbell looked at Wolf meaningfully.

Wolf shook his head. 'He had not got that far.'

'Bastard,' cursed Campbell.

'Aye, he's that all right,' agreed Wolf.

Down the road, the last trace of Kempster disappeared into the distance.

Campbell turned to Wolf. 'What now?'

'Now we continue on to London.'

'But Miss Meadowfield…Is she recovered enough to travel? Maybe we should wait a few days before—'

But Wolf cut him off. 'We need to finish this job, Struan. Get it over and done with, take the money and get clear of the whole damn mess.'

Campbell looked hard at Wolf. 'You're no' really gonnae force that lassie on to a horse the day, after what Kempster did to her, are you?'

'We'll travel post-chaise. You seem to be forgetting that

Miss Meadowfield is a felon in our custody. She ran off willingly with Kempster.'

'And you're forgetting that she went into a burning stable to save a wean. The boy would have burned had it no' been for her.' Campbell looked at him. 'What is this about, Wolf?'

But Wolf did not want to reveal the sense of betrayal that he felt at Rosalind Meadowfield's flight. He did not want Campbell to know that when it came to her he could no longer trust himself to think straight; more than that, he thought angrily, that he, who had spent his life hating the likes of Rosalind Meadowfield, had feelings for the woman.

'Having second thoughts about bringing her in?' asked Wolf in a quiet voice.

'Sometimes you can be a hardnosed bastard, Wolf.'

'Just sometimes?' queried Wolf, and raised his eyebrows.

Campbell shook his head in disbelief.

Wolf turned back into the inn, walking across the floor of the public room towards the stairs.

'Wolf,' Campbell's voice sounded softly.

He stopped, glanced back.

Campbell's gaze met his, and he could see the concern in it.

He gave a grim nod of acknowledgement, knowing that Campbell was asking him to be gentle with Rosalind Meadowfield. But what was simmering inside of him was not in the slightest bit gentle. It was an explosive mixture of hurt and anger and desire. She had played him, and he had been a fool to allow himself to listen to her, to begin to trust her. She did not want him, but only to escape the justice Evedon had waiting for her. All else was lies, manipulation—just as he should have known. The echo of his mother's tortured words sounded from the past, words of darkness and injustice, words of warning…and his own whispered promise from so long ago: *Vengeance upon the gentry; sweet vengeance for a life destroyed.*

And then he climbed the stairs that would take him to the bedchamber in which he had left Miss Meadowfield, determined, despite all of Campbell's words, that she would face the consequences of her actions in full.

She would tell him, she had decided. All of it, every last sordid detail. He had saved her from Kempster. Maybe if he knew the truth, he would save her from Evedon too. For all of his harsh exterior, he had proved to be the true gentleman. It was Kempster, with his smooth pretty gilding, that had been the rogue. Her heart was telling her to trust Wolf, and, for once in her life, Rosalind would not choose the sensible safe option, she would listen to her instinct.

A knock at the door.

Rosalind stared at the door, her heart skipping a beat. A pause, before it swung open to reveal the man that stood framed in the doorway.

'Wolf.' His name escaped her lips before she could stop it. She was on her feet and moving towards him, smiling— before she saw the expression on his face. All trace of gentleness had vanished from him. He was once more the Wolf who had met her from the coach on Munnoch Moor. The smile slipped from her mouth. Her steps checked, and she halted, looking at him with uncertainty.

Wolf stepped into the room and closed the door behind him.

She stood where she was, unsure of what to do.

He stood in the shadow by the door. 'You are recovered?' he asked; his voice had all of the same old harshness to it.

In that moment she knew that everything had changed, that this was not the same Wolf who had kissed her with such tenderness, the man who had saved her from Kempster. The wash of despair was so great that she could have wept had she allowed herself to. Fanciful hope shattered; he would not save her from Evedon, and Rosalind knew she would tell him nothing.

She nodded, not trusting herself to speak.

'And are you well enough to travel this day?'

'To London?' Her heart rate accelerated as she awaited his answer, even though she already knew what it would be.

'Where else?' he said.

She glanced away that he would not see the truth of her feelings.

The silence hissed between them.

'When do we leave?' She forced herself to meet his gaze squarely, to stand up straight and proud and strong as if she cared not one jot.

'As soon as you are ready.' He stepped out of the shadow and into the sunlight that flooded the room. The battered leather hat held within his hand brushed against his thigh. His hair was ruffled, as if he had just run his hand through it, its strands glinting golden in the sun, and his eyes were a pale mesmerising grey against the honeyed tan of his skin. His face was lean and rugged and, for all of its severity, much more handsome than the pretty-boy looks of Pete Kempster; she thought that she had never seen a man to match him.

She took a deep breath. 'I am ready now.' The calmness of her voice made her words all the more convincing. It was a lie, of course. She would never be ready to face Evedon.

He stood there, looking at her, and she looked right back at him, and the tension pulled tight between them.

'The little boy from the stables—how is he?' She hoped that he would think the hoarseness of her voice due to the effect of smoke.

'Why would you care?' A short hard sentence, uttered like a whiplash of contempt.

'I care,' she countered.

'You care so much that you ran off with Kempster rather than stay to help the lad.'

It was the truth and the truth hurt. Yet it was not just that which she baulked at; he made it sound as if she had eloped with Kempster, as if there had been something between them. She ignored his comment.

'The boy?' she asked again.

'The boy is recovering.'

She nodded. 'I am glad to hear that.'

'Are you?' he said harshly and stepped closer, a blaze of fury flaring in his eyes. 'Are you really, Miss Meadowfield?'

'Of course!' She sighed and, massaging her fingers against the gathering knot of tightness in her forehead, turned away to the window. 'I should not have gone with Kempster,' she said quietly, almost to herself, and did not know why she was admitting any such thing to Wolf. 'But I was desperate.' She swung round, facing him with renewed defiance. 'I do not want to hang.'

'Enough of this pretence. Were you some common housemaid, you would swing from the end of a scaffold all right, but they'd not hang a gentlewoman. Evedon wants your theft kept quiet. It's an unfair world, Miss Meadowfield; surely you know that?'

Unfair? Rosalind thought of them hanging her father and all that had happened to her family. She thought of the diamonds being found in her chamber, and of Evedon and his damnable letter. And she pressed her lips firm that the words would not spill.

Wolf's gaze was hard and judgemental. 'And what of Kempster?'

'He offered me a way out. He said he would take me to the next coaching inn and leave me there.'

'Just like that.' She could see the hardness around his mouth.

'Yes,' she said. 'But he lied.'

'As did you.' His voice was deathly quiet. And just for a second, the most incredible searing hurt flashed in his eyes before the harsh anger masked it. 'And there was me believing you were telling the truth.'

'I am telling the truth.'

'Really?' Wolf shook his head cynically, disbelievingly, and digging in his pocket, pulled out a fold of banknotes. 'Thirty pounds, Miss Meadowfield. We found it on Kempster.' He thrust the notes towards her. 'Yours.'

She stared at the money and then up at Wolf. 'You believe Kempster that I bribed him,' she said slowly.

'Where else does a footman get thirty pounds?'

Her gaze held his. 'Where indeed?' she retorted angrily. Wolf believed Kempster's lies. He did not deserve to know.

'Then you do not deny it?'

She stared at the notes, feeling the blast of Wolf's icy contempt. She could tell him every last word of the truth and still he would not believe her. Then damn him, for she would tell him nothing.

His eyes narrowed at her silence. 'Go on, take it.'

It seemed like there was a heavy weight pressing against her chest, making it hard to breathe and she felt the ominous prickle of tears behind her eyes. She would not cry, not in front of him. Anger forced the tears away as she faced him with a defiance to match his own.

'Take it,' he said, and there was a ferocity in his voice. 'The money from the emeralds, I presume. You think that you can buy anything, any*one* for the right price. Anything to save yourself, without the slightest thought for what happens to those who get in your way. Well, not this time. I'll see to that, Miss Meadowfield.' His eyes were dark and stormy and filled with fury.

He turned and left without a further word. And the white paper banknotes fluttered down to scatter over the wooden floorboards where he had stood.

Chapter Twelve

They did not leave that morning after all. For all that Wolf had relented and given them a day's rest, he slept poorly that night. His thoughts centred constantly on Miss Meadowfield. He saw again the way her eyes had lit up when he had entered her room, her instinctive move towards him and the shyness of her smile. He remembered, too, her terror and fear and anger at Kempster's hands within the alleyway. And her stubborn refusal to take back her thirty pounds, leaving Struan to collect up the notes, from where they still lay upon the floor, when he had delivered her dinner tray. And even knowing all he knew of her treachery—that she had bribed Kempster in order to escape him—Wolf still wanted her, still cared for her. Fool. She was a liar and a thief. She had stolen the emeralds and sold them. Where else could she have obtained the money to pay Kempster? If she even was as poor as Kempster had said. She had done all of these things, and none of it made any difference.

He still remembered her kindness to the little beggar lad, and her bravery in risking her own life to save the child. He remembered the feel of her mouth beneath his, the look of surprise and innocence and guilty desire within her eyes when he had kissed her, the raggedness of her feet from walking endless miles without complaint. He should hate her, should despise her, God only knew had he not been raised for just such a purpose, but he could not. There was something about Miss Meadowfield that seemed to reach through all the barricades he had erected over the years. She affected him, for worse or for better. He wanted her; he wanted her as he had never wanted any woman. And his dreams were filled with the fire, and the fight with Kempster, but most of all, with Miss Rosalind Meadowfield.

'So a chaise'll no' be available until the end of next week? We cannae delay that long, for all the lassie's fears.' Campbell was leaning against the wall in the yard surveying the stables.

'We cannot,' agreed Wolf. He was tired this morning, not so much from lack of sleep, but from the constant dilemma that raged within him.

The cold grey morning sky seemed to reflect both his mood and Campbell's.

'She's no gonnae like it.'

'Tough. We'll ride easy with her; it's the best we can do.'

'You do realize that she'll have to ride wi' you. That wee mount they've given me cannae take two up.'

'Have my horse. I'll ride yours.'

'It wouldnae make a difference. Still too small.' Campbell looked round at Wolf. 'What's the problem wi' you taking her?'

Wolf flicked him a glance. 'There's no problem.' He did not want to lie to Struan, but he had no wish to start explaining the exact nature of the problem, not when he did not really understand it himself.

'No problem save what's between you and Miss Meadowfield,' said Campbell quietly.

Struan never did miss much. 'There's nothing between us,' Wolf countered too quickly.

'Really?' Campbell arched a dark eyebrow.

'Really,' said Wolf curtly, wishing that his friend would just leave the matter alone.

'But you dinnae want to take her pillion.'

'I'll take her pillion.' Wolf said a little too heatedly. 'It is no matter to me.' Another lie. Just the thought of having Rosalind Meadowfield pressed against him raised a storm of warring emotions.

Silence followed his words.

'We dinnae have to take her back,' said Campbell slowly and looked thoughtfully at Wolf. 'We could just let her go free and be done with it. You did say that you had your doubts over Evedon's story.'

Like hell would Wolf give in to this weakness. 'We're damn well taking her back to Evedon, Struan.'

'Aye,' said Campbell softly beneath his breath as he ambled back into the inn, 'but what the hell state are you gonnae be in by the time she reaches him?'

There was no chaise, Rosalind learned. Instead they rode that day just as they had done before, with Rosalind sitting up by Wolf on his great horse. Except it was not the same as when he had brought her back from the bluebell wood; everything had changed between them, she could feel it in the tension in the strong arm settled around her waist, and

see it in his eyes when their glances accidentally met…
and sparked.

The day was as sombre as the mood that hung over them.
A bleak grey sky across which the chill wind blew a thick
padded lining of cloud. It had already rained twice, only
showers that did nothing to slow their pace. The horse did
not bother her so much now. She knew that Wolf was a
good horseman and that he kept the horse under control.
She could even relax a little into the monotony of the canter,
feeling her body heavy and aching from lack of sleep and
her struggle with Kempster. She longed to rest her head
against Wolf's chest and close her eyes, but she could never
do that. He thought her a thief. He thought her a liar.

London was only a few days away, according to Campbell. Not long now before she must face Evedon. And for all
that Wolf believed, she knew that Evedon would not allow
her to live knowing what she knew about him. The chafe
of the letter against her ribcage was a constant reminder
of that; fool that she was to have taken it. Every step of
Wolf's horse was taking her closer to that fate. Her stomach
clenched at the thought and her palms grew clammy with
fear.

The image rose in her mind of the black silken noose
swinging between Evedon's fingers that night in his study,
and of his fury and panic at the sight of the letter dropping
through the air to land beneath her fingers. And she knew
that she was not ready to die, that she could not just sit here
so meekly before Wolf and let him take her to her death.
For a moment, she contemplated telling him the truth, of
appealing for his mercy. Her body was warm from the shelter of his, and she imagined that she could feel the steady
beat of his heart against her arm. She dared a glance up at
him. He sensed her movement. The silver eyes met hers,
and despite all their angry words of that morning, some-

thing else still flared between them. She could feel it in the strange warm sensation that shimmered low in her belly.

Wolf held her gaze for only a second more, then looked away.

The time passed in tense silence.

A noise sounded from behind, something thudding down upon the ground that broke the quiet monotony. The horse checked its stride. Wolf glanced back and brought the beast to a stop. He slid Rosalind down before dismounting himself.

She saw Wolf's saddlebags lying some paces back up the road, and watched while he walked back to retrieve them. He crouched down on the road, examining the strapping before hoisting them over his shoulder and coming back to where she stood with Campbell now by her side.

'The straps look undamaged. You fastened them on this morning; was there any problem?' Wolf asked Campbell.

Campbell shook his head. 'I thought I had buckled them up good and fine...'

'No harm done,' said Wolf and began to fit the bags back on to his horse.

'I'll take the lassie up and keep going while you sort your baggage. It'll save time and you can catch us up easily enough and take her back. My horse should manage the both of us over a short distance.'

Wolf gave a nod.

'Unless you've an objection to riding with me, Miss Meadowfield, and prefer to wait for Wolf.' There was something of a knowing look upon Campbell's face.

'No,' she said too quickly. 'I have no objection, Mr Campbell. What difference does it make with whom I ride?'

Campbell cocked an eyebrow. 'Indeed.' And when he mounted his horse and reached his hand down to her, she took it.

Campbell rode as easy as Wolf, the horse resuming a steady canter on down the road. She was careful not to look back at where Wolf remained.

They rode on, and with every minute that passed, Rosalind expected to hear the gallop of Wolf's horse behind them, but none came. She waited and waited, listened and listened, and at last could not resist a glance back. There was no sign of Wolf. Had they really travelled so far?

Campbell rounded a corner, and brought the horse to a stop. To wait for Wolf, she thought, and knew that she should not care. Was it not better that she rode with Campbell when there was so much sparking friction between her and Wolf? But Campbell slipped her down on to the road, and stayed in the saddle. He stared down at her and there was a pensiveness about his face.

'Still want to escape, Miss Meadowfield?'

She looked up at him, confused and more than a little suspicious.

'Or have you grown accustomed to the idea of returning to Evedon?'

'Of course I wish to escape.'

'Then here's your chance. Start running.'

'You are letting me go?' She stared at him incredulously.

'That's precisely what I'm doing.'

'Why would you do such a thing? I thought Evedon was paying you a lot of money to capture me.'

'Dinnae remind me what I'm giving up here, lassie.'

'Does Wolf know what you are doing?'

'What do you think?'

She shook her head.

'I'm no' blind, Miss Meadowfield. I see what's between the two of you.'

'There is nothing—' she began, but he cut her off.

'That's what Wolf says too, but you're rotten liars, the pair of you.' He smiled a fleeting smile. 'Wolf has dragged himself up from the gutter. He's done what he had to to survive. You have no idea of where he's come from, of the life that he's had to lead, of the things he's had to do. He's overcome what would have killed other men. But his desire for you is making him question all that he believes in, that which has kept him going through the long hard years. Put simply, Miss Meadowfield, you will destroy him. And I'll not stand by and watch that happen.' He shook his head.

'No,' she cried, 'it is not like that. There is nothing between us.' And in her heart she knew that she was lying. There had been something between her and Wolf from the very start.

'Is there not?' He produced a small purse from his pocket and threw it down to land on the ground before her. 'Best no' to take any chances. There is the thirty pounds. Take it this time, Miss Meadowfield.'

She stared at the purse in disbelief.

He gestured to the surrounding countryside. 'There is your freedom.' His expression was the most serious that she had ever seen it. 'Take the money and go, miss, for you'll no' have another chance like this.'

She could not believe what he was saying, what he thought of her.

'Your thinking is quite wrong, Mr Campbell.'

'I dinnae think so.'

She forced her chin to stay up, forced her gaze to remain steady on his.

'Cut across that field over there. There are hills and woodland at the other side. Stay in the woods and head north. I dinnae want Wolf finding you. Do you understand?'

Without another word, she turned away, leaving the purse where it lay.

'The money, Miss Meadowfield,' Campbell called after her.

Rosalind ignored him and began to run.

Saddlebags fastened securely back in place, Wolf pushed the stallion on hard, making up the distance that separated him from Campbell and Miss Meadowfield. He was still angry, her flight with Kempster still lodged like a fishbone in his throat, sharp enough to draw blood. Yet he craved the feel of her body perched on the saddle before him, ached for the fragrance of her hair and the softness of her arms around him. Even though he knew that he should not, he was desperate to have her from Campbell and back with him.

'Fool,' he muttered to himself. Why was he allowing the woman to affect him like this? He should teach Rosalind Meadowfield a lesson, he thought savagely; he should pull up her skirts and ease his hard swollen flesh into hers. Maybe then this torment would end. He swallowed hard, his body reacting to just the thought.

He knew as soon as he saw Campbell that something was wrong.

'Where is she?' he asked, guiding his horse right up to his friend.

'She's gone, Wolf.'

'What the hell do you mean?'

'Just that. I nipped behind a hedge to have a quick pee, left her with the horses, and when I came back she was gone.'

There was silence.

Wolf felt the pulse begin to hammer in his neck. 'You let her go, didn't you?'

Campbell said nothing.

'Didn't you?' demanded Wolf, staring at Campbell with undisguised fury. 'The same as you left the strapping for my saddlebags loose. You planned this whole damn thing.'

'It's for your own good, Wolf.'

'My own good?' His voice was harsh with incredulity. 'She's worth a bloody mint.'

'A hundred guineas, and were it two hundred I'd still do the same. Your life's worth more than that. Besides, you dinnae need the money.'

'Have you run mad?'

'I should have done it sooner. Look at the state she has you in; she's all that you can think of night and day. You burn for her, yet you'll no' just have her and be done with it. She's under your skin, inside your head. This craving for her is tearing you apart. She's no' of our world, Wolf. She's one of them: a gentlewoman, a bloody ladies' companion. She's trouble, Wolf, that's what she is.'

'She's just a job like all the others. A capture. All I'm doing is delivering her to Evedon.'

'Stop lying to yourself, man!' Campbell shouted. 'I'm no' blind; I see how you look at her, however much you deny it. I see what she's doing to you.'

'She's doing nothing.'

'Do you deny that you want her?'

'Aye, I want her,' snapped Wolf. 'But it does not mean I'll take her. I'm not ruled by what's beneath my breeches.'

'Listen to yourself. You want her, and yet she's everything that you shun. She's of the gentry, Wolf, and nothing you do is gonnae change that. And you cannae change your past no matter how much you will it.'

Wolf's brows lowered, his expression became hard and deadly. 'Were it anyone else saying that…'

'I'd be dead,' finished Campbell. 'You've been like a brother to me. You saved my life so I'll no' let you destroy yourself over a bloody woman. Hardnosed bastard or no', I still care about you.'

There was a small silence. Wolf placed his hand upon Campbell's shoulder.

'I know you do, Struan, and that's why you're going to tell me exactly where she went.'

Campbell sighed and shook his head. 'Wolf…'

'I cannot let her go, not like this. She'll not survive out there alone; you know she'll not.'

Campbell massaged his fingers against his temples.

'Please, Struan.'

'I'm as much a bloody fool as you,' said Campbell. 'Come on, I'll show you. But if she's reached the woodland then I dinnae think that we'll find her.'

'We'll find her,' said Wolf grimly. 'We have to.'

Rosalind had almost reached the beginning of the woodland when she saw the two riders in the distance. She knew without seeing, the identity of the horsemen: Wolf and Campbell. The grey horse was spurring on in the lead, its rider dressed in a long dark brown overcoat. And it seemed she could see across the vastness of the field to the man's lean hard face, a face without a single line of softness in it anywhere and yet burned upon her mind for all eternity, so that she could imagine the steady focus of those silver eyes, and the utter determination that they held.

'Wolf,' she whispered.

And it seemed that he heard her for he seemed to look directly at her. He pointed in her direction.

Time stilled. She knew that he was coming. She whirled and ran the distance to the trees.

She continued running, dodging a path through the woodland, unmindful of her wet stockings or the worn soles of her boots through which the ground seemed to tear at the remnants of her blisters. The rain pattered on to the pale green canopy above, dripping through the leaves to wet her as she ran. It was raining in earnest now, so that the soil beneath her feet was growing softer and deep dark brown in colour. And the air was filled with the scent of rain and the dampness of earth. Her ankle turned on an exposed tree root sending her sprawling down, but she scrambled up at once and kept on running. Running and running, until her lungs were burning for air and no matter how hard, how heavy, how fast she breathed, there was not enough air to fill them. Her side was aching with a stitch and the soles of her feet were burning as if on fire. But none of it mattered. Rosalind forced herself on, knowing that this was her last chance. Knowing that, after this, she dare not face Wolf again.

The birds were not singing. There was no sound save for the rhythmic pelt of the rain. For all that sunset was far off, the light had dulled so that the woods seemed chilled and sombre, all of the lively colour of spring washed a dismal grey by the rain. Once she thought she heard Wolf coming through the woods behind her, but it was hard to hear over the loud ragged pant of her breathing; but when she held her breath and tried to listen, the sound was gone. She kept on running until she could run no more.

It was the river that stopped her; a river flowing fast and broad and deep across her path. The water was grey, frothed with white where it gushed and dropped over rocks, none of which were of any use as stepping stones. Rosalind's gaze scanned frantically, seeking a way across, but there was none. Over to the left was a great slope of soil, sheer in its increment but with bushes and trees growing upon its slope. She could see it was flat at the top. River or slope, she thought grimly, not much of a choice. But as she could not swim nor did she have a change of clothing with her, the choice was already made. She hurried to the bottom of the slope and began to climb.

She used the bushes and woody tree roots to pull herself slowly up the sheer incline, taking her time to gingerly test the strength of each root before leaning the whole of her weight upon it. The sweat was trickling down her back, prickling beneath her arms, but still she kept on climbing— glancing frequently down to check that Wolf had not yet caught up with her—until the river below looked very far away and she felt a sense of nausea so that she did not look down again.

There was not so very much further to climb, one more yard to the top. And for all that her muscles were aching and burning and crying for relief, she knew that she could keep going for that little distance. She reached for the last branch, ready to pull herself to safety, feeling the dampness and solidity of the wood beneath her fingers as her hand closed around it. One quick glance down below. No one. Thank God, she thought, and heaved herself towards the top. There was an almighty crack as the branch fractured into two. She started to slide back down the slope. A single piercing scream rent the air and Rosalind did not realize it was herself who made the sound.

Her hand flailed wildly, clawing until it fastened upon the thin wiry branches of a scrubby bush and she grabbed at the leaves. Everything stopped. The silence echoed amidst the hush of rain. She hung there, secured by only the grip of a single hand, swaying in the lilt of the wind. Cautiously, she probed with her feet, seeking something, anything on which to find purchase, scared to move too much lest she loosen her grip. But there was nothing to be found. She shifted her weight, inch by tiny inch, until she could reach up with her other hand and anchor it too to the bush. There was nothing else within reach between her and the top of the incline, nothing else upon which she might climb. No way up, and only the land so far away below.

Rosalind's arms trembled already with the strain and she knew that she would not be able to hold on for much longer. She was going to die, but she was not panicking, not as she panicked about horses and everything else of which she was afraid. Indeed, she was strangely calm. And she realized as she hung there that she had spent most of her life afraid. So much fear, and for what? Death was coming just the same, and in that thought was a peculiar freedom so that she thought again of Wolf: Wolf with his strength and his anger, all fearless and confrontational and passionate, the very antithesis of herself, and underneath it all, hurting just the same.

She was running from him, just as she had run from everything in her life. Running away when she wanted to run towards. She could already feel her grip beginning to weaken. Soon the thin wiry branches of the bush would slip right through her hands, and she would fall back down below. Below, where the river rushed so fast. Below, where Wolf would find her. And a pain seared in her heart for what might have been, for realizations come too late. The branch began to slip beneath her fingers.

'Hold on, Miss Meadowfield!' she heard him shout, and when she looked up to the top of the slope there was Wolf.

Chapter Thirteen

$\mathbf{W}$olf saw Rosalind clinging so precariously to the sheer face, and his heart seemed to still in his chest at the shock of seeing her in such danger. A whisper from death, he thought, and then thought no more.

'Look up at me, only at me,' he shouted. 'Hold on.'

Her face was stark white. 'Wolf,' she whispered. Her eyes never left his face.

His gaze shifted to where her hands still gripped the bush with bloodless fingers, and he saw the strain in them and how easily her fingers would slip as the branch became wetter, and he knew that he must act right now if he was to save her. He pulled the rope from within his greatcoat before stripping off his coat and jacket. One end of the rope he secured to the closest tree, the other he tied around his waist.

'Please hurry,' she cried, and he could see the infinitesimal movement of the branches through her fingers.

'Hold on, Rosalind, just a few seconds more.' He spoke

calmly, trying to allay her panic, as he backed off solid ground on to the slope. He half climbed, half slid down the sheer face, striving to reach her as quickly as possible. He could hear her laboured breathing, hear the tumble of pebbles and soil cascading down, rolling to land too far below. And the thought that Rosalind Meadowfield might follow them was unbearable so that, for the first time since he was a child, he prayed.

Dear God, save her, he willed. *Take me in her stead, and save her. Please.*

He heard her sudden gasp of air. He heard her body begin to slide. 'Wolf!'

And he was there, catching her in his arms, pulling her tight against his body, holding her secure.

'Rosalind, I have you.'

She clung to him, burying her face against his chest.

A heartbeat, and then another.

'Wrap your arms around my neck and your legs around my body. I'll get us out of here.' Heaven only knew how much he did not want to let her go, not for one second, but he knew what he had to do.

She did as he instructed, holding tight to him.

Wolf focused, shutting every sensation out, single-minded, determined, ruthless. He climbed up the rope with his most precious cargo, and only when they were both safe, away from the precipice, did he release her long enough to unfasten the rope.

She stood before him, exactly where he left her, not moving, not shifting her gaze from his.

'I thought…I thought that I would…'

'I know,' he said, and pulled her back into his arms. 'I know,' he said again and stroked the strands of loose hair back from her face. 'But you are safe now.'

She nodded and closed her eyes against him. 'I had

to run,' she whispered, 'I had to try. You understand, do you not?'

'I understand.' He rubbed a hand against her back. And God help him, but he did. She must really believe that Evedon would hang her, if she was willing to risk her life like this to flee him.

'Evedon will not hang you. I was telling the truth when I said that he is most adamant in wanting the whole affair hushed up.'

She glanced away towards the slope's edge, staring at it as if it held her mesmerized.

'Rosalind,' he said softly, trying to turn her from it.

She looked up at him then, her face pale, her eyes a dark mossy brown and shimmering with unshed tears. 'I have not told you the truth of this matter and neither has Lord Evedon.' She paused, taking a deep shaky breath.

'It is of no consequence right now; let us speak of it later when you are recovered.'

'No.' She shook her head and her hair, all loose and flowing from their chase, swept against her face. 'I need to tell you, Wolf. I want you to know.'

He nodded, feeling his chest tighten, and waited.

'I *am* a thief. I *did* steal from Evedon, not the dowager's jewels but…something else, something of which he does not wish the world to know. He believes me guilty of both crimes, but I swear to you, I took neither the diamonds nor the emeralds.' She glanced away and bit at her lip. 'I did not know whether you knew of the…' she hesitated '…of the other item.'

'Evedon employed me to bring you back for jewel theft, nothing else.'

Her eyes met his once again. Such dark troubled eyes, filled with sincerity and with pain.

'What did you steal?' he asked as gently as he could.

She bit her lip again, harder this time, so that he saw the tiny trickle of blood. 'A letter. I did not mean to take it…but there seemed no other option.' She swallowed and stared up into his eyes. 'Please do not ask me,' she said softly. 'For all that Lord Evedon thinks, I will not betray him. Not for his sake, but for the sake of another. I know his secret. I have the proof, and because of that, he *will* kill me.'

And this time when she said the words, he believed her.

'Wolf,' and in that one word was both relief and fear. 'What am I going to do?'

He could feel the tremble that raged through her body.

'I'll not let him hurt you; I'll not let anyone hurt you.' He pulled her to him, holding her as if he would protect her from the world, and dropped a single kiss to the top of her head.

And she believed him. For the first time in such a long time, she felt truly safe. He was strong and invincible, nothing could overcome Wolf she thought, as he wrapped his arms around her and just held her. Beneath the press of her cheek to his chest, she could feel the strong steady beat of his heart. A man of iron, so ruthless, so hard, and yet beneath, such gentleness; a man that fought for what he believed in, a man in whom she could trust.

Deep inside, an overwhelming tenderness for him welled up and overflowed, so that the tears spilled down her cheeks and she began to weep for everything that he was and everything that she was and all that could not be. Wolf held her and stroked her and whispered that he would keep her safe, until all her tears were cried and she rested against him spent and empty. He wrapped his greatcoat around her and gathered her up into his arms as if she were a child. And she let him carry her through the trees and the teeming rain. There would be no more running. It was time to stop hiding from the truth.

They rode through the grey sheet of rain, Wolf careful to keep his horse at a slow steady pace for the sake of Rosalind who was riding pillion before him. She sat quiet and exhausted; the trauma of her ordeal seemed to have sapped all of her energy. After an hour of riding, he felt her relax against him, her head lolling into him as she dozed.

'Well?' said Campbell at last. 'Are you still gonnae tell me that she's just a capture?' He looked pointedly down at where Rosalind was sleeping in Wolf's arms.

'It's more complicated than you think,' said Wolf.

'Aye, I think I can see exactly what kind of complicated it is.'

Wolf drew him a look.

Campbell stared back unrepentant. 'Are we still taking her to Evedon?'

Wolf deliberately avoided the question. 'She says that she did not steal the jewels.'

'She's been saying that all along.'

Wolf glanced down at the where Rosalind lay against him. 'And maybe she's been telling the truth all along.'

'Maybe.' He could hear the cynicism in Campbell's voice.

'She says she stole a letter belonging to Evedon, and it's the letter that he's after, rather than the jewels.'

'Does it make any difference? She's still a thief.'

'Aye, it makes a difference. Evedon lied to us. Maybe there never was a jewel theft. This whole thing could have been about the letter all along.'

Campbell looked away, rubbed at the back of his neck and when he looked round again, his expression was grim. 'What kind of a letter?'

'One worth a hundred of Evedon's guineas,' said Wolf.

'And does she still have this letter?'

'I believe so.'

'Easy enough to check,' said Campbell and looked at him meaningfully.

Wolf gave no reply. He knew what Campbell was suggesting. Searching Rosalind would be no hardship. A vision of her naked flashed in his mind. He closed his eyes to dispel the image.

'If she has the letter, then Evedon's strange insistence that we search neither Miss Meadowfield nor her baggage makes sense.'

'As I said before, maybe he wants an excuse to do the searching himself,' said Campbell. 'Maybe there's more between Evedon and the woman right enough, just as Kempster said.'

'Kempster's a damned liar.'

'Maybe he didnae lie about everything.'

It was a small horrible thought that Wolf did not want to dwell upon, for his imagination could reckon all too easily what might have passed between Evedon and Miss Meadowfield. He gritted his teeth and clamped down hard on his jaw.

Campbell slid a glance across at him. 'So which one is playing us, the woman or Evedon?'

'I think that Rosalind is telling the truth,' said Wolf.

Campbell crooked an eyebrow. '*Rosalind*, now, is it?'

Wolf scowled as he felt his cheeks warm at Campbell's tone.

'And what if she's lying? What then? Will you hand her over to Evedon?'

'I don't know, Struan.' He pushed the thought away and looked across at Campbell. 'We need to make a few enquiries of our own about Evedon's jewels. We're not so very far from London: a couple of days at most by mail. Will you travel on alone and visit some of our old acquaintances? Find out if anyone's fenced some emeralds in the past few weeks.'

Campbell gestured his head towards Rosalind. 'And what about you and Miss Meadowfield?'

'I'll keep Rosalind at the inn we're headed for, until we know what's going on.'

Campbell nodded and his eyes met Wolf's. 'While you're there bed her and be done with it, Wolf. Bed the lassie and get her oot your system. Do it for both our sakes.'

Wolf said nothing. Maybe Campbell was right. Maybe if he bedded Rosalind, this craving he felt for her would be sated. The confusion clouding his mind would be gone. Life would be simple once more, everything black or white, no more shades of grey. Life would go back to as it had been before Rosalind Meadowfield. He looked down at the woman he held secure against his body and wondered if that would ever be possible.

They rode on in silence.

Rosalind awoke to find herself being handed down into Campbell's arms. The day was a dark dismal grey and the rain was still falling steadily from the skies. She stumbled to her feet.

'Forgive me, I did not mean to sleep.'

'Dinnae fash yersel', lassie. We rode the quicker for it.' Campbell said, not unkindly, but he did not smile.

She glanced between Campbell and Wolf, not sure of Wolf's reaction to her, or if Wolf was aware of Campbell's part in her escape. Wolf was staring moodily ahead, and she could not gauge either matter. The afternoon air was cool and the atmosphere between the men heavy and brooding. She shivered in the heavy dampness of her clothes, even though Wolf's greatcoat was still wrapped around her.

She did not understand what this thing was between her and Wolf, this force that had bound them from the beginning. He was her captor and she his prisoner. Was he still taking her back to Evedon? His whispered words from the cliff-top echoed in her head: *I'll not let him hurt you. I'll not let anyone hurt you.* Promises of safety and reassurance that no one else had ever uttered, his arms strong and protective around her. She turned away, and began walking towards the inn door.

The murmur of voices sounded behind her, Wolf's and Campbell's and then she heard the blast of the mail coach's horn and the rushed gallop of hooves entering the inn's yard. Her heart stuttered in a moment of panic.

'Wolf?' She swung round, suddenly afraid that he meant to abandon her.

But Wolf was standing where she had left him. It was Campbell who climbed on to the top of the mail coach. He raised his hand in a half wave, half salute at Wolf before the coach rolled through the gateway and disappeared out on to the road from which it had just come.

Her eyes cut to Wolf, the question hanging unspoken between them.

'He has business to see to,' he said.

'Is he coming back?'

'In a few days.' He picked up his saddlebags and walked towards her. 'Just you and me tonight, Rosalind,' he said quietly, before he moved to open the inn door.

Her heart gave a flutter, and a shiver stroked from the nape of her neck to the base of her spine. She followed Wolf into the inn.

It was a comfortable room, much more expensive than any that they had stayed in during their journey. A fire blazed on the hearth, warming the gloom. Wolf dumped the baggage on the rug by the doorway and drew the dark heavy curtains across the window, shutting out what was left of the day and causing shadows to flicker against the pale blank walls.

She stood there motionless, the rain still dripping from his greatcoat that was wrapped around her.

Just the two of them alone in a bedchamber. The tension was so tight that he could almost feel his body spark with it. Rosalind could feel it too; he could see it in her face, in the parting of her lips, the slight heaviness of her breathing and the dark dilated pupils of her eyes.

He swallowed hard, his mouth dry with a sudden unexpected nervousness. His body ached for her. He stepped closer.

She did not move away, just stood there, her gaze never leaving his. And in her face was such trust, such warmth, such goodness that he felt a heavy ache in his chest where his heart would have been—if he still had a heart. And he knew then that he could not do it. He would not bed her, no matter how his body willed it, nor for any words that he and Campbell had spoken. It was not her fault that he wanted her. She did not know the dark deeds of which men were capable. He would not ruin her to satisfy his own lust.

He opened his mouth to say the words. But it was Rosalind who spoke first.

'You saved my life today. Had you not arrived…' Emotion thickened her voice and she caught at her bottom lip with her teeth, holding it back until she was once more composed.

'I did not thank you.' Two steps and she was right there before him, staring up into his face. 'Thank you, Wolf,' she whispered, 'for today, for Kempster, for everything.'

She reached up and cupped her hand with the utmost tenderness against his scarred cheek.

'I'm the last person you should be thanking.' His voice was hoarse and gritty. 'I'm the heartless bastard that's dragged you the length of the country.' He knew that he should move away from her caress, but he could not.

The rain had rendered his fair hair dark and sodden, running in rivulets down his cheeks to drip from his stubbled chin. He slicked his hair back from where it hung against his face, and she slipped into his arms and wrapped herself around him, and to Wolf nothing had ever felt so right. She laid her palm against his chest, covering his heart.

His hand closed over hers. 'Rosalind,' he whispered and tried to guide her hand away.

'Not heartless,' she said and kept her hand where it lay. Beneath her fingers, his heart beat hard and fast. 'Never heartless.' She stared up into his face, and he wanted nothing other than to save her from the world.

He could not help himself. He lowered his mouth to hers and kissed her.

It was a kiss to salve every hurt Rosalind had ever been dealt, a kiss to chase the cold and the fear from her veins. Gentle, coaxing, tender. And when he eased away, taking his mouth from hers, she reached up and guided him back down. He kissed her, harder this time, his mouth hot against hers, his tongue stroking and delving and teasing.

He kissed her and kissed her until her head was dizzy and her skin tingled with the need for his touch. Her heart thumped fast and hard, her blood hot and rushing, as ever it did when he was close. She breathed in the familiar masculine scent of him and felt heady with it, faint with the need for him. She wanted him, only him, wanted the kiss never to cease. There was no Evedon, no fear, no worry.

There was only Wolf and this moment and the magic of what was between them.

Her arms wound around his neck, pulling him closer as her body moulded itself to his. Her body hummed with excitement and sheer life, as if she had only now been woken from a lifetime of slumber. His kiss deepened, intensified, and his hands stroked a magic against her back, her shoulders, her neck. And even though he was not touching them, the soft skin of her thighs seemed to burn.

'Rosalind,' he whispered, and she could hear the desperation in his voice, as needful as that which surged through her. She kissed him harder, wanting so much more of him.

'Wolf, oh, Wolf,' she gasped, and it seemed that she could think of nothing other than him and this overwhelming urgency between them.

His greatcoat slipped unnoticed from her shoulders landing in a pool of leather upon the floor, and she was tugging at his jacket, trying to push it down over his arms, while he worked at the buttons on her dress. She could feel the tremble in his fingers and hear the raggedness of his breath as he struggled to free each fastening. And then he was pulling the bodice of her dress down, sliding it and her skirt from her. Her petticoats followed until she wore only her corset and shift.

He shrugged out of his jacket, while she pulled his shirt out from where it was tucked into his trousers, slipping her hands beneath to glide over the smooth bare skin of his chest. Her hands were shaking as she stroked his lean tight muscle. She marvelled at her audacity in undressing him, in touching him, even looking at him so. Yet she could not stop; she wanted to see, to feel the man that she loved.

He threw off his shirt then tugged at the ribbons of her corset, unfastening them with more ease than she ever had done, and the corset dropped to land forgotten on the floor with the rest of her clothing. She stood there in the thin linen shift, her breasts, peaked and sensitive, nosing at the flimsy fabric.

He stilled for just a moment. Stood there with his breath as loud and ragged as if he had been running. 'We should not…*I* should not—' And then he reached to the ribbon around the neck of her shift…and pulled.

The shift slipped down her body to gather in a froth around her ankles. She heard his intake of breath and, not understanding, she tried to hide her body with her hands.

'Oh, Rosalind,' he whispered, and then he lifted her into his arms and carried her to the bed.

He laid her in the nest of warm covers as if she were the most precious of jewels, then pulled off his boots and stockings and climbed upon the bed to lie by her side. He stroked her arms and her back, and kissed her again as if he loved her with every ounce of his being, so that there was nothing of embarrassment left.

She breathed in the scent of him and let her fingers explore the hard bulk of the muscle that lined his body. He was nothing of softness—all hard, and long and lean. In the amber light of the fire, his skin was golden as honey; her hand where she stroked him, so pale and white in comparison. Her fingers traced the paths of ancient silvered scars.

His fingers cupped her breasts, plucked at her nipples before putting his mouth to her.

He lapped against the delicate skin of her breast, licking around it until she cried out with delight and tried to thrust her aching nipple into his mouth. He teased at the swollen bud with his teeth, before taking it into his mouth and sucking it. While his mouth catered for one breast, his fingers worked upon the other, until she was moaning with excitement, reaching for him, pressing him to her, wanting it never to end.

Her eyes were dark with desire, her breasts swollen and sensitive to his every caress. And with every stroke, with every touch, he loved her. He traced a trail of kisses down over the smooth white skin of her belly, feeling her gasp as he reached the dark curls of her womanhood.

'Wolf! You cannot—'

'Trust me,' he whispered, and slid lower, placing his hands on her inner thighs and opening her to him. The skin was silky soft and flushed hot with desire. He kissed each thigh in turn, hearing the small gasps and moans that she tried to suppress.

'Wolf…'

He touched his mouth to her, tasted her, and kissed the essence of her womanhood.

She jerked and tried to pull away, but he held her firm, wanting her to know only pleasure and nothing of pain.

He kissed her until she was crying out aloud, straining for her climax. He reached up and rolled her nipples between his fingers and thumbs, while his mouth stayed busy below. Until at last, she shuddered beneath his tongue and he felt her pulse.

Such things Rosalind had never even imagined. She was floating in sheer ecstasy. A sunburst of pleasure shimmered throughout her body, warm pulsating waves of utter bliss. Wolf took her into his arms and stroked the tendrils of hair from her forehead and kissed her eyebrow and the tip of her nose and her cheek. And he held her with such loving tenderness that reality seemed far away. This was paradise. This was love. And she thought her heart would burst with the joy of it. She loved him, utterly, completely. She snuggled closer as he pulled the covers over them and drifted off to sleep in his arms.

* * *

The hour was late when Wolf awoke. He knew that, without the need to part the curtains and look out at the inky darkness of the sky. The fire upon the hearth had been reduced to a small flicker of flames and the heat within the room was waning. He lifted the coal tongs as quietly as he could and, taking care not to wake Rosalind, built the fire once more.

He glanced across at the bed. She lay where he had left her, cosy and warm beneath the sheets and heavy woollen covers, her hair long and sprawling temptingly over the pillows. Such hidden passion, he thought, and smiled as he remembered their lovemaking. He had wanted so much to pleasure her, to hear her cry his name in ecstasy. That his own desire had gone unsated was irrelevant. He knew that he would do the same a thousand times over.

Across the room their clothes lay in a crumpled pile where they had discarded them earlier. He could see the arm of his greatcoat, still dark and damp from the rain. He smiled again, remembering their urgency in undressing, and moved to retrieve the garments.

Having grown up with nothing, Wolf took care over his possessions, and besides, he had no wish for either of them to don damp clothes in the morning. He hung his greatcoat on the hook on the back of the bedchamber's door, and then set the chairs before the fireplace and draped Rosalind's dress and petticoats over them. He laid his shirt flat upon the floor and propped both their boots close to the hearth. Only Rosalind's underwear remained. He hooked her shift over the end of the curtain pole, the thought of its thin sheer material draped over her body stirring his interest too easily. He shook his head at how he responded to her, smiling, and moved to gather up her corset.

The ribbons were smooth and sensual beneath his fingers.

He thought of his fingers untying them, of his easing the corset from her, of the revelation of her breasts all firm yet soft, their pale rounded beauty nestling in his hands, while her heart fluttered in a fury beneath. He untangled the ribbons and opened the corset up that he might hang it from the other end of the curtain pole…and saw then the small linen package that had been stitched into the corset's inner lining.

Wolf crouched there still and silent, the corset and its secret lying on the floor before him, exposed and enticing. The truth, his to be had, if he just reached out and took it. What were Evedon's secrets to him? Nothing. But Rosalind's secrets, now they were worth knowing. What was it that she carried so close to her heart? Evedon's letter…or the dowager's emeralds? The answer lay temptingly before him. He did not move, and his breath was quiet and shallow. And for all the coolness of the room sweat prickled beneath his arms.

Chapter Fourteen

Rosalind could not be sure what woke her. The room was in silence, and lit in a soft golden hue from the flames on the hearth. Where Wolf had lain within the bed was empty. She sat up, a sudden apprehension gripping her.

He was standing by the window, still as a statue, clad only in his trousers and staring out into the darkness of the night. And across his back, she saw what she had not, earlier that evening: a terrible scarring as if the skin had once been cut to ribbons.

'Wolf?'

He did not look round.

From one finial of the curtain pole her shift hung, limp and drying. Across the room, the rest of her clothes and Wolf's had been arranged before the fire so that they might dry. On the table lay her corset, and by its side she could see the glint of Wolf's knife…and the letter—unfolded and read.

Her heart plummeted with dread and hurt and rage. She

climbed from the bed, pulling the top cover around her nakedness.

'You searched my clothes!'

'I sought only to dry them.' His voice was flat, dead in tone.

'You had no right!'

'No right at all,' he agreed and still he did not look round, just continued to stare out of the window.

The glow of the firelight danced against the darkness outside so that in the glass of the window she saw their reflection—Wolf standing there, so still and unimpassioned, and herself in the background, eyes flashing with anger, body tense and quivering with indignation.

'You read it, after all that I told you. Why, Wolf?'

He gave no answer, just stood there in silence, unmoving, not even looking round at her.

'You did not believe me, did you? That is why you had to see the letter for yourself.'

He gave no response.

'Look at me, Wolf. Tell me to my face.' Her voice was loud and she did not care. The anger was burning in her soul, raging through her blood, anger that he had used her, anger that he had made her believe that he cared, anger for not believing in her. 'That is what it was about, was it not? You…you seduced me, so that you might find the letter!'

'No!' He looked at her then, and what she saw caught the words from her tongue, for in Wolf's eyes was the darkness of tortured despair. 'Never think that, Rosalind. What happened between us was nothing of seduction. I could not—' his voice fractured, and he would have turned away had she not caught him back and made him face her.

'Wolf?' she whispered, and all of her rage ebbed away and in its place was only concern for him. Something was very wrong. 'What is it? What is wrong?'

He shook his head. 'The letter.'

'It proves Evedon did not tell you the truth.'

He smiled, a bitter smile. 'Evedon is not Evedon at all. His father was not Evedon, but Veryan.'

'The letter names his father as a Lord Keddinton.'

'Robert Veryan, Viscount Keddinton, one in the same.'

'You have heard of this man?'

'Aye,' said Wolf quietly, 'I've heard of him.' And something of the hatred and steel was back in his eyes.

'Then the dowager…' She stopped, unwilling to criticize the woman who had helped her so much. 'For some years now she has been haunted by something from her past, imaginings of a man that distress her greatly, a man she calls Robert. I think that it must be this Robert Veryan… the Lord Keddinton from the letter.'

'No doubt.'

She reached across and touched his hand. 'Does this matter remind you of…of the circumstances of your own birth?' She thought she understood why the letter seemed to have had such an affect on Wolf.

'I am hardly on a par with Evedon,' he laughed bitterly, and in it she heard his pain. 'But, yes, it reminds me of things I would rather forget.'

'Would it help to speak of them?' she asked gently.

'I have gone a lifetime and never spoken of them. What good are words? They cannot change the past.'

'They can help release you from its binding. I told you of Elizabeth and the horse, and just in sharing the memory, the pain and fear begins to heal.'

'It is not the same thing.'

The curtness of his words stung her. She dropped her hand from his and looked away that he would not see the hurt in her eyes.

'Rosalind,' he sighed and raked a hand through his hair. 'Forgive me, I do not mean to hurt you.'

She nodded.

He glanced away and then back at her. 'Do you really want to know? Shall I tell you the sordid truth of my parentage?' Through his despair and torment, she could hear the edge of bitterness.

'Only if you wish it, Wolf.'

There was silence, and then Wolf turned back to the window, staring out into the darkness beyond, as if he could see his past there, and he began to speak.

'My mother was the daughter of a rich gentleman. She was courted by a young man of good standing, a man with a promising future, a gentleman. He told her that he loved her, that he meant to marry her. And then he seduced her before abandoning her to marry another girl whose father was richer and had more influence.'

'How dreadful,' she whispered.

'That is not the best of it,' he said with a bitter smile. 'When her father discovered that she was with child, he disowned her and threw her out of the house. She went to her lover, my *father*—' he spoke the word with so much hatred that Rosalind shivered '—to ask for his help, but he sent her away without so much as a farthing, to whelp on the streets. We travelled to York in hope of a better life, but there was none to be had.' He did not tell her what his mother had been reduced to for survival. 'She died when I was ten years old, but she had raised me to hate—as she hated—all of those who call themselves gentlefolk.'

'I am so sorry.' She understood now the anger that burned in Wolf, the anger that had been as much a part of his life as fear had been in hers. 'What happened to you when your mother died?'

'I survived,' he said simply, and Rosalind knew those

two words hid a lifetime of suffering. He looked round then at her, and she saw that his face was wet with tears. 'So you see what I am, Rosalind, the whole ugly truth of me.'

She felt his pain resonate through her own heart. 'I see,' she said softly and slipped her hand around his.

She drew the curtains again, then led him to one of the armchairs and sat him down upon it. With gentle fingers she wiped away his tears. 'I see all of you, Wolf,' she said, and she stroked his hair and kissed his scar. 'And I love you.' Then she moved her lips to him and began to kiss him, and in that kiss was all of her love, all of her acceptance, everything in her heart. She kissed him until he wrapped his arms around her and kissed her back. Her heart felt as raw as his. And she understood at last that they were the same, him and her. Each a broken half, together a whole. The blanket slipped from her shoulders.

'I need you, Wolf,' she said quietly, 'and I think that you need me too.'

'Aye, lass,' he whispered, 'more than life itself.'

Their eyes stayed locked as he carried her to the bed. He laid her beneath the covers and stripped off his trousers before climbing in by her side. There was no need for words. He kissed her, and stroked her and touched her, until her breath was ragged and there was an ache between her legs that she knew was all for him. And when his body moved over hers, nothing had ever seemed more right. She was his woman, and he, her man.

The rigidity of his manhood probed at her woman's place and she opened her legs to him, wanting him and all it was that he could do to her, trusting him, needing him.

He moved in a slow rocking rhythm, rubbing against her sensitivity just as his mouth had done earlier that evening, until she was pressing herself to him, rocking with him in this dance that would unite them. His manhood stroked and slid, and her breath was hard and heavy as she rocked faster and faster against him. And then something changed, the slightest adjustment of his angle and there was a hard pressing sensation and a sudden pain. He caught her cry with his kiss. And then the pain was gone, and their bodies were as one in truth.

And after a while, he began to move again. They moved together, their skins slick with sweat, the hard muscle of his chest stimulating the flushed sensitivity of her nipples, his manhood working such pleasure within her. Her fingers closed over his buttocks pulling him all the harder to her, panting with exertion, groaning with needful delight, until she felt him withdraw quickly and suddenly and his manhood convulsed against her thigh, flooding her skin with the warm wetness of his seed.

He collapsed down to lay by her side, eyes closed, pulling her to him, and kissing her forehead.

She lay in his arms, her cheek against his chest, listening to his heart beat. Nothing could undo what had passed between them this night. She loved him and he loved her. Nothing else mattered, in comparison to that. Not Evedon, or her fear of horses, or even what they had done to her father. There was only love.

Sunlight was creeping into the room when Wolf awoke, its bright light turning the dark curtains a glowing rich red to cast the whole room in a subtle rosy light. He glanced down at the woman by his side and felt his heart expand with tenderness. She knew the truth of him and yet she had shown nothing of hate or revulsion. Instead she had accepted him for who he was and what he was, as if all of the darkness of the past made no difference. And now, in truth, he felt its power wane. She had given herself to him with such gentle love as to draw out the poisons from his soul. Her love healed his heart. The pain and darkness had gone. And all because of Rosalind. He wanted this time to last for ever, wished with all his heart that they might stay here together, away from the world, and never leave.

She stirred as he watched her, opening her eyes to look up at him and smile.

He smiled back, and for the first time that Wolf could remember, life felt good.

He dropped a kiss to her lips and showed her all over again just how very much he loved her.

It was midday by the time they were dressed and eating the tray of food that Wolf had ordered. Bread, cheese, cold ham and a bottle of the finest red wine the innkeeper had in his cellars.

'Last night…' Rosalind started, and stopped as a rosy blush spread over her cheeks.

Wolf glanced up from the wine he was pouring into two glasses; he smiled in very wicked way.

She blushed all the harder. 'Are we celebrating?'

'I hope so.' And he truly did.

'And what of Evedon?'

'Leave Evedon to me.'

She bit at her lower lip, and he saw the concern that crossed her face. 'He will be livid with you. I do not trust that he will not harm you.'

He could not stop from smiling. She was worried not for herself, but for him! 'There's nothing to worry over,' he said and smiled again. He reached across the table and took her hand in his. His heart began to race and there was a dryness in his mouth. Before the fear could take hold, he said the words he had never thought to say.

'You have stolen my heart, Rosalind Meadowfield. Will you marry me? Will you be my wife?'

'Yes,' she cried in joyful surprise. 'Oh, yes!' And she was across the table, on his lap and in his arms, laughing and crying at the same time.

He kissed the tears from her face. '*Now* we are celebrating, sweet lass.'

He held his glass to her mouth, and she lapped at it; some of the wine spilled down her chin, the ruby liquid sensual in its trickle over her skin. He caught the droplet with his finger, before kissing her again.

He wanted to marry her. He loved her and she would be his wife. Rosalind had never felt such happiness. Her joy was such that she felt dizzy with it. They would live together for ever more in happiness. There would be no more Evedon, no more running. Her past would stay where it was. Far away. No more hiding. Soon she would be Mrs Wolversley and there would be nothing left of the shame she had left behind. There would be only Wolf and their love. The bright spring sunshine bathed them in its light, and when Wolf began to kiss her in earnest, she thought she would melt with the utter joy of it.

A knock sounded at the bedchamber door.

Wolf ignored it and carried on kissing her.

She disengaged her mouth from his, smiling and still stroking her fingers through the hair above the nape of his neck. 'There is someone at the door.'

'There is,' he said, and kissed her again.

She pulled away, laughing. 'You cannot just ignore it. We have to answer it, Wolf.'

'If you insist.' One last quick kiss and he let her up from his lap.

Wolf moved to open the door, while Rosalind fixed her shawl in place and tidied her hair. She was smiling, wondering if Wolf would make love to her again this afternoon. From where she stood she heard the mumbled words.

'For the lady, from the gent outside,' said a boy's voice.

'Which gent?' asked Wolf, but the boy was already gone.

The door closed.

And through her whispered a foreboding so strong that she feared to look round. She turned then and saw what it was that he held in his hand: a rolled-up newspaper tied with a black silken rope, just like the rope she had seen in Evedon's study on a night from a lifetime ago. All of Rosalind's joy shattered in that instant. She froze, unable to think, unable to act, unable to do anything save stare at that terrible object.

'No!' And she did not know whether she cried the denial aloud or whispered the word in her head.

'Rosalind?' Wolf was already walking towards her, concern upon his face.

She moved then, ran to the window, staring out wildly, searching for Kempster. But it was not Kempster that she saw.

There, on the road before the inn, was a man dressed all in black astride a black stallion. A gentleman. The dark stranger of whom Kempster had spoken.

He saw her quite clearly, and it seemed to Rosalind that he had been waiting for her. He smiled, and even across the distance she could see his straight, white teeth and his eyes as black as the devil's. His gaze held hers boldly, almost flirtatiously. Rosalind stared and could not look away.

In two strides Wolf had reached Rosalind's side. He watched as the horseman tipped his hat at him and galloped off down the road. Unease weighed heavy on him, for Wolf recognized the man from years back…a Gypsy gem trader who, like Wolf, had often operated beneath the law. Why should such a man have sought out Rosalind? He did not want to think about the obvious implication: that Rosalind had taken the jewels. And even if she had lied, what did it matter when he loved her?

Rosalind's face was ashen. She still stared across at the empty road. 'The man that Kempster said paid him to steal Lady Evedon's jewels,' she whispered.

'You never told me that of Kempster,' he said.

'If I had, would you have believed me?' Her gaze swung round to meet his own before dropping to the newspaper in Wolf's hand. 'This is his work.'

'Kempster's?'

'The dark stranger's.'

'The man is a gem merchant.' Wolf slipped the newspaper free of its binding, before unfurling the paper and flattening it out so that it might be read. 'Do you wish me to read it first?'

She shook her head. 'I have to read it, even though it cannot be anything of good news.'

He passed the newspaper to her, and stood there while she scanned through its pages, until she found the one that she wanted.

He had thought her pale before, but as she read her skin seemed to bleach a bloodless white. The paper trembled within her hand. She read and read, until Wolf thought he could bear the tension no longer. And then, at last, she raised her eyes to his and in them was such pain that it made his heart ache.

'Here.' She held the newspaper out to him. 'Take it and read it. You may as well, now that all of London knows.'

Dread clenched his stomach tight, but he took the paper

and began to read. And as he read, he could scarcely believe
the words printed upon the page.

> *We can exclusively report that there is a scan-*
> *dal of immense proportions within Lord Evedon's*
> *household. For it can be revealed that a certain gen-*
> *tlewoman, posing these past seven years as the dow-*
> *ager Lady Evedon's companion, is a liar and a thief.*
> *Indeed, this newspaper has learned the shocking*
> *truth that she is not Miss Rosalind Meadowfield, as*
> *purported, but Miss Rosalind Wardale, eldest daugh-*
> *ter of the infamous Earl of Leybourne, who, as some*
> *of our readers may remember, vilely murdered his*
> *friend and fellow peer, Lord Framlingham in the year*
> *1794. It was indeed a most dishonourable crime. By*
> *Act of Attainder Lord Leybourne was stripped of his*
> *peerage and lands and was thus executed by hanging*
> *with a silken rope on account of his noble station.*
>
> *Not only has Miss Wardale hoodwinked Earl Eve-*
> *don and his mother, but she has foully exploited her*
> *position with the dowager to steal the lady's most*
> *exquisite and costly jewels and has fled with them to*
> *Scotland. It is believed that Lord Evedon has made*
> *his own private arrangements to have this most*
> *shameful daughter of a murderer retrieved.*
>
> *-The London Reporter, 19th May 1815-*

'Is it true? Was Leybourne your father?' He was expecting her to deny it, to say that it was all lies and nothing of
truth.

'Yes, he was my father.' Her voice was soft, the words
barely louder than a whisper.

He did not know what to say, what to think. 'You are
an earl's daughter!'

'You read what they printed—my father was stripped of his title and lands.'

'That makes no difference,' said Wolf. She was still of noble birth. The words whispered through his head. 'Why did you not tell me, Rosalind?'

'I...' She shook her head.

'Did you not think that I had a right to know? I asked you to be my wife, for pity's sake!' He, a whore's bastard, and she, an earl's daughter. And she had known the truth of him, and let him fall in love with her and believe in happiness. He could have laughed with the absurdity of it, had his heart not been breaking.

'I could not tell you.' The breath shook in her throat. 'Had you known who my father was, it would have changed everything.'

'Yes,' he said, unable to lie to her. An earl's daughter could not marry a bastard from the back streets of York, regardless of what her father had done.

She seemed to still, as if her very heart had paused. 'If you wish to withdraw your proposal of marriage...'

'Rosalind...' He sighed and raked a hand through his hair, forcing words he did not wish to say to his tongue. 'There can be no marriage between us...not when our stations are so very distant. You are an earl's daughter, and I am...well, you know exactly what I am.'

'I...I understand.' Her head was held high, but her hands gripped together so hard that her knuckles shone white.

'Rosalind...' He reached for her, but she stepped back.

'I said that I understand.' Her voice was tight with emotion yet she did not weep, and he was glad of it. He did not know if he could have borne her tears without weeping himself.

He cleared his throat, gathered his strength. 'Kempster said you were an orphan…'

She shook her head, confirming the lie. 'My mother made me sever contact with her and my sister so that my position with Lady Evedon would be safe. Had anyone learned my true identity…I need not tell you of the consequences.' She swallowed. 'It was a decision made of necessity, not choice. We had little option; there was not enough money to support us all, and my brother had disappeared. So when she learned that the dowager Lady Evedon was looking for a ladies' companion, my mother wished for me to apply. I kept the details from my sister at my mother's insistence; she thought it better that Nell did not know of my whereabouts in case she sought me out and our secret was discovered. I consoled myself with the thought that the money would go further with one less mouth to feed.'

'Where are they now?'

'I do not know. Our old lodgings were the first place I went when I ran from Evedon. It was the address to which I had always sent my forbidden letters, and the only one I had for them. The tenants told me that my mother and Nell had long since left.' She turned her gaze to look directly into his eyes. 'What happens now? Do you take me back to Evedon?'

How could she ask such a thing when he loved her? Yet he could not tell her, he must not tell her; it would only make their parting all the harder. Better that he leave her with the fire of hate in her heart than sadness.

'I'll sort matters with Evedon over the jewels and letter. Then I'll find your mother and sister and take you to them.' He switched off his emotions, the part of him that felt hurt, just as he had learned to do such a long time ago. It was for the best, he told himself. She deserved better than him. And because he loved her, he would do what was best for her, not for himself. He would sacrifice his heart, give up his happiness, for Rosalind's sake.

She nodded, her jaw tight. 'If that is what you wish.'

'I have money—'

'I do not want your money, Wolf.'

Yet she would have it just the same, he thought. He would not leave her or her family penniless. And he could only be thankful that he had taken care during their love-making not to spill his seed within her. At least she would be able to find herself a husband without the fear of his child growing within her. His fists clenched at the image that thought conjured.

He lifted the newspaper and its rope from where it lay on the rug, noticing for the first time that the rope had been tied to form a small noose. Some sick bastard really wanted to hurt Rosalind, and Wolf resolved to discover the gem merchant's role in it. He threw both paper and rope into the fire, taking Rosalind's hand in his and making her stand there and watch while they shrivelled and burned, until there was nothing left of either.

Wolf slept on some blankets on the floor that night, leaving Rosalind alone in the bed. She had known, as soon as she caught sight of that slim black silken rope tied around the newspaper, that something terrible was about to happen. Her whole future destroyed in a single moment. And she thought as she lay there sleepless through all the long hours of the night, of how she had spent her life ever fearful that the secret would be learned. A bitter smile curved her mouth at the irony of it, for now the whole of London knew the truth of her. What her mother had sought to prevent all of the years had come to pass: Rosalind was ruined, utterly, completely. All the fear, all the hiding and keeping secrets had been for nothing. But she did not care about the newspaper nor that she was ruined. They seemed as nothing compared to Wolf's rejection.

She had not thought him to be a man so shallow. He did not want her, because the world thought her father a murderer. He did not want her, yet she could not stop from loving him. And she remembered his words: *Our stations are so very distant*—an excuse rather than tell her that he did not want her because of something they said her father had done. She had thought Wolf the bravest, strongest man in the world, but in reality, he was as much a coward as she.

All of her hopes had gone, all of her dreams shattered. She was alone once more. Under cover of the darkness, the tears slipped silently down her face. Better that Evedon would have called the constable than to have been captured by Wolf. Better to have told Evedon the whole wretched truth herself, than to have fallen in love with her captor. She wept, as quietly her heart broke.

Chapter Fifteen

They left for London the next day, catching the early mail coach and arriving late in Stamford where they stayed overnight in the George Inn. She slept in the bed, while Wolf took the chair. Barely a word passed between them. And then they were up early the next morning and on the mail that took them to London.

Her father's crime had driven a wedge between them. It was as if their love had never been. Wolf's expression was as hard and determined as the night that he had first collected her on Munnoch Moor, his jaw clamped tight with self-control. But his eyes had changed since then, they were softer, sadder; she could see it on the rare occasions that his gaze met hers.

He led her through the busy streets, keeping hold of her arm, as if he feared that she would run away again. But he need not have worried, she thought bitterly, she was done with running. He was careful to maintain a distance between their bodies, yet beneath his gentle grip; her skin burned. He seemed to be shielding her with his body as he pushed slightly ahead keeping her a little behind, as if clearing a path through the crowds. He blocked a shove, parried a push and waylaid a pickpocket's hand.

He finally stopped in a smart London crescent—Cumberland Place. Built of honey-coloured sandstone, the houses were large and elegant in design. Their window frames were all painted an immaculate white and their heavy panelled front doors, a glossy ebony black adorned with gleaming brass door knockers. A liveried coach and four was being walked up and down the cobbles as the coachman waited for his passengers to appear from one of the houses.

Suspicion prickled at Rosalind's scalp. She eyed Wolf warily, wondering if he had brought her here to hand her to Evedon after all.

'You said that we were going to your home.'

He did not look round, just began to climb the steps leading up to one of the front doors. 'I did that.'

'Wolf!' Rosalind stood where she was.

He looked at her then, his eyes a searing silver as they seemed to reach in and search her very soul.

'Is Evedon within?' she asked with trepidation. 'Do you take me to him?'

'The expression on his face was closed, just as it had been since learning of her father, so that she could not read what he was thinking, what he was feeling. The seconds lengthened and his gaze did not waver until at last he spoke. 'This *is* my home, Rosalind.'

Surprise widened her eyes. 'But I thought…' She gasped, and then recovered herself. He could not possibly be telling the truth, could he?

'Thought what?' He waited.

She shook her head and gave a tiny shrug of her shoulders, unwilling to say the words.

The door at the top of the stairs at which they stood suddenly opened, and Rosalind was amazed to see a butler standing there.

'Mr Wolversley,' the butler intoned.

'Good evening,' replied Wolf.

Rosalind's mouth dropped open.

Wolf looked at her again. 'Until I have spoken to Evedon, it would be better if you did not linger on the street.'

She nodded and wordlessly followed him inside.

The house was large and luxurious. The hallway was all white marble and sweeping staircase, pristine and austere. Wolf dumped the baggage he had been carrying on to the Italian tiled floor, and strode on, tall and confident, his long greatcoat tails kicking out, oblivious to how out of place his mud-splattered attire appeared in such surroundings. She supposed her own shabby appearance must be equally incongruent. She hurried along behind him, not entirely convinced that he was telling the truth.

He led her into a drawing room decorated in cool pale greys and blues, its furniture plain but clearly of quality. The large bow windows revealed a view of the fading light in the street outside. He indicated for her to sit.

She glanced all around the room, half expecting Evedon to appear, and then perched herself on a large blue armchair.

'You honestly live here, in this house?'

'I do.'

'I am surprised. I had thought your address to be elsewhere.'

'In one of the rookeries, perhaps?' he asked. 'Or a flea-ridden doss-house?'

'A conservative room in a lodging-house,' she answered, feeling her anger rouse. 'You misled me, Wolf.'

He raised his eyebrows at that, the look in his eyes clearly throwing the accusation back at her for all his mouth did not utter the words.

She blushed, knowing that she was being unfair. He had told her of his background, revealing the pain and bitterness that drove him on and made him the man he was today. He had bared his soul, and she remembered the wetness of his tears beneath her fingers, their saltiness upon her lips. A strong fierce man exposing his very vulnerability, while her own secret festered dark and untold. She had no right to chastise him. She was the one who had done the misleading. She was the one who had lied.

'I did not mean that, I just thought…After all you said of the gentry…'

'It is all true, every last word. I might be rich, Rosalind, but I will never escape the restrictions of my birth, nor do I wish to.'

'But you were penniless. You were on the streets…'

'I was. But not any more. I am a very wealthy man. Business has been good, and I am a shrewd investor. I earned every penny of my money, unlike the others who live in this street. And my neighbours hate me for it.' He smiled, the same bitter smile of old, as if he did not care, but Rosalind knew better.

'Then why did you take the job with Evedon, if you do not need to work?'

'It is what I must do, Rosalind. It's not about the money; it was never really about the money, although I'm well aware of the importance of money, having gone without it for much of my life.'

'Wolf…'

He turned away and stood looking out of the window, his

face once more hard and determined. 'I will make imme-
diate enquiries as to your family, as I promised. You may
stay here for how ever long it takes to find them. Treat the
house as your own. Make your stay comfortable. If you
wish for anything, anything at all, speak to Haddow and
he will arrange it.'

'Haddow?'

'My butler,' he said.

Wolf did not want her to speak to him. That hurt. She
held her head higher, her back straighter.

'Stay inside the house, unless you wish to attract press
interest and have the newspaper men camped on our
steps.'

'And Evedon?'

'I will speak to him.'

She nodded.

There was silence, punctuated only by the tick of the
clock upon the mantel.

'Haddow will show you to your room.'

He was a fake and a fraud, every bit as much as she,
pretending to be one thing while underneath was something
else. He professed to hate the gentry for their money and
their power, while all along he was rich as Croesus himself.
She had believed in him; she had loved him.

Wolf opened the door and the butler appeared.

She rose from her seat and followed Haddow as he
limped from the drawing room, without so much as a
backward glance at Wolf.

The next morning, Rosalind stood by the window in
the pristine front bedchamber that looked as if it had never
been used, looking out at the empty road. The front door
slammed and she watched Wolf's tall figure hurry down
the steps and disappear along the street.

Damn him, she thought, damn him to hell. And her anger swathed the crack in her heart.

He did not return until much later in the day, when she was sitting in the small dressing room that led from the bedchamber in which she had slept. She heard the thud of the front door closing and knew it was him. The last hours had been spent in a contemplation of the situation in which she now found herself, and her anger had grown to a fury. That which she had spent a lifetime fearing had come to pass, and just as her mama had warned, once the knowledge was out it had changed everything. One hint of the scandal, and the man she loved had withdrawn his offer of marriage. Wolf was using the fact that her father had been an earl as an excuse. Rosalind knew the real reason he could no longer stomach their alliance. She would be for ever branded a murderer's daughter. There would never be any escape from it, no matter how much she did to hide it, no matter whether her father had been guilty or innocent.

She thought again of the dark stranger who had paid Kempster to steal the jewels and plant them within her chamber. She remembered the look on his face after he had delivered that horrible newspaper and the salacious story printed within its pages. All of it hedged in truth but told in such a way as to render it obscene. Little wonder that Wolf did not wish to marry her after reading it. No man would. She wondered why this gem merchant should wish so much to ruin her. Who was he? She had seen the way that Wolf had looked at her after seeing him, with the faint glimmer of suspicion in his eyes. How dare he?

She pressed her lips firm. Yes, she had lied. Yes, she had not revealed her past, but little wonder when his reaction justified everything that she had feared. And now she had no money, and no where else to go. She was ruined beyond redemption, shunned by all of polite society. Her family were lost, her life still at risk from Evedon, and goodness knows what else the dark stranger was planning. Wolf had said he would help her. He would find her family and speak to Evedon and sort all of her problems…all save her broken heart. But she did not want his help. She did not want to be dependent on his charity.

She was angry with everything that had happened in her life. So angry that all of those years were lost to fear and timidity and forever hiding the real Rosalind Wardale. And all of the anger welled up until she could not stand it any longer. She rose to her feet and strode purposefully out of the room and towards the stairs, determined to unleash exactly what she thought of Wolf's duplicity upon his head.

Haddow was in the hallway. 'How may I assist you, Miss Meadowfield?'

'My name is Wardale, not Meadowfield, Miss Rosalind *Wardale,* and I would be much obliged if you would direct me to Mr Wolversley. I wish to speak with him.'

The butler's face was weathered and scarred in a way that she had never seen in any butler before, yet it remained completely impassive, showing not the slightest shock at the revelation of her true identity.

'Mr Wolversley is not at home, miss.'

'I heard him return, not ten minutes since.'

'I repeat: Mr Wolversley is not at home. Is there something else with which I may help you, some tea perhaps?'

Rosalind's jaw clamped stubbornly. 'No thank you.' She walked back to the stairs and began to climb, slowly, stiltedly. She was on the first landing when she heard the butler's uneven footsteps recede. A door opened and closed. There was silence.

Rosalind turned on her heel and ran quietly back down

the stairs. She began opening each of the doors that led off from the hallway, quietly so that Haddow would not hear, and peeped inside each room. The third door was lucky. It opened into a small room. In contrast to the rest of the house, it was shabby in appearance, its dark mahogany panelling and heavy dark velvet curtains that were drawn against the daylight lending it a snug air of secrecy. Although the day outside was fine, a fire burned on the hearth, casting the room in a warm amber hue. If she had expected book shelves, there were none. A small desk and a single rickety-looking chair was tucked in the corner of the room, and by the fire a couple of high backed armchairs, their leather worn and saggy with comfort, and a small mismatched table between them on which perched a bottle of brandy. Wolf's den.

The room seemed well-suited to him. She could imagine him in here relaxed, guard down. Everything about the room seemed to be imprinted with his presence. Even his scent hung about the place, so that she knew that this little room, so unlike the rest of the house, was where Wolf spent most of his time.

She wandered over to the desk. It too was made of mahogany, darkened by age to a deep colour, a campaign desk by the look of the design. It was badly damaged on one side, as if a knife had hacked at it leaving that small part battered and gouged. She touched a finger to one of its scars, tracing its path across the surface. Battered, but still strong; marked, yet all the more handsome for a character revealed. Rosalind thought of Wolf.

A noise sounded from across the room.

She started, and turned quickly to confront Wolf, her heart hammering hard, her mouth strong and ready, her nostrils flaring with determination.

But it was not Wolf.

Campbell was standing by the chair, a glass filled with brandy in his hand. He must have been sitting in the chair with its back towards her, so that she had not seen him upon entering the room.

'Rescued from a French colonel during battle.' He gestured towards the desk. 'Do you like it?'

'Mr Campbell.'

'Miss Meadowfield, or should I address you as Wardale?'

'Then you know,' she said, no question.

'Aye, lassie, I read what they wrote within the newspaper.'

'No more pretences,' she said. 'All of London knows who I am. A most dishonourable murder they called it, as if any murder could be honourable. They named my father a murderer and me a murderer's daughter.'

'I am sorry, miss.' Campbell's eyes were shadowed, his voice gentle.

'Not as sorry as me, I assure you, Mr Campbell.' She smiled, a bitter smile. 'My ruination is quite without redemption.'

'Come tomorrow, it will be yesterday's news. People forget.'

'Not Wolf.'

'What do you mean, lassie?'

She shook her head, as if it were of little consequence, as if she did not care so very much. 'He said that he hated the aristocracy, the gentry, those with money, the corrupt, the powerful. I believed him. I believed everything that he said. And then I discover that he lives here—' she gestured around her '—Cumberland Place, in a house grander than that which was my father's town house. He has servants, money… He is not what he appears, Mr Campbell.'

'None of us are, Miss Wardale.'

'Wolf is as much a liar as me.'

Campbell's gaze met hers directly, and his eyes flashed with anger. 'Wolf has earned every last penny of his fortune, through his own skill, through the strength of his character and fist and sword. He might have risen from the gutter, but he has never forgotten those that were there with him. The servants you speak of are people from his past, men that served under him in Wellington's Army who were named useless because they can no longer fight. Men who lost limbs and eyes for their country, men who would be begging out on the street were it not for Wolf. He employed them, gave them back their respect, their ability to care for their families. He pays his staff twice the going rate of any of the tightfisted gentlemen on this street, and he's a fair master.'

She remembered Haddow's pronounced limp, the footman with a folded and pinned sleeve where an arm should be, the silver hip flask…Lieutenant Will Wolversley, 26th Regiment of Foot. Her anger drained away.

'Aye, he has a grand house, a fine carriage and four, and plenty money, but it doesnae change who he is…and it doesnae take away his pain. He's a hard man, Miss Wardale, hardest of all with himself. But he's no liar and I'll not hear you call him such.'

The silence that followed his words seemed to ring loud.

'I did not know,' she said.

'Well, you do now.' Campbell had not moved. His gaze stayed trained upon her.

From outside they heard the sound of booted footsteps upon the stone stairs and then the opening and shutting of the front door and the hush of voices. The door to the den opened, and she did not need to look round to know that it was Wolf that had come into the room. She turned, her gaze meeting his. The firelight danced off the silver in his eyes. He glanced from Rosalind to Campbell and back again, and she could see the question in his eyes.

She did not know what to say. The anger had all gone, and where it had been was only hurt, hurt that her pride would not let him see.

'Please excuse me, Mr Campbell, Mr Wolversley.' She held her head high, kept her shoulders back, and with as much dignity as she could muster, swept from the room.

Wolf waited until the door closed before he spoke. 'What the hell just happened in here? Rosalind looks like you just slapped her in the face.'

Campbell set his still half-full glass down and, lifting the bottle of brandy, filled a second glass. 'The lassie was under some misapprehensions. I set her right, nothing more.' He lifted his own glass once more, leaving the newly filled glass where it was on the table, and sat down in the chair. 'You didnae bed her, then.' Campbell sounded doleful.

Wolf sighed and rubbed the heel of his hand against his temple before coming to sit in the chair opposite Campbell's. 'Don't go there Struan.' He lifted the filled glass from where Campbell had left it and took a large swig of the brandy. 'I take it you received the message I sent?'

Campbell nodded. 'I didnae like how the lassie got under your skin, but she didnae deserve that. Is it true what they printed in the newspaper?'

'Aye, she's Leybourne's daughter. A bloody earl's daughter.'

'Said in the paper that he was stripped of his title.'

'It makes no difference. She's still of noble birth,' said Wolf and there was an ache in his chest as he said the words. He looked away, staring into the fire, trying to get a grip of himself.

There was a short silence.

Campbell cursed and it hissed quiet in the room.

Wolf did not even look round.

'It's more than what's in your breeches; you have feelings for the lassie,' Campbell accused.

Wolf looked round then, and he could see the concern in Campbell's eyes. 'I love her, Struan. Asked her to marry me, before I knew the truth of who she was.'

'Marriage?' Wolf could hear the slightly horrified tone of panic in his friend's voice.

'You need not worry. The newspaper changed all that. An earl's daughter cannot marry the bastard son of a whore.'

'She shunned your offer?'

'No. She accepted me wholeheartedly.' Wolf smiled through the pain and bitterness. 'It was me who withdrew the offer.'

Campbell stared at him. 'You love her. She agrees to marry you. And yet you refuse to marry her because her father was an earl?'

'You know where I come from, Struan. You know what I am.'

'It doesnae make any difference, if you love each other.'

'It does to me.' He finished the rest of the brandy in one gulp and poured himself another. 'And it does to her. Besides, I didn't ask you here to speak of this. What did you discover of the emeralds?'

'You're no' gonnae like it.' Campbell watched him a moment longer before speaking. 'They were fenced the night of the theft by a servant from Evedon's household.'

Wolf glanced round, his eyes sharp, waiting.

'It was Kempster.'

'Hell,' Wolf muttered beneath his breath. 'The stones will probably end up with Beshaley.'

'Beshaley?' Campbell glanced up suddenly, alert. 'You mean the Gypsy, Stephano Beshaley? The gem trader?'

'One in the same,' confirmed Wolf. 'Beshaley's at the centre of this whole mess. I couldn't place his name at the time, but a few discreet enquiries today soon revealed his identity. Beshaley is the gentleman from the inn that I wrote of, the one who delivered the newspaper to Rosalind. The same one that Kempster told Rosalind had paid him to steal Lady Evedon's jewels and plant them in her bedchamber. Beshaley went to a lot of trouble to scandalize Rosalind's reputation.'

'Who the hell is Rosalind Wardale to him?'

Wolf's eyes narrowed and he shook his head. 'Rosalind said she did not know him.'

'And you believe her?'

'Aye, Struan, I do.'

'And Kempster, the sneaky wee rat that he is, was double-crossing Beshaley. He stole both sets of stones, but only planted the diamonds; the emeralds he sold to line his own pocket, little realizing Beshaley's trade. Beshaley will find him out, if he hasnae already done so.'

'Beshaley will not care. This is some kind of vendetta against Rosalind. We need to find the link between them.'

'Where does Evedon fit into all this?'

'He doesn't,' said Wolf. 'Beshaley was just looking for a way to ruin Rosalind. When he thought that the jewel theft was going to be hushed up, he resorted to publication of the story. Evedon is a bystander victim in all of this.' He thought of the letter that Rosalind had carried within her corset, that now lay neatly folded and safe within the pocket of his jacket.

'Some victim. Did Rosalind steal Evedon's letter as she claimed?'

'She did.'

'And?' Campbell waited, a look of expectation on his face.

'It's naught we need worry over, Struan.' He downed the rest of the brandy and set the empty glass on the table. 'See what you can find on Beshaley. I've an appointment with Evedon to keep.'

'Rather you than me. Evedon's no' gonnae be happy. Nae lassie, nae emeralds, just a poxy letter.' Campbell smiled and got to his feet.

Wolf returned the smile in full. 'The poor bastard will be happy enough with his letter.'

Rosalind heard the front door shut as Campbell took his leave. Five minutes later, there was a tap at her bedchamber door and Wolf's voice sounded.

'Rosalind?' He waited where he was, even though it was his house and the door was not locked.

His expression was uncertain when she opened the door to him, as if he could not be sure of her response.

'You are well?' He stood there, and she could sense the slight discomfort about him.

'Very well, thank you,' she said politely.

He nodded, and cleared his throat, but still stood where he was, making no move to enter the room.'

'The bedchamber is to your liking?'

'Yes,' she lied. The bedchamber was grand and elegant, dressed in whites and creams and furnished with expense, yet it held no comfort. It was like the rest of the house, austere and luxurious, but with nothing of a home about it, all save Wolf's small shabby den. She liked that room.

'I am glad of it.' His eyes held an uneasiness. 'Haddow said you wished to speak with me.'

She looked at him; he seemed as awkward as she was with this mask of manners to disguise the truth of what lay between them. 'Campbell told me you were in the Army. Lieutenant Will Wolversley.'

'He had no right to tell you that.'

'I read the inscription on your flask, that day by the stream in the bluebell woods, the day I rode pillion with Kempster.'

'The day you ran away.'

'And you fetched me back.'

Their eyes met and held, so that she felt a shiver tingle across her skin.

'What happened? England is still at war with France, yet you are no longer in the Army.'

'Did not Campbell tell you the rest of it?' he asked harshly, and then he shook his head and glanced momentarily away before looking back at her. 'Dishonourable discharge. I was flogged until there was no skin left upon my back. I'm damned lucky that the sentence was so light; by rights I should be dead.'

She remembered the scarring she had seen that night in the inn. 'Why?' she caught her teeth at her lip, afraid of the answer but needing to hear it all the same.

'I killed a fellow officer.'

Her eyes widened.

'You are shocked.'

'A little, but I am sure you had good reason for…for the action you took.'

He smiled at that, and something of the awkwardness vanished. 'Through his own pomposity and stupidity, he led good men to be butchered and nigh on would have destroyed the company had I not disobeyed his command.'

'And you killed him in punishment?'

'I killed him in a duel to which he challenged me. I meant only to injure the fool.'

'Wolf…'

He shook his head as if to stay what she would have said. 'It is all of it in the past now.'

'Yes,' she said quietly.

'That day in the inn, the man who delivered the newspaper, you said that you did not know him.'

'I have never seen him before.'

'He is called Stephano Beshaley.'

She shook her head slowly. 'The name means nothing to me.'

'There must be some connection between the two of you, for he was most determined to see you destroyed.'

Her eyes met his again and another shiver ran through her.

'You need not be afraid Rosalind. You are safe here, and I mean to discover what Beshaley is about.'

'And Evedon?'

'I have an appointment with Evedon in half an hour. You have nothing more to fear from him.'

'You…you have the letter?'

He gave a nod. 'I have the letter.'

They looked at one another for a moment, and the tension seemed to wind tight between them. So many words unspoken; so much found, then lost. For all that had gone, she did not want him to face Evedon alone.

'Let me come with you.'

'It is better if I see him alone.'

She swallowed hard. 'Better for whom?'

'For us all, Rosalind.'

'You do not know what he is like.'

'I think I can hazard a good-enough guess.'

'I am trying to warn you of the danger,' she said with exasperation.

'I know, lass,' he said softly, 'and I thank you for it,' and leaning in, dropped a kiss to her cheek before he turned and was gone.

Rosalind stood alone in the bedchamber and heard the banging of the doors and the ensuing silence that seemed to echo through the house, and her cheek, where his lips had touched, burned.

Chapter Sixteen

Wolf declined the chair that Evedon offered, preferring instead to stand within the earl's library. Evedon's face was flushed, as if he had been drinking heavily even though the afternoon hour was not late.

'Where is she?' Wolf could see the fear that lurked behind the anger in Evedon's eyes. 'Thief, and murderer's daughter—she has quite ruined my mother's reputation… and mine.'

'No person's reputation is ruined save Miss Wardale's own,' said Wolf.

'You were supposed to keep this quiet. That was the deal. A hundred guineas to bring her back unnoticed. And instead, you sold the story to the press. What the hell did they pay you? Was not my money enough for you?'

'The newspaper story was not of my doing.'

'Kempster said that you fancied her, that you were bedding the little trollop.'

Wolf walked right up to Evedon, keeping on going even

when the older man backed away. 'Watch your mouth, Evedon. I'll not have you speak of Miss Wardale in such terms.'

'Then he was right,' murmured Evedon and turned away to pour himself another drink.

Wolf knocked the glass from his hand, the finely engraved crystal falling to smash upon the hearthstone. 'You've had enough to drink this day. Kempster is a liar, a thief and an arsonist. It was Kempster that stole the dowager's jewels, not Miss Wardale.'

Evedon gaped at him. 'You are lying, because you are bedding her.'

Wolf grabbed him by his cravat and hoisted him close. 'You best tell Kempster to run, because I'll kill the little coward when I get my hands on him. He was paid to steal Lady Evedon's jewels in order to implicate Miss Wardale as the thief. He hid the diamonds in her chamber as directed, but his greed meant that he could not resist selling the emeralds for himself. Where is he now?'

'Gone,' croaked Evedon, his face flushing redder from where Wolf held his cravat tight. 'Asked for his character and left as soon as he returned from Scotland. Some sort of family trouble I understand.'

Wolf's expression was hard, unremitting, but he released Evedon, pushing him away from the table on which the servant's bell sat.

'Ring that and I'll have a bullet through your heart before the first footman is through the door.' Wolf touched a hand to the bump where his pistol lay beneath his coat.

The earl regarded him sullenly. 'You have come without the girl. What do you do here, Mr Wolversley? Surely you do not expect payment?'

Wolf slipped the letter from his pocket and sat it on the table between them.

Evedon's face paled before burning redder than before. He stared first at the letter and then at Wolf. He wetted his lips and swallowed nervously. 'How much do you want?'

'I want your oath, sir.'

Evedon's breath caught. He stared all the harder with suspicion. 'My oath, Mr Wolversley?'

'That you will ensure all London knows of Kempster's guilt in the theft of the jewels.'

Evedon's face lifted in surprise. 'That should present no problem.'

'You will not seek out Miss Wardale or contact her by any means. Nor shall you speak ill of her to any person. Your mother shall write her a favourable character. That is all.'

'And if all of your demands are met…'

'The letter is yours, sir, to do with as you wish. Neither Miss Wardale nor I shall speak of it.'

'You do not want money?'

Wolf gave a hard laugh. 'I do not need your money, Lord Evedon; I have more than enough of my own.'

Evedon's face coloured a deeper hue. 'Kempster was right. You do want the woman.'

Wolf ignored the comment.

The earl's gaze met Wolf's. The two men watched each other as the seconds ticked by. Evedon gave a nod.

'Very well, Mr Wolversley. I will do all that you ask. I give you my word.' He extended his hand and Wolf grasped it firm, pulling the earl closer, so that his words, when uttered, were soft by Evedon's ear.

'Renege on any part of it, and I will come after you and ensure that all of England knows your secret.'

Wolf could see the sheen of sweat across Evedon's brow and on the bridge of his nose. He released the man's hand, pushing him back as he did so.

Evedon's breathing was shaky and his face stained ruddy, yet he said nothing, just stared across the distance that separated them once more.

Wolf pushed the letter across the table's smooth, highly polished surface.

Evedon reached for it. The letter trembled within his hands, as he touched the seal and then scanned the contents. Satisfied, he folded it once more and slid the letter into the inner pocket of his jacket.

'Thank you, Mr Wolversley. That will be all.'

'Not quite all,' said Wolf. 'There is something I have yet to tell you, something that concerns us both.'

The earl swallowed hard and held his hand defensively over the pocket in which the letter lay. He edged towards the bell that would summon his footmen.

Wolf smiled a hard smile and stepped easily to block Evedon's intent. 'Somehow I do not think this is something you'll be wanting your servants to hear.' He steered Evedon towards his desk. 'Best sit down, Lord Evedon.'

Alone within the ivory bedchamber, Rosalind could not rest. She flitted nervously from one chair to another, paced anxiously and stared endlessly from the window, willing Wolf's safe return. She knew how angry Evedon would be, and she could not imagine that Wolf's confrontation with her past employer would be as straightforward as he seemed to think. Simply returning the letter to Evedon would not be enough. Evedon would know that she had read it, and Wolf too, and neither of them would be safe.

Wolf did not seem to appreciate the danger into which he had plunged. She knew that he was trying to protect her. Had he not promised her that he would sort the matter with Evedon, and if any man could do such a thing it was Wolf for he was darkly dangerous in a way that the earl could never be. But even knowing this, even trusting him as she did, she could not relax the knot of tension in her stomach. She should have gone with him despite his protestations; it would have been better than sitting here and worrying.

Lord, keep him safe. Protect him. She whispered the prayer to herself, saying the words again and again, like a mantra that would act as his talisman. And walked again to the window for the hundredth time to check for his return.

It could have been little more than an hour later when she heard at last the opening of the front door. Her heart beat fast. She hurried across the bedchamber, flinging open the door and running to the stairs.

Wolf was shrugging off his coat in the hallway. He glanced round at the sound of her footsteps.

She slowed, coming to a halt in front of him, suddenly embarrassed by her behaviour. She saw the amusement upon Haddow's face before he hid it behind his butler's mask, and she blushed at her own impetuosity.

'You are unhurt?' Her hand moved to touch Wolf, and stayed itself just in time. Her eyes scanned the whole of him checking for any sign of injury.

'Completely,' he said with a smile. He led her into the nearby drawing room before speaking further. 'It is done. All is well, Rosalind.'

'Are you certain?'

'Absolutely. Evedon shall not bother you again.'

'It was done so easily?'

'Easily enough.'

She smiled her relief. 'Thank you.' She touched her hand to his and felt his fingers entwine with hers.

Wolf's gaze shifted to their clasped hands before raising once more to meet her eyes. She saw the desire in the shimmering silver, saw how he leaned his face down to hers as if he would kiss her. And then he stopped, and something of the light dimmed in his eyes, and she thought she saw bleakness move in its place.

His fingers loosened from hers and fell away. His smile vanished and the lines of his face grew hard once more and edged with sadness.

All of the tension was back winding tight and awkward between them.

'I should go. There are things to be attended to.'

'You have not eaten. The hour grows late.'

'Your family must be found.'

Did he really wish to be rid of her so quickly? 'Yes,' she said, 'you are right.' She stepped back, increasing the distance between them, determined to show nothing of the hurt she was feeling.

His gaze held to hers, and she could not look away no matter how much she tried. She saw the muscle tighten in the squareness of his jaw as if he clenched his teeth in determination.

'Rosalind,' he said, and his voice was hoarse as though the word was wrung from his lips against his will.

She saw the sudden darkening of his eyes, from pale luminescent dove grey to smoky slate.

There did not seem to be enough air in the room; her breathing grew short and ragged. She wetted her lips.

He gave a groan of submission, and then she was in his arms and his mouth was hard upon hers, kissing her. His lips were like the thrum of her own blood—hot and hard and needful. He tangled his fingers in her hair, as his tongue entwined with hers so that she felt the heat of passion sear her thighs. But even as she melted against him, she felt him slip away.

He stared into her eyes for a moment longer. 'Forgive me. I should not have done that.' And then he was gone, leaving only the slam of the front door and the thump of her heart echoing in his wake.

The butler showed Wolf into a small reception room of the large town house in fashionable Bruton Street and left him there alone. It was the room used for trade and for servants, but Wolf was used to such treatment. He did not speak like a gentleman. He did not dress like a gentleman. In truth, he was no gentleman. He did not sit down on one of the plain wooden chairs as the butler had indicated but, instead, stood by the small high window peering out on to the stables. He did not have to wait long before the tall dark-haired man he had come to see joined him.

'Lord Stanegate,' he nodded an acknowledgement.

'At your service, Mr Wolversley. You said in your note that you had news of my wife's sister.'

'Indeed. I come seeking the whereabouts of Mrs Wardale and her youngest daughter, that they might be reunited with Miss Rosalind Wardale.'

Wolf did not miss the flicker that crossed Lord Stanegate's face before he schooled his expression once more to impassivity.

'Mrs Wardale passed away several years ago, but Lady Stanegate, her daughter and my wife, has been most anxious to hear of her sister. We read the newspaper account…' He let the sentence trail off unfinished.

'All of London did, but you need not fear, my lord: Miss Wardale is no jewel thief, despite all that the papers have been saying. You understand the nature of malicious gossip, sir.'

'I do, but what I do not understand, sir, is your connection with Miss Wardale.'

'I am a friend, sir.'

'A friend, sir? I have heard you are something of a thief-taker, Mr Wolversley. Employed by Evedon to capture Miss Wardale.'

'That is so.' Wolf met Stanegate's gaze unflinching, and saw the concern behind the suspicion that he was accustomed to seeing in the aristocracy's eyes when they looked at him. 'Miss Wardale has suffered enough. If you seek to deal her further censure, then speak now.'

'I wish for nothing other than my wife's happiness. Knowing her sister is safe and well would do much for that. The lady is welcome here.'

Wolf nodded. 'Then I will bring her to you.'

'Sir—'

But Wolf was already walking towards the door. 'Ensure that she is treated kindly, Lord Stanegate.'

From the expression upon his face, Stanegate was not accustomed to taking orders, especially not in his own house—not that Wolf cared one iota for that.

A single nod and Wolf was gone. His mission was accomplished. He already knew from his research that Stanegate was a decent man and that he doted on his young wife and child. And Wolf was confident that Stanegate would take Rosalind into his household and care for her. Rosalind would be safe in a place that she belonged, with people that loved her.

But as he strode through the streets, his heart was heavy and there was a hard lump in his throat that would not shift no matter how he tried to swallow it down. People that loved her, he thought again, and knew that none of them loved her as much as he did. But he had first to tell Rosalind the news of her mother's death. He headed to the Red Lion tavern to delay what must be done.

It had moved from evening to night when the knock sounded on Rosalind's bedroom door. Only ten of the clock, but already she was in her nightdress and in bed, lying beneath the clean freshly ironed sheets wide awake in the darkness. She knew instinctively that it was Wolf outside her door.

When she opened the door, she could not see his face; he was a dark silhouette against the brightness of the wall sconces in the hallway. But she could smell the cold night air and the faint sweetness of brandy that emanated from him.

He turned slightly so that the light caught his face, and she saw his gaze take in the thick white cotton of her night-clothes. 'Forgive me, I did not mean to wake you. It can wait until tomorrow.'

'No.' She put out her hand to stay him, then drew it back fast at the feel of his bare fingers beneath hers. 'I was not asleep.' There was an awkward pause as she found her eyes meeting his again. It was night time and he had come to her bedchamber. Her heart was beating too fast. But when she looked into his eyes, she saw not the tell-tale darkening simmer of desire; she saw pain and dread and resolution to a task. She felt the cold hand of premonition touch to her shoulder and she shivered. The churning dread was back in her stomach.

'You have some news, sir?' The question was polite and her voice flat and unemotional, revealing nothing. It was the voice of Rosalind Meadowfield, not Rosalind Wardale. She could feel herself retreating back beneath the safety of the familiar guise.

'Indeed.' He nodded, and his grim expression did nothing to allay her fears.

Bad news. About Evedon? About the dark stranger? Or her family? She tensed in preparation. She made no move to invite him in, just kept him standing in the corridor. It was all she had left she thought, her pride, and she held her head up and looked him directly in the eye.

'I have found your sister. She has been married these eighteen months to Marcus Carlow, Viscount Stanegate.'

'Nell!' All pride was forgotten. Rosalind thought only of her sister. 'She is well?'

Wolf nodded.

'Where is she?'

'She was living with her husband in Stanegate's father's residence in Albemarle Street, but following the arrival of their baby, they have moved to their own town house in Bruton Street.'

'She has a child? Nell has a baby?' Rosalind laughed with relief and joy. 'I thought for an awful minute that you meant to bring me bad tidings. I am so pleased to hear it. Did you see her? How did she look?'

Wolf did not smile. His face was both stern and filled with sadness, and all of her joy that had bubbled up stilled and grew cold.

'And what news of my mother?'

Wolf reached out and took her hand in his. She knew then, before he even said the words.

'I am sorry, Rosalind. Mrs Wardale died some years past.'

She heard the breath escape her throat as a gasp. 'It cannot be,' she whispered.

'Consumption took her.'

'She cannot be dead. I was saving my money. I was to go back to them when I had enough. I was going to buy us a cottage somewhere nice. I would find my brother, Nathan, and he would come back to us.' She glanced up at him, wide-eyed at the sudden new fear that struck her. 'Nathan?'

'I have no news yet of your brother, Rosalind.'

She nodded and turned as if she would go back to the bed, yet in truth her mind was reeling and she could not think at all. Wolf's hand was warm around hers. He did not release her.

She shook her head as if to deny the words he had uttered, as if by doing so all would be as it was before and her mother alive and well. She pulled free and walked back into the room, to stand before the fire, and all the while, the words whirled in her head and she could believe none of them.

The golden flames danced bright, revealing the dark shadowed form of Rosalind's body beneath the thick cotton of her nightdress. She looked not at him, but into the flames, and he could see from the set of her body, from the way that she held herself, her bowed head, the droop of her shoulders, the blow her mother's death had dealt her. He could feel her pain as raw and aching as if it were his own and could not bear to see her hurt.

'I am sorry,' he said quietly. And he wished more than anything that he could undo all that had happened and magic a perfect happy ending for her. But life was grim and painful and harsh. He thought back to his own selfish arrogance in wanting to teach her that lesson. And now she knew it, knew it as well as he, and it gave him no pleasure, only a pain that ripped at his heart so that it was raw and aching. And had he the power to take her suffering on to himself, he would have done so in an instant.

'Rosalind,' he whispered, but still she did not look round. The truth had not yet sunk in. It would soon enough, and her pain would be all the worse for it. He had seen such reactions a hundred times over when men lost those around them—on the battlefields of King George's Army, on the streets of London and of York.

He turned her to him and took her gently into his arms. For all that she stood so close to the fire, her body felt chilled, her fingers where they touched him, frozen to the bone.

She looked up into his face and there was the tiniest flicker of hope. 'You are certain, Wolf? I mean, might you not be mistaken in your enquiries?'

He did not want to douse that last glimmer, but to do anything other would be cruelty for the sake of his own relief. He shook his head. 'I am sorry, Rosalind, but I had the news from Lord Stanegate himself.'

She nodded, and smiled bravely, a smile that was everything of misery and disbelief and feigned acceptance. She pushed away from him, then stumbled over to the small armchair, and there she sat, her face white, her eyes staring with disbelief.

'Thank you, sir,' she said through stiff cold lips. 'I will call upon my sister in the morning. You have done all that you agreed to do, and more. I thank you.' She turned away as if she had dismissed him and he was already gone. But Wolf closed the door and sat quietly in the neighbouring armchair.

They sat in silence, with only the crack and the ripple of the flames upon the hearth and the heavy tick of the clock upon the mantel.

Rosalind could not move, could not speak, could not think. She knew that she should tell Wolf to leave before she climbed back into the big white bed, but she could not bring herself to do so. Her mama was dead, and the hope of reuniting her family that had sustained her through the long, difficult lonely years was gone. How could her own mother have died and she, who had loved her, not known? Surely she should have felt something? A feeling, a sense, a dream even? But there had been nothing. Her thoughts ran on. If Mama had died, what had become of Nell? Had her little sister married her viscount before their mother's death?

So many questions and beneath them all, this sense of emptiness. A nothingness that seemed almost to paralyse her. She did not know how long she sat there staring across at the fire. And when the flames burned low, Wolf rose and trod across the room to feed them with fresh coal.

She should visit Nell. She should check that her sister was well. She should discover the details of her sister's life and all that had happened to their mother. She should find Nathan. So much to be done, and yet still Rosalind could not move. So alone and empty, and yet she was not alone. Wolf was there, his silent presence supporting her. She looked across at where his tall figure sat. And in his silver eyes was such strength and compassion to comfort her wounded heart. Their chairs sat side by side, separated by a small table. She laid her right palm flat on the table, her fingers pointing towards him. And slowly, ever so slowly, her fingers edged towards him, moving at most an inch before they stopped.

Wolf laid his hand gently on hers, resting it there for a moment or two. It felt so warm, warm enough to chase the chill from her soul. She turned her hand over beneath his, so that their palms met and touched and lay together, before he threaded his fingers through hers and took her hand within his own. And it did not matter that he had withdrawn his offer of marriage; it did not matter whether he loved her or not; nothing mattered in that moment except that he was there.

She was so cold and just wanted to be warm. Wolf was warm, and he could fill the emptiness that gaped within her. She was on her feet and did not remember standing.

She walked to the bed and heard him follow. And when she climbed beneath the covers, Wolf discarded his jacket and boots and did likewise. He took her in his arms and held her, just held her, through the long hours until at last she said to him, 'Love me, Wolf. Love me this one last time.'

He shook his head. 'I cannot, sweet lass, for both our sakes.'

She touched her lips to his and kissed him gently. Tomorrow she would be gone to Bruton Street and there would be Nell but no more Wolf, not ever. She kissed him harder with all the aching need that was in her heart.

'Love me…please,' she said.

And when he stripped the shirt from his body, she knew that he would do as she asked.

He kissed her and stroked her until she was quivering for him.

'Wolf,' she whispered.

And when at last he slid into her, the relief was overwhelming until he began to move, their bodies rocking in unison in the most ancient of all rhythms between a man and a woman, and a new desire began to build. She moved her hips to meet each of his thrusts, delighting in his possession but knowing that it was not enough, that there was still something more. And she was striving for it, reaching for it, and this man whom she loved was loving her with every shred of his being, with every breath in his lungs.

She heard his gasp and felt him shudder within her as the whole of her body and mind exploded in a shimmering shower of ecstasy. And there was the thud of her heart and of Wolf's, and love, only love. He collapsed down on to her, his body slick with sweat.

'You will always be my love, Rosalind. Always.' And he stroked her hair and kissed her and held her to him as if he would never let her go.

* * *

He took her in the carriage the next morning to Viscount Stanegate's house. The awkwardness was back between them. Neither spoke during the short journey. She looked strained and pale, and he berated himself that he had gone to her bed last night. A gentleman would not have, but then Wolf was no gentleman, and never would be no matter how hard that he tried. Last night was yet more proof as to why he was all wrong for Rosalind and why he was doing the right thing returning her to her family. He loved her, and because he loved her, he would do what was best for *her*, even if that meant breaking his own heart.

After today it was unlikely that he would see her again. He had already seen the suspicion with which Lord Stanegate regarded him and, in all truth, he could not blame the man. Were he in Stanegate's shoes, he too would have wondered just what the hell was going on if such a shady character turned up on his doorstep with his wife's sister in tow.

He wanted the best for Rosalind, but now there was the added complication of their lovemaking last night. He knew that he could not just let her go and say nothing. If there was to be a child, it would change everything: all of his best intentions and Rosalind's chance for a better life.

'Rosalind…' he started.

'All is said between us, Wolf,' she said, but did not shift her gaze from the houses passing in the window.

'Not quite.' The carriage rolled smoothly along.

She glanced round at him then.

'Our actions of last night…if a child should result—' He had been careless, so caught up in his love for her that he had lost control. He had already spent the morning chastising himself that her future could be ruined because of it, for, undoubtedly, that is what marriage to him would do.

'I shall love and care for it,' she finished.

'You do not understand how Society will treat you were you to bear a child out of wedlock.'

'I understand enough,' she said. 'Am I not already ruined?'

'A bastard's fate is not an easy one, Rosalind. You will let me know if there is a child.'

'Why?' she snapped and her eyes flashed with anger. 'So that you might marry me?' Her cheeks scalded red. 'I will not have you, sir.'

He felt the sting of her words and knew that he deserved them. Seeing her distress, he did not pursue the matter. If Rosalind was with child, he was sure that he would discover it. One step at a time. He would deal with that matter if it arose.

Rosalind was angry and miserable by the time they arrived at Bruton Street. It did not matter that this morning, for the first time since she had met him, Wolf had taken a care over his appearance. Gone were the casual work clothes and in their place was an outfit befitting a wealthy gentleman of the *ton*. The black coat that he wore was tailored by London's finest and fitted to perfection. Beneath it, and attached to his matching waistcoat, she saw the glint of a pocket watch. His dove-grey cravat, that matched the colour of his eyes, was understated yet elegant, and, had she not known better she would have thought, tied by the hand of the most masterful valet.

His fitted buff-coloured breeches served only to emphasize the length and musculature of his legs and the shine on his black knee-high riding boots would have been the envy of the Prince Regent himself. His hair had been combed to a tidy style and his rugged jawline had been scraped clean of stubble to be smooth and infinitely kissable. Wolf presented a most handsome and formidable sight. This was not Wolf the thief-taker, but Wolf the gentleman.

The transformation made his rejection all the harder, yet all the more understandable. He was trying to be a gentleman, and marrying a woman branded a murderer's daughter would ruin any chance of that. Despite all that he had claimed, it seemed that Wolf did care for his reputation after all.

She let him escort her into the foyer, but was careful not to touch him. They were shown into a drawing room that rivalled the one in Wolf's house. She sat tense on the sofa, her fingers gripping nervously together. Wolf stood by the window, his face harsh as he stared out at the empty street.

She wished that it would not end like this; not after all they had been through; not when she loved him.

The door opened and a tall well-dressed man entered. She could tell at once from his bearing that this was the viscount. He was dark-haired and handsome in a conventional way. His face was serious, austere almost, and she had the impression that he was a man that did not smile often. When his gaze moved to Wolf, a frown wrinkled between his eyes making him seem even more forbidding. She wondered as to her sister's happiness married to such a man.

Rosalind was seized with sudden panic. Here she was, about to cast herself on the viscount's charity. This was his house, his life she was imposing herself upon. What if Nell did not wish to see her? The presence of a scandalous sister was sure only to be an embarrassment. What if Nell had not told him of their father, what if Rosalind was risking Nell's secret by being here? Rosalind rose swiftly, ready to plead her excuses and escape, but then the door opened once more—and there stood Nell.

Nell with her beautiful face and golden-brown hair, and eyes filled with such excitement and kindness and love—just as Rosalind remembered her from across the years.

Nell was hurrying across the room towards her and throwing her arms around her.

'Rosalind! Rosalind, it really is you!'

All thoughts fled Rosalind's mind save that this was her beloved little sister. The years seemed to roll back in those moments, and they stared from their women's eyes at the girls they once had been.

'I am so very glad to see you, so very glad indeed.'

And they were laughing and crying and hugging all at once.

Wolf watched Rosalind and her sister together and knew that he had done the right thing for once in his life. The pain of his sacrifice was small in comparison with Rosalind's happiness at finding her sister. This was where she belonged: in this grand house, with these grand people.

Wolf could see that the two woman shared the same hazel eyes. Indeed, from the physical resemblance between them, it was clear they were sisters, although his Rosalind was not as tall and her hair was darker than Lady Stanegate's. *His* Rosalind? She was not his any longer. He wondered if she ever really had been. He took his leave of Stanegate and made to slip away. He was at the drawing room door when Rosalind saw him.

'Wolf.'

He stopped, reticent to look round, not wanting to make this any harder for himself than it already was. There was little choice. He turned to face her. 'Miss Wardale,' he said carefully.

'You are leaving?' The colour that had flushed her cheeks on seeing her sister seemed to fade.

'I am,' he said. 'My job is done. You are returned safely to your sister.'

She caught her teeth at her lower lip as if to stay the words that she would have spoken. She was staring at him, and just for a moment, the mask of politeness upon her face slipped and he saw there hurt and loneliness and devastation—just for a moment—and then it was gone, hidden quickly away. But Wolf had seen her pain, and the thought that he had caused it was like a rock in his gullet.

She recovered herself, her fingers smoothing out imaginary wrinkles upon her skirt. 'I thank you, sir, for all of your assistance.'

A single nod of his head. He knew he must go, but she was still looking at him and he thought that the image of her standing there so pale and still, yet with such gritty pride, would be etched upon his memory for ever.

'Goodbye, Miss Wardale,' he forced the words out.

She hesitated, her eyes still clinging to his. 'Goodbye, Mr Wolversley.'

His heart was aching. He turned away while he still could and left Rosalind at Bruton Street—to her sister, to the life to which she was born…without him.

Chapter Seventeen

It was five days since Wolf had gone, and Rosalind was only just starting to accept the finality of their parting. For those first few days, she had been unable to rid herself of the notion that he would come back for her. Now, she knew that he would not.

She was delighted to be reunited with her sister, but no matter how she denied it to herself, she missed Wolf. She smiled across at where Nell rested upon the sofa, and lifted the baby on to her knee. William was a sturdy boy of nine months with chubby pink cheeks, a cherubic little mouth and his father's dark grey eyes. William wriggled on her knee. She dropped a kiss on to the top of his fine golden hair and slid him down that he might play once more with the rag doll at her feet. The sun shone in through the windows of Nell's private apartment making the room bright and warm.

'I am sure that we can make you a good match, Rosalind. Marcus has so many contacts.' There was an excited twinkle in Nell's eyes.

'But I do not wish to make a match. I am quite happy to stay here and help you with baby William, and—' she glanced towards Nell's stomach '—the new little one, when he or she arrives later this year.' A sudden thought struck her. 'Unless you would prefer that I did not, that is.'

'Of course I wish you to stay, dearest sister.' Nell smiled, and Rosalind could see her sister's sincerity. 'We have so much still to catch up on. But we must consider what is best for your future. Marcus is quite convinced that he can find you a man that would make you happy.' Rosalind noticed how her sister's face lit up and her voice softened when she spoke her husband's name.

'As Marcus makes you happy?' she asked.

'Oh, yes,' Nell sighed. 'More happy than you can imagine. There is such joy to be found in marriage, Rosalind. I cannot imagine my life without Marcus. He saved me.'

'Saved you from what?' Rosalind asked. 'Will you not tell me what happened, Nell, after Mama died and you were alone?'

But Nell shook the question off just as she had done every time that Rosalind had tried to ask it. She laughed and said in a mock scolding voice, 'Do not seek to change the subject; I know what you are about, Rosalind Wardale. I mean to find you a husband that will make you as happy as Marcus makes me.'

'Nell, there is no need. I am too old for such nonsense and decidedly happy upon the shelf.' She wondered if she would ever be happy again. 'I shall be an old maid and help you with your nursery of children.' She said it with laughter in her voice, but her heart was heavy beneath the pretence.

'Tush!' said Nell sternly. 'You are but five and twenty, plenty young enough to be a bride. We could have a summer wedding at Stanegate Court, Marcus's country house. It is in the most delightful location on the edge of the Chiltern hills and overlooking the vale of Aylesbury. It would be wonderful.'

Wonderful was not what Rosalind was thinking, but Nell's face was animated with excitement. She chattered on before stopping suddenly, her expression more excited than ever. 'Why did I not think of it before? There is Hal, Marcus's younger brother. He is a major in the Dragoons, and is very dashing, and almost as handsome as Marcus—' she smiled '—but not quite. He is currently with his regiment in Brussels but I am sure that he shall be returning home soon for a visit.'

'Nell—' Rosalind tried to interject.

'He is perfect for you, and he would have no objections to our friendship.' A tiny frown wrinkled Nell's nose. 'But he does have a rather wild reckless streak.' She chewed at her lip. 'He quite worries Marcus to death with his exploits. And I seem to recall from his last letter to Marcus…' A faint flush rose in her cheeks and neck. 'But—' she hesitated '—never mind that.'

'Nell—'

'All rakes can be reformed, and I am sure that his reputation is much exaggerated. I will speak to Marcus—'

Rosalind could not let it continue. 'Please do not; I cannot marry Hal. I cannot marry any man.'

Nell stopped and looked at Rosalind. 'Forgive me, I had no wish to distress you.'

Rosalind shook her head. 'It is I who should beg your forgiveness. You are only trying to help.'

Nell's eyes were too seeing, her thinking too like Rosalind's own. The small silence seemed to stretch.

'Who is he, Rosalind, this man to whom you have already given your heart?'

'You are mistaken, sister. There is no one.' But the hot blush on Rosalind's cheeks gave lie to her denial.

Nell swung her slippered feet on to the rug and sat upright. There was another short silence before she spoke quietly, with certainty in her voice. 'It is Mr Wolversley, is it not?'

'No!' Rosalind's heart began to race. 'Of course not. Mr Wolversley is…Mr Wolversley…' She began again but she could think of no words.

'The day he brought you here, I saw the way he looked at you. I saw too the way you looked at him. Like lovers.' She gave a soft laugh. 'How could I not have realized?'

Rosalind should have been denying it. She should have told Nell that Wolf was nothing to her, but she could not speak the lie. The seconds ticked by until she said quietly, 'Yes…like lovers.'

'You have given yourself to him?' Nell asked.

Rosalind nodded, and the memory of their loving was strong in her mind.

'Then there could be a child…'

'And if there is, I shall love it and care for it the best that I can.'

'Oh, Rosalind,' her sister said softly.

'Are you appalled that I am a fallen woman? I will understand if you wish me to leave your house.'

Nell shook her head. 'Foolish sister, you are going nowhere. I have lost you once and will not do so again.'

Rosalind felt her heart well with love and gratitude.

There was a small silence.

'A match could be arranged between you and Mr Wolversley. Indeed in the circumstances—'

'No.' The word was categorical and irrefutable.

'But if there was to be—'

'Mr Wolversley has made it clear that he does not favour

an alliance with me, and I would never use a child to force him to a union he does not want.'

'Mr Wolversley's affections did not appear that way to me, Rosalind.'

'I assure you that it is the truth,' said Rosalind, and she could not keep the edge of anger from her voice.

Nell said nothing. This strong, angry Rosalind was quite unlike the meek sister she had known.

Rosalind reached for her sister's hand. 'I am sorry, Nell. I do not mean to hurt you. I should not have spoken of Mr Wolversley. Let us not speak of him ever again.'

Nell nodded, but there was a thoughtful look upon her face.

Inside the murky interior of the Red Lion, Wolf sat alone at a table in the corner of the taproom. It was a shabby tavern and a popular haunt of old soldiers, with enough of a dubious reputation to guarantee an evening free from the company of gentlemen. The usual crowd were in tonight but Wolf kept to himself, his expression enough to warn away any company. He sipped slowly at his ale, knowing that he needed to keep a clear head. There was the crack of logs on the small fire, and the buzz of low level conversation.

Wolf had kept himself busy these last days, anything other than allow himself time to think of Rosalind. Yet she was in his head now, just as she ever was. Across the room, he saw the burly figure of Campbell duck his head to pass under the door lintel. The Scotsman took a few moments to readjust his eyes to the tavern's gloom before heading over to Wolf.

He slipped his hat from his head, smiling broadly as a tavern wench brought him over a tankard of ale. He took a swig and sighed his appreciation as if the cheap watery ale were the finest brandy.

'My, but that tastes good.'

Wolf smiled. 'Only when you have not had it for a while.'

Campbell laughed.

Wolf did not ask. He knew that Struan would tell him soon enough.

Campbell set the tankard down and looked across the small scrubbed table at Wolf. 'Johnny came back wi' the information you were asking for.'

Wolf smiled again.

'You were right about Stephano Beshaley and Stephen Hebden being one in the same. But that isnae the best of it. It seems that Hebden's got a history. His father was Christopher Hebden…' Campbell paused for effect.

'Get on with it.'

'Lord Framlingham,' said Campbell with a smug expression.

'And?' *Framlingham.* A faint recollection whispered through Wolf's mind. 'Framlingham,' he said aloud, and he knew where he had heard the name before—where he had read it, to be precise: in the newspaper article delivered to Rosalind. Framlingham was the man that Rosalind Wardale's father had murdered. 'Oh, hell,' he muttered.

'Hell, indeed,' said Campbell. 'It looks like your man Beshaley has something of a score to settle.'

Wolf felt the dread whip through him. 'Maybe ruining Rosalind's reputation isn't going to be enough for Beshaley. If he's watching her, he'll know that we did not take her back to Evedon.'

'She should be safe enough with Stanegate.'

'She should be, but best not take any chances. We better warn Stanegate about Beshaley. Besides, if Beshaley's targeting Rosalind, there's every chance that he'll go after her sister and brother too. If he hasn't already.'

'You'll be paying Lord Stanegate a wee visit in the morning then?'

'Aye.'

'And what of Miss Wardale? Will you be seeing her at Bruton Street?'

God only knew how much Wolf wanted to see Rosalind. He wanted it so much that it was like a physical ache. But Rosalind was beyond his reach now. 'No. I'll speak to Stanegate. He'll see that she's kept safe.' His eyes met those of Campbell. 'It's for the best.'

'If that's what you think, Wolf,' but Campbell's dark gaze was dubious. He lifted his tankard and drained it before calling the serving wench over to refill both his and Wolf's cups once more.

It was too early in the morning for Nell to have risen. Rosalind faced Marcus Carlow across his study. The viscount was seated at his desk reading through papers.

Rosalind had slept poorly since her arrival at Bruton Street, waking before dawn each morning. Today she was taking advantage of her early rising to speak to Marcus without her sister. There were questions that she needed to ask, questions that were too distressing to Nell.

Marcus raised a single disapproving eyebrow at the sight of her and then continued with his writing. 'Nell is still abed. I suggest that you come back later.'

'It is you to whom I wish to speak.'

The eyebrow raised further still. His writing stilled and he laid down his pen before fixing her with an eye that could hardly be described as encouraging. Not so long ago his manner would have intimidated Rosalind, but the past weeks had changed her, perhaps more than she wished to admit.

'I have come to ask if you know of my mother's burial place. I would like very much to visit her grave. I have tried to ask Nell, but the subject of my mother's illness and death distresses her greatly and I have no wish to cause her suffering.'

'I am relieved to hear it,' he said, and Rosalind could see how very protective he was of her sister. 'Nell had Mrs Wardale buried in the graveyard of Christ Church in Spitalfields.'

'Is the grave marked by a stone?'

'It is now. Nell was penniless at the time of your mother's death and could afford nothing more than a pauper's grave. After we were married, we had a gravestone erected.'

'Thank you,' Rosalind said. 'So you met and married Nell after my mother's death?'

'Yes.'

Rosalind took a deep breath. 'The time when Nell was alone…she will not speak of it.'

'That is her prerogative. She will tell you of it when she is ready.'

'I am worried as to what she suffered.'

'Nell is safe now, and I do everything in my power to see that she is happy.'

There it was again, that word 'safe', which only made Rosalind worry even more as to her sister. She had the distinct feeling that something terrible had happened, some past threat to Nell's safety. But neither Nell nor Marcus were going to tell her. 'I have never seen her happier, sir.'

Marcus gave no response, but his face softened and the hint of a smile played about his mouth as if he were think-ing of Nell. And then the smile was gone, and he was looking at Rosalind again. 'If there is nothing else, Miss Wardale…Rosalind, I have much to attend to.'

Rosalind blushed at her overt dismissal. 'Of course, sir, and I thank you.' She hurried from the study and almost collided with a sleepy-looking Nell crossing the hall.

'Rosalind, have you been breakfasting with Marcus?' Nell smiled, but she was looking rather pale. 'I swear I cannot look at food this morning.'

'You should go back to bed and rest.'

Nell chuckled. 'You are beginning to sound like Marcus. I am here to check that my dear husband is not working too hard. He has been up since the crack of dawn, and would be every morning if I did not stop him.'

Rosalind knew by her sister's words that Marcus must share Nell's bed each night. The study door opened and Marcus popped his head out. Rosalind marvelled at how his face seemed to light up at the sight of his wife.

'Darling Nell, what are you doing up? Return to bed at once.'

Nell drew Rosalind an 'I told you so' look and, with a warm, liquid smile, ignored her husband's command and walked towards him. Rosalind nipped up the staircase, glancing back to see Marcus and Nell locked in a passionate embrace in the threshold to his study. Their love for one another was so radiant that it seemed to fill the whole house.

Rosalind reached her bedchamber and locked the door behind her. She stood by the window looking out at the start of what promised to be a day of fine weather. The sky was a cloudless blue, and sunshine flooded through the panes of glass to cast the room in bright warm light that shimmered and sparkled upon the crystal chandelier and cast rainbows on the soft feathered bed beneath. Such a beautiful day in such luxurious surroundings, Rosalind should have been happy. She was safe from Evedon and reunited with Nell. Yet she had never felt more miserable.

She loved Nell and was happy for her sister, but Nell and Marcus's happiness, their love, reminded her too much of what she had lost and would never regain. Wolf was gone and he would not be coming back. According to Nell, even their brother Nathan had found love and was happily married. She could begrudge neither Nell nor Nathan their happiness, but her own heart was still wounded and sore. She heard the thump of footsteps striding past her door and a stifled giggle before Nell's whispered warnings that Marcus would drop her and that Rosalind would hear.

'I do not care if the whole world hears,' came Marcus's reply, and then the door to their chamber shut and Rosalind heard nothing more. She thought of Wolf and of their own sweet lovemaking…And forced herself to stop. This would not do at all.

She slipped on a dark green pelisse to match her dress, fitted on her brown bonnet and blue kid gloves that were rather the worse for wear from her journey down the length of the country, and slipped quietly from the bedroom. She tiptoed down the stairs to the black and white chequered hallway, where she asked a passing maid where she might catch a hackney coach to Spitalfields, before leaving. The front door closed silently behind her. She had ghosts to lay to rest and her mind to clear, and neither could be done in this house.

The clock in the hallway struck ten.

Wolf glanced at his pocket watch before descending from his carriage. Eleven o'clock. He wondered again if the hour was too early to call upon Lord Stanegate, but dismissed the thought, knowing that he had been up since seven chafing to get here. Stanegate needed to be warned for Rosalind's sake, and there was always the chance that Wolf might catch a glimpse of Rosalind while in Bruton Street. A spur of excitement pricked him at that thought. Rosalind. He doubted he had gone five minutes without thinking of her, no matter how hard he tried not to.

Stanegate was still tweaking his cravat into place when he entered the same trade reception room in which Wolf waited.

'I had not thought to see you again, Mr Wolversley.' Stanegate raked a hand through his tousled hair. He had the look of a man who had just got out of bed, Wolf noted somewhat sourly.

'I am here on a matter of importance, to give you warning concerning a particular man. Some know him as the Gypsy, Stephano Beshaley, others as the gentleman, Stephen Hebden.'

'Beshaley!' Stanegate's gaze shot round.

'Do you know of him?'

'Oh, yes. Beshaley and I have had dealings in the past.'

'Then he has already come after your wife?'

'His vendetta has encompassed more than Lady Stanegate.'

Wolf's face hardened. 'Nice of you to warn Rosalind.'

'We did not know of Miss Wardale's whereabouts. My wife lost contact with her many years ago.'

'And after the newspaper article was published about Rosalind?'

'I made my own discreet enquiries,' said Stanegate coldly. 'There was nothing that could be done until she was found.'

'You should have warned her of Beshaley. And you should have warned me.'

'Pray tell me why on earth I should tell you aught of

this family's business, for it is certainly none of yours, sir. I know who you are. I know *what* you are. And I resent your overfamiliar tone when speaking of my sister-by-marriage.'

'Do you indeed?' Wolf's eyes were like flint. 'Then maybe I should tell you that Beshaley was the man behind the jewel theft in which Rosalind was framed.'

Stanegate's brow rose at that.

Wolf ignored it and continued on. 'He was the man behind that damnable scandalmongering newspaper article. He has sought to ruin Rosalind completely and utterly. And I am not certain that he will be content with how matters have ended.'

'Beshaley is indeed a dangerous man, Mr Wolversley, but Miss Wardale is safe with us. Beshaley would not dare show his face round here again.'

Wolf's gaze was hard. His words were low, but the threat contained in them was unmistakable. 'Then I hold you responsible for Miss Wardale's safety.'

Stanegate's manner was positively icy. 'The lady's welfare is none of your concern, sir.'

Wolf stepped closer to Stanegate and spoke quietly. 'On the contrary, my lord, it is everything of my concern, as you will discover should aught befall her while she is within your care.'

'Are you threatening me, Mr Wolversley?' Stanegate asked with incredulity.

A knock at the door sounded and Lady Stanegate appeared. She smiled and Wolf was instantly reminded of Rosalind.

'Mr Wolversley.' The smile deepened and she held out her hand to him.

The atmosphere within the small room was rank with animosity, but Lady Stanegate appeared not to notice that

he and her husband were facing each other like two dogs
with hackles raised. Wolf looked at her hand. He was not
sure if he should kiss it or shake it. He plumbed for the
latter, but felt suddenly awkward. The awkwardness intensified with the lady's next question.

'Are you here to visit Rosalind?'

To deny it would seem rude. To agree with it, worse still,
given the lay of the land between Stanegate and himself.
Given that the lady had already been Beshaley's target he
thought it prudent not to mention the villain's name in her
presence. He cleared his throat. 'I am here on a matter of
business with your husband.'

'But you will surely wish to see my sister while you are
here?'

Temptation beckoned. Wolf wanted it more than anything. He struggled to recall why he had deemed that he
and Rosalind should not meet again.

'Mr Wolversley was just leaving,' said Stanegate
coolly.

'I am sure that he can spare some few minutes to take
a little tea with Rosalind,' his wife countered.

'Lady Stanega—' Wolf began.

'Indeed, I insist upon it.'

'Nell…' Stanegate said with a warning look.

She met her husband's eye, and Wolf could see the
unspoken message pass between them. A plea and a promise that she knew what she was doing. Stanegate gave a
barely imperceptible inclination of the head.

'Do join my wife, Miss Wardale and myself for tea.'
The dark grey eyes met Wolf's.

'Please do,' added Lady Stanegate.

There was no way out without delivering a slight to
Stanegate's wife, and whatever Wolf thought of Stanegate,

he was not about to do that. He thought again of Rosalind. 'Thank you.'

But when Rosalind was sent for, she could not be found.

Wolf grew uneasy, suspecting that Rosalind knew he was here and did not want to see him. He could not blame her for that, but it still hurt. But then it emerged from a small chambermaid that Miss Wardale had left the house earlier that morning having asked directions to Spitalfields.

'Mama's grave,' uttered Lady Stanegate.

'I am sorry, Nell,' said Stanegate. 'She came to me this morning asking questions. I had no idea that she meant to visit the grave alone and today.'

'She should be safe enough, should she not?' Lady Stanegate's words were spoken with more hope than belief. 'There is no one around who should desire to hurt her, is there?'

Wolf met Stanegate's gaze with hard piercing thoroughness until the viscount finally glanced away at his wife.

'It seems that Stephano Beshaley has been up to his old tricks again. He is in London, Nell.'

Lady Stanegate's eyes widened. 'But he cannot know where she is. He cannot try to hurt her…'

'He already has,' said Wolf.

Lady Stanegate gave a little cry and the colour seemed to drain from her face. Stanegate moved to support her.

'Do not worry, dearest. I will send the carriage to Christ Church immediately.'

But Wolf stepped forward. 'There is no need, Stanegate. I will go.'

'Look here—' Stanegate started to say.

His wife took his hand in her own. 'Let him go, Marc. He will bring her back safely to us.'

Wolf was already gone, the tread of hurried booted footsteps echoing through the hall, and the heavy front door slamming in his wake.

'There is something you should know about Rosalind and Mr Wolversley,' Lady Stanegate said softly to her husband.

Chapter Eighteen

The hackney coach drew up outside Christ Church in Spitalfields. Rosalind paid the driver the last of her money and climbed down to gaze upon the huge white columns that fronted the building. It was a large church, built during the reign of Queen Anne, with an angular spire that projected into the cloudless blue sky. She walked through the deserted columns, her footsteps echoing on the bare stone paving, and headed into the graveyard. She was quite alone, not another living soul to be seen, yet that only seemed to add to the serenity of the place.

She wandered along the gravel pathway past the gravestones and the unmarked paupers' graves and the leafy saplings planted nearby. She read the name on each stone, her feet carrying her onward until, at last, she came to the one that she sought: a small, white-marble stone with the epitaph engraved with black letters. It said simply:

Catherine Wardale,
Beloved mother
Died 12th January 1810, aged 47

Nothing more.

She stood there quietly, head bowed, thinking of her mother, remembering, praying, until at last she felt a sense of acceptance, and in that knowledge was a certain comfort.

A quiet tread sounded behind her and Rosalind knew that she was no longer alone. And strangely, for someone who had spent most of her life hiding and running and afraid, she felt no fear. The thought flashed in her head that it was Evedon come to get her after all. She turned to face him.

The man stood behind her some little distance away, dressed all in black. A finely tailored coat, black breeches and long black riding boots. A black waistcoat and cravat tied as if he were attending the most fashionable of events, and a shirt that was so pristine white as to appear that he had just had it delivered that morning. And from one ear-lobe came the glint of a small gold hoop. Not Evedon, but the dark stranger. The man Wolf had named Stephano Beshaley. The man who had gone to such lengths to destroy her.

'Good morning, Miss Wardale.' His voice was arrogant, indolent almost, with something about it that struck her as strange. The lightest hint of a foreign accent perhaps, or maybe just a lilt to his words.

She looked up into his face, seeing him at close range for the first time.

'You!' she whispered.

'At your service, Lady Rosalind.' He affected a mock

bow, and smiled a smile that had nothing of friendship in it and yet was so compulsive that she could not look away. His skin was olive, his eyes as black as his hair, set in a face that was undeniably handsome. His body was lithe; his movements smooth, unhurried. He was sleek and wary and watchful as a great black cat. His hands were uncovered, a pair of black leather gloves held carelessly in one grip.

'We meet at last.' He reached his hand out, his long brown fingers lifting her hand to his mouth. She felt the warmth of his lips touch to the back of her hand, and the caress of his breath over her skin. The dark eyes met hers; there was something in them that both shocked and fascinated her.

'You are not afraid?' he asked.

'No.' It was the truth, she realized.

He smiled again in that darkly dangerous way, and she felt the shiver ripple through her, from the core of her belly to the tips of her breasts.

'Why are you doing this to me?' she asked; her voice was quite calm, nonchalant even.

'Did not your sister tell you?'

'Nell?' And suddenly those cryptic references to safety made by Nell and Marcus made sense. 'You tried to ruin her too.' She stared up at him, unable to hide her horror at the realization. An awful possibility made itself known to her. 'And Nathan?'

'And Nathan,' he confirmed with a lazy smile. 'There are too many secrets in families. Too much shame to be hidden.' And she had the sensation that it was not only her family of which he spoke.

He winced and pressed his fingers to his forehead as if he was in pain.

'Dear Lord,' she whispered.

'He shall not help you,' Beshaley said. 'He certainly never helped me, no matter how much I prayed.'

She did not know how to respond to that.

In the silence that followed, she could hear the melodic song of a blackbird and, glancing over at the budding bushes from where the call sounded, saw the small dark movement dart beneath the branches. When she looked at Beshaley again, there was a silver pistol in his hand and it was pointing at her. She could not help noticing the exquisite workmanship of the pattern engraved upon its barrel, and the fine ivory handle.

'Are you going to kill me?' No panic, not even the slightest fear. Part of her wanted to laugh with the irony of it.

'No. I merely wish to finish what I started. Evedon's prosecution will mean that you cannot climb so easily back into favour by virtue of your noble relations. We are for Evedon House.' He moved, taking her arm in his, with the deadly pistol held low within the other. 'My carriage is not far.'

Her eyes scanned the church yard seeking a means of escape, but found none.

A dark unmarked carriage sat parked at the side of the road. As they neared it, she resolved to take her chances but Stephano Beshaley seemed to sense it and she felt the soft press of the pistol's muzzle against her belly.

She had little choice other than to climb up the steps that the exotic-looking manservant kicked down into place, and enter into the coach.

Compared to the bright sunshine outside, the carriage interior was dim and gloomy. She noticed that the thick black velvet curtains had been closed across most of the windows to block out the majority of the light.

Beshaley took his seat opposite her, before the door

thudded shut and the coach moved off with only the gentlest of sways.

'If you are taking me to Evedon, then do you not think that you owe me an explanation as to why you have sought to hurt me and my family?'

'I owe your family nothing but hurt,' he retorted, then fell silent, staring down at the floor below, so that she thought that he would tell her nothing. Then he looked at her again, shifting forward in his seat to lean towards her. 'Do you not know who am I?'

'Wolf told me you are a gem merchant, Mr Beshaley.'

'Ah, Wolversley,' he sighed, 'the thief-taker who would save my little thief.' And his dark eyes glittered in the gloom of the carriage. He laughed softly, and she sensed in him the same underlying danger that was in Wolf, that same feral unpredictability. He was shorter than Wolf, narrower but lithe; she did not doubt his strength.

'I do not know you, sir. I do not understand what this is all about.'

'The sins of their fathers, Rosalind—' he sounded almost tired '—for which the children will pay.'

'My father is dead, sir.'

'Hanged,' he said and the dark eyes were on her once again. She remembered the black silken noose that had swung from both Evedon's and Wolf's fingers. 'For murder.'

'So they said.' She watched him carefully, not understanding where this was leading.

'Whom did he kill, Rosalind? Who was his victim?'

She shook her head as if to deny it.

'Do you even know?'

'A man by the name of Framlingham.'

'Lord Framlingham—Christopher Hebden,' said Beshaley. 'My father.'

She stared at him, eyes wide, pulse racing. 'But your name is Beshaley.'

'Beshaley was my mother's name; she was Romany and my father's mistress; I was born Stephen Hebden and raised for the first seven years of my life as a Hebden in the family home.'

She stared as if she could not believe what she was hearing.

'Your father murdered mine and, by so doing, he cost my birth mother her life and ruined mine. I was cast out of the Hebden family. They left me in a foundling home, from where I ended up living on the streets before my mother's people found me and took me in.'

'I am sorry.'

'Are you?' he asked. And when those dark eyes met hers, she felt the shiver pass right through her body.

'Of course,' she said. 'You were a child the same as me. We none of us deserved what happened.'

'It is too late. What was foretold cannot be undone. The blood of all those with a hand in what happened is cursed—the Hebdens, the Carlows, but most of all, the Wardales, for it was your father who did the deed. You cannot escape it; you are cursed to be ruined by scandal, Miss Wardale. That is why I cannot let Wolf save you.'

'I am utterly ruined. You have seen to that. What need had you for the newspaper article? What need have you to do more now? The theft alone was enough to ruin me, if that is what you wanted.'

'Alas, my sweet girl,' he said, 'it was not. Evedon was going to hush the whole thing up. I had to force his hand, so to speak, with the newspaper. And as for now: Stanegate is not without connections. A year in the country while the scandal dies and then you would be back as if nothing had ever happened.'

'You know it would not be so,' she countered.

'If Wolf has his way, it will.'

'Are you going to kill me?' she asked again, not trusting that he meant to take her to Evedon. She was not panicking. Indeed she felt strangely calm as she faced him in the carriage.

As he reached across to her, she saw the worked-silver band that surrounded his wrist. He stroked a single long brown finger down the side of her cheek, so gently, with such sensuality, that she gasped aloud at the sensations it wrought. 'The murderer's blood is in your veins, Rosalind,' and her name was like a caress upon his lips, 'not mine.'

She jerked her face away from his hand. 'Then what shall you do with me?'

His eyes flickered over her as if he could see through all of her clothing, and brought a hot blush to her cheeks. 'What would you like me to do?'

She blushed all the harder, angry at herself that he could have such an effect on her. 'Release me. Let me go free.'

He smiled in that same dangerous way, and she thought again of Wolf.

'Persuasive though you are, Rosalind, I fear I must fulfil my destiny and deliver you to Evedon. And then there is the small matter of Mr Wolversley and the trouble he has caused me.' His eyes glittered, and his face, in the shadows, was as harsh as Wolf's.

Her heart seemed to stop before kicking suddenly to a frenzy. 'You have no quarrel with Wolf.'

'Only over you.'

'No, I beg of you, sir, do not hurt him.'

She saw Beshaley's expression change, saw the surprise in his eyes. 'You care for him,' he said as if stumbling across the discovery.

She looked him directly in the eye, unafraid, unashamed, 'I love him.'

'Have you forgotten that Wolf is the villain that caught you? He is a bastard, shunned by all Society.' And she thought she caught the whisper, 'Like me.'

'A bastard maybe,' she said, 'but a finer man I have never known. The whole world might shun him and it would still make no difference.'

'Kempster was right. Wolf did bed you.'

She held her head high. 'I am not ashamed of loving him. I will go with you to Evedon, sir, on the condition that you stay away from Wolf.'

'You are coming with me regardless.'

'I could make this very difficult for you, Mr Beshaley.'

He laughed and produced the pistol from his pocket. 'I do not think so, Miss Wardale.'

'Then you think wrongly, sir.' She looked at him, and now the fear was back with her, not for anything that he could do to her, but rather for what he might do to Wolf. And no matter how strong, how fast, how able Wolf was, she knew that he and Beshaley were too alike and she feared for what Beshaley could do to him. So she reached out her hand and closed it gently over the muzzle of the pistol.

Beshaley's eyes registered his surprise. 'My, but you must truly have a care for your thief-taker.'

She said nothing, just stared at him with more determination than she had ever felt in her life and kept her hand steady where it was.

'He is a bastard, a man from the streets, who has carved his own path through this world. A man cast out from Society,' he said.

'He is all of these things, and still a giant amongst the

men who would condemn him. He is a good man, sir. There is none better.'

'Make no mistake, Miss Wardale, if I fire this pistol you will die. Your hand will not stopper the ball. Do you understand that?'

'I understand it perfectly.'

'And yet if I say that I will not pursue my grievance with Wolf then you will accompany me willingly to Evedon?'

'If I have your word on Wolf's safety,' she said.

'My word?' His brow raised as if he could not believe that she would value such a thing.

'Your word, sir,' she said firmly.

'You would give yourself up to Evedon. You would even risk me shooting you dead. And all for this Wolf of yours.'

'Yes, I would.'

Beshaley was staring at her, and something of the hardness had gone from his face. He uncocked the pistol, drew it back from her hand and slipped it once more into his pocket. Then he reached up and banged his cane on the ceiling and the carriage drew to a stop. He drew the curtain briefly aside and dropping down the window shouted an instruction up to the coachman. The carriage rolled on, but Beshaley no longer spoke. He was staring ahead in the gloom as if he no longer noticed that she was there; despite everything, there was such a sadness about him, a weariness, that Rosalind could almost feel sorry for him.

Eventually the carriage came to a stop, and the door was opened by the small swarthy man that had helped Rosalind into the carriage. Outside did not look to be the steps of Evedon House. She craned her head and saw the front of Bruton Street. Her heart rate quickened.

The brightness of the daylight flooded the carriage interior, showing Beshaley's features in stark detail.

'Your part in this is over. Fate is a cruel mistress, leading us down a path we would not choose to take, and all in the name of vengeance.'

Vengeance. It lay at the heart of this man's endeavours and of Wolf's.

Out in the street the sun was bright.

Beshaley gestured outside, and there coming out of the front door of the house was Wolf. Rosalind heard the door slam. Her heart skipped a beat. Butterflies flocked in her stomach. She moved towards the carriage door, then hesitated and stared round at Beshaley suddenly wary that this was some kind of a trick.

'Go. For what it is worth, Rosalind, I would that you were not William Wardale's daughter.' He smiled, and in the darkness of his eyes was the pain she had seen before. 'Go to your thief-taker,' he said.

Wolf was running down the steps towards her as she stepped down into the sunshine. And then she was running to him, and she was in his arms.

He swung her round behind him, pulling a pistol from his pocket as he turned to face the carriage once more. Rosalind saw his intent and grabbed at his hand.

'No! Let him go. Please, Wolf. He did not hurt me.'

Wolf's aim was knocked askew.

The carriage door thudded shut and the black curtain was drawn back from its window. Stephano Beshaley looked directly at Wolf and drew him a salute as if they were brother warriors. Then the carriage was gone, leaving Rosalind and Wolf standing alone on the steps to Bruton Street.

He made the pistol safe, then dropped it into his pocket before turning to her, and pulling her into his arms. 'Thank

God, you are safe,' he said and crushed her to him. 'Thank God,' he said again, and buried his face in her hair. 'I thought that he…' His words were so quiet as to scarce be above a whisper. 'I thought…' But again he could not say the words.

'I am safe, Wolf. Unharmed.'

He drew back enough to look into her face. 'He did nothing to hurt you?'

'No. He intended to take me to Evedon.'

'Yet he brought you here, to your sister.'

'He brought me to you, Wolf.'

She saw the flicker in the tense line of his jaw at her words. And the concern that filled his eyes.

'Then what is his game? Rosalind, he is Framlingham's bastard son.'

'I know who he is, Wolf.'

'He is seeking vengeance.'

She shook her head. 'He sees himself as the hand of fate, seeking redress for past injustices. We all face the consequences of our father's actions, Wolf, however unfair it may be.' She smiled wryly and took his hands in hers.

'I am so sorry, Rosalind.'

The sun shone lights through the fairness of his hair that ruffled softly in the breeze. His face was strong and handsome, his jaw clenched with emotion.

'Sorry for what? For saving my life? For breaking my heart?'

He winced.

'Were it your father the murderer, Wolf, I would love you just the same. The sins are those of the father, not the son…or the daughter.'

'Rosalind,' He stared down into her face. 'You think that I let you go because of what your father did?'

'Why else?'

'You were raised as an earl's daughter, and I as a whore's bastard.'

'Will you make us both suffer for it for ever? You and Beshaley are not so dissimilar, after all.'

His jaw clenched tighter and she saw the shock and hurt and realization in his eyes. He was staring at her with such intensity as if he could see into her very soul. 'Would you marry a damned fool?' he asked.

Her gaze held his. 'I might if he were to ask me.'

'Marry me, Rosalind.'

'Are you going to change your mind this time?'

'Never.'

'Then, yes, I will marry you, Wolf.'

He laughed, and slid his arms around her, and kissed her in such a way that she could not doubt his love.

'We had better go in and tell Nell and Marcus.'

Wolf grinned. 'I think they might already know.' He glanced towards the house.

Rosalind followed his gaze to see Nell and Marcus standing by the window of the study. Nell was smiling broadly while Marcus's face held an expression of shock.

Wolf smiled, and kissed her again. 'Just for good measure,' he said, 'so that they will understand the need for a hasty wedding.'

Rosalind and Wolf were married five days later by special licence in a quiet ceremony in Wolf's grand house. The guest list was short: Nell and Marcus and baby William, Struan Campbell and, Wolf's wedding gift to Rosalind—Nathan and his wife, Diana. A family reunited once more. A love found for ever. Tears of joy escaped her cheeks as Wolf slid the gold band on to her finger and her heart welled with love for this man who was now her husband.

And afterwards, when everyone had gone and they were

alone on a shabby chair in the snug comfort of Wolf's den, there was one small question that still lay unanswered at the back of her mind.

'I was wondering, Wolf,' she said.

'Mmh?' he murmured as he kissed the tender skin at the nape of her neck.

'About Evedon.'

He raised his face from his nuzzling. 'Evedon shall not trouble us again. I promise you that, Rosalind. You need think of him no more.'

'But how can you be so certain?' She wriggled round on his lap to face him. 'He has the letter. We have no means to prevent whatever he might wish to do.'

He shook his head. 'Sweet Rosalind,' he whispered, and stroked a gentle finger to her cheek. 'There is something I have not told you, something that perhaps I should have before I asked you to be my wife.'

He felt her body still and tense beneath his hands, afraid of what he would tell her.

'Evedon will keep his word because…' he hesitated, 'because he is my brother,' he finished.

'Your brother?' Her brow wrinkled in puzzlement. 'But how can that be?'

'The letter that you took from Evedon named Robert Veryan, Viscount Keddinton, as Evedon's true father. Keddinton cuckolded Evedon's father. And it was Keddinton who seduced my mother and ruined her.'

Rosalind gasped. 'Keddinton is your father?'

'Unfortunately so,' he said, but the bitterness and fury and shame that he normally felt on thinking of the man were no longer there. His love for Rosalind had rendered such feelings small and inconsequential. Her love had freed him from his past. 'So Evedon will do nothing to stir up that hornet's nest.'

'You are right.' Her expression was serious. 'Wolf…'

He tensed, waiting for what she would say.

She smiled. 'I still love you,' and she plucked a small kiss from his lips.

'As I love you, lass, as I love you.'

Down in Bruton Street, Nell and Marcus were snuggled together on the sofa in Nell's little parlour.

'I am so glad that Rosalind and Wolf are happy at last. He loves her very much you know.'

'He does,' said Marcus, and slid his arm around Nell's shoulders. 'I did not know what game he was playing initially. And upon first impressions he is…' Marcus tried to find the right word to describe Wolf.

'Rather excitingly dangerous,' supplied his wife.

'That is not exactly what I was going to say, but yes, he does have a dangerous wolfish presence about him.' He smiled down at Nell. 'But I think he will look after Rosalind very well indeed.'

They sat in silence for a little before Nell remarked, 'I am glad that this business with Beshaley is over at last. At least Hal is safe from him over in Brussels.'

'Safe fighting the French,' said Marcus wryly.

'Oh, you know what I mean; Beshaley cannot reach him there.' She smiled. 'Before I knew about Wolf, I had thought that I might make a match between Rosalind and Hal.'

'You grow as bad as Mama. She despairs of Hal ever settling down with a nice girl. Indeed, I am afraid to confess that a nice girl is the last thing for which Hal is looking.'

'Poor Hal,' murmured Nell. 'But at least I need worry no longer over Rosalind.'

'Hurrah to that,' said Marcus.

Nell raised her glass of lemonade and touched it with a

small clink against Marcus's snifter of brandy. 'To Rosalind and Wolf, that they might know happiness like ours.'

'To Rosalind and Wolf.'

* * * * *

*See below for a sneak peek from our classic
Harlequin® Romance® line.*

Introducing DADDY BY CHRISTMAS by Patricia Thayer.

MIA caught sight of Jarrett when he walked into the open lobby. It was hard not to notice the man. In a charcoal business suit with a crisp white shirt and striped tie covered by a dark trench coat, he looked more Wall Street than small-town Colorado.

Mia couldn't blame him for keeping his distance. He was probably tired of taking care of her.

Besides, why would a man like Jarrett McKane be interested in her? Why would he want to take on a woman expecting a baby? Yet he'd done so many things for her. He'd been there when she'd needed him most. How could she not care about a man like that?

Heart pounding in her ears, she walked up behind him. Jarrett turned to face her. "Did you get enough sleep last night?"

"Yes, thanks to you," she said, wondering if he'd thought about their kiss. Her gaze went to his mouth, then she quickly glanced away. "And thank you for not bringing up my meltdown."

Jarrett couldn't stop looking at Mia. Blue was definitely her color, bringing out the richness of her eyes.

"What meltdown?" he said, trying hard to focus on what she was saying. "You were just exhausted from lack of sleep and worried about your baby."

He couldn't help remembering how, during the night, he'd kept going in to watch her sleep. How strange was that? "I hope you got enough rest."

She nodded. "Plenty. And you're a good neighbor for

coming to my rescue."

He tensed. Neighbor? *What neighbor kisses you like I did?* "That's me, just the full-service landlord," he said, trying to keep the sarcasm out of his voice. He started to leave, but she put her hand on his arm.

"Jarrett, what I meant was you went beyond helping me." Her eyes searched his face. "I've asked far too much of you."

"Did you hear me complain?"

She shook her head. "You should. I feel like I've taken advantage."

"Like I said, I haven't minded."

"And I'm grateful for everything…"

Grasping her hand on his arm, Jarrett leaned forward. The memory of last night's kiss had him aching for another. "I didn't do it for your gratitude, Mia."

Gorgeous tycoon Jarrett McKane has never believed in Christmas—but he can't help being drawn to soon-to-be-mom Mia Saunders! Christmases past were spent alone…and now Jarrett may just have a fairy-tale ending for all his Christmases future!

Available December 2010, only from Harlequin® Romance®.

HARLEQUIN®

A Romance

FOR EVERY MOOD™

Spotlight on

Classic

Quintessential, modern love stories
that are romance at its finest.

See the next page
to enjoy a sneak peek from
the Harlequin® Romance series.

Bestselling Harlequin Presents® author

Julia James

brings you her most powerful book yet...

FORBIDDEN OR FOR BEDDING?

The shamed mistress...

Guy de Rochemont's name is a byword for wealth
and power—and now his duty is to wed.

Alexa Harcourt knows she can never be anything
more than *The de Rochemont Mistress*.

But Alexa—the one woman Guy wants—is also
the one woman whose reputation
forbids him to take her as his wife....

Available from Harlequin Presents
December 2010

USA TODAY bestselling authors

MAUREEN CHILD

and

SANDRA HYATT

UNDER THE MILLIONAIRE'S MISTLETOE

Just when these leading men thought they had it all figured out, they quickly learn their hearts have made other plans. Two passionate stories about love, longing and the infinite possibilities of kissing under the mistletoe.

Available December wherever you buy books.

Always Powerful, Passionate and Provocative.

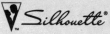

Sparked by Danger, Fueled by Passion.

RACHEL LEE
A Soldier's Redemption

When the Witness Protection Program fails at
keeping Cory Farland out of harm's way, ex-
marine Wade Kendrick steps in. As Cory's new
bodyguard, Wade has a plan for protecting her—
however falling in love was not part of his plan.

*Available in December
wherever books are sold.*

Visit Silhouette Books at www.eHarlequin.com

SRS27705

REQUEST YOUR FREE BOOKS!

 HARLEQUIN® HISTORICAL:
Where love is timeless

2 FREE NOVELS PLUS 2 FREE GIFTS!

YES! Please send me 2 FREE Harlequin® Historical novels and my 2 FREE gifts (gifts are worth about $10). After receiving them, if I don't wish to receive any more books, I can return the shipping statement marked "cancel." If I don't cancel, I will receive 6 brand-new novels every month and be billed just $4.94 per book in the U.S. or $5.49 per book in Canada. That's a saving of 20% off the cover price! It's quite a bargain! Shipping and handling is just 50¢ per book.* I understand that accepting the 2 free books and gifts places me under no obligation to buy anything. I can always return a shipment and cancel at any time. Even if I never buy another book from Harlequin, the two free books and gifts are mine to keep forever.

246/349 HDN E5L4

Name _____ (PLEASE PRINT) _____

Address _____ Apt. # _____

City _____ State/Prov. _____ Zip/Postal Code _____

Signature (if under 18, a parent or guardian must sign) _____

Mail to the **Harlequin Reader Service:**
IN U.S.A.: P.O. Box 1867, Buffalo, NY 14240-1867
IN CANADA: P.O. Box 609, Fort Erie, Ontario L2A 5X3

Not valid for current subscribers to Harlequin Historical books.

Want to try two free books from another line?
Call 1-800-873-8635 or visit www.morefreebooks.com.

* Terms and prices subject to change without notice. Prices do not include applicable taxes. N.Y. residents add applicable sales tax. Canadian residents will be charged applicable provincial taxes and GST. Offer not valid in Quebec. This offer is limited to one order per household. All orders subject to approval. Credit or debit balances in a customer's account(s) may be offset by any other outstanding balance owed by or to the customer. Please allow 4 to 6 weeks for delivery. Offer available while quantities last.

Your Privacy: Harlequin Books is committed to protecting your privacy. Our Privacy Policy is available online at www.eHarlequin.com or upon request from the Reader Service. From time to time we make our lists of customers available to reputable third parties who may have a product or service of interest to you. ☐ If you would prefer we not share your name and address, please check here.

Help us get it right—We strive for accurate, respectful and relevant communications. To clarify or modify your communication preferences, visit us at www.ReaderService.com/consumerschoice.